Edge of the Future

by

Andria Stone

Table Of Contents

PROLOGUE

After the last war, most democratic countries on Earth united, combining their forces into one universal military. This led to a pooling of military funds, resulting in the construction of a new Space Station, spacedock and shipyard. The military quickly became the primary spacefaring entity.

The moon, now officially named Luna, was colonized with three underground military bases. Next, world leaders elected to discard the old nomenclature "Earth" meaning dirt or soil; formally christening the planet Terra, with Terran Military Defense (TMD) as humanity's dominant armed forces.

Chapter 1

The Emergency Warning siren blared from every comm system throughout the research facility. Lights dimmed to a flashing red. The PA system crackled with static, announcing, "This is not a drill. The CAMRI facility is under attack. All systems are under full security lockdown. Shelter-in-place."

Captain Mark Warren froze for a moment. Looking up from his microscope, he scanned the room for his lab partner, Dr. Coulter. She wasn't there. He didn't remember her saying where she was going, either. He'd been so absorbed in his experiment he hadn't paid any attention. He instinctively rushed to the door of their small Xenobiology laboratory and tried to twist the knob. *Nope. Not opening. Damn.* He hurried to the desk and checked the vid screen for information. *Black nothingness.* He grabbed his tablet to check for data. *Dead.* He tapped his comm for any voice message. Silence.

The headache-inducing siren stopped. Only the red warning lights continued flashing. Mark ransacked the cabinets for anything useful. He found a MedKit, a fire extinguisher, but not so much as a box cutter to defend himself. And if someone wanted to hide—there wasn't even a closet.

All hell broke loose. Mark flinched at the sounds of automatic weapons' fire coming from several different directions. An explosion ripped through the air. The whole room shuddered. *Shit, shit, shit.* Mark found the darkest corner in his small lab and hunkered down to wait for the end. *Oh, hell.* He should have stayed in Portland; nothing ever happened in Portland, or any one of a dozen different places he'd been. Like Paris. Yes, Paris, with Juliette, now only a memory. Long distance relationships with beautiful French women were short-lived. Instead, he'd let the

Terran Military recruit him, then snooker him into a tour in the isolated Canadian wilderness, all for the sake of research. If it hadn't been for his love of science—wait—he remembered an earlier briefing about some fanatics. A faction of global anti-technology extremists had been very vocal lately; making threats. Today they were making good on those threats with bombs and guns. Mark wondered where the soldiers were that should be guarding this place.

***

The Terran Military troop transport ship hovered scant inches above a cold North Dakota spaceport tarmac, while the tactical assault group boarded.

Sergeant Axel Von Radach was the last to jump through the airlock hatch. He headed straight for the pilot's cabin. He knew the drill; he rapped on the bulkhead and poked his head inside to confirm the coordinates. He recognized the call signs emblazoned in red on both pilots' helmets. Axel had personal history with both these women.

"Well, hello, ladies. We having lunch in Canada this afternoon?"

To his left, Boss Lady continued tapping the screens on her flight console. "Affirmative. Don't worry your pretty little head, Sergeant. We'll be there before you know it." She tossed him a look over her shoulder, winked, and puckered her lips.

In the Nav seat, Tiger Lily flashed him a smile then gave him a thumbs-up. She tapped the ship's comm, and announced, "Okay, people, harness up. Ten seconds to liftoff."

Axel backed out, slid around the bulkhead into the nearest empty harness station, and strapped himself to the hull.

As they became airborne, the interior lighting switched to deep blue. The same color glowed in the twin light strips on the floor. Today, his transport held one platoon of thirty soldiers. Mostly men, some women, all with buzz cuts or shaved heads. Each outfitted in urban gray tactical combat armor, gear, and pulse weapons. They were divided into two squads sitting opposite each other.

Lieutenant Monroe always positioned himself in the middle, facing the hatch. Inside his helmet, Monroe's mouth moved, and his head bobbed. Axel knew he was conversing with HQ. Sergeant Russo, of Bravo Squad, sat centered along the back, updating his people in subdued tones.

Axel commed his squad. "Listen up. Terrorists have attacked CAMRI, a joint Canadian-American Military Research Installation outside Churchill, Manitoba. We received an alert when their systems went offline. An unknown number of heavily armed militants have been onsite now for fifteen minutes. CAMRI's onsite forces have gone dark, so we have no news on casualties or damages. Our orders are to eliminate any and all threats. We knew this was a military research installation, but now suspect it may house classified biomaterials. I say again, classified biomaterials. Use extreme caution in any laboratory areas. I don't want anyone bringing back a deadly pathogen. Am I clear?"

In unison, fourteen voices responded, "Yes, Sergeant."

Axel continued, "They're dropping us onto the roof. The structure is two levels of twenty-four laboratories, each. We'll split up, sweep it from the top down. Bravo Squad is taking the ground floor." Axel grinned. "Neutralize all the bad guys—not any of the good guys—and do not go blowing holes in things for the fun of it—unless you want them billing us for the damages."

Again, fourteen voices responded, "Yes, Sergeant."

The ship's comm buzzed. Tiger Lily warned, "Okay people, lock and load. Hot LZ in twenty seconds."

***

A massive explosion detonated somewhere close in the corridor outside Mark's lab, followed by weapon fire, yelling and screaming, then silence.

Mark got to his feet, feeling that fight-or-flight epinephrine surge through his body. He stared at the door handle as it began to glow red-hot. A force hit the metal door. He flinched. It burst open. He stumbled backward.

An armored soldier erupted into the room. He looked straight at Mark, and turned to drag in a wounded soldier. Both their helmets had red TMD insignias.

"Who are you?" The soldier's helmet turned his voice into a raspy growl.

"Captain Mark Warren, Terran Military, Exobiology Research & Development."

"Good, you can help me." He handed the wounded soldier's sidearm to Mark. "Guard the door." He pulled a packet from a hidden seam on his bicep, tore open the wrapper, dropped to one knee next to the injured soldier, and jabbed him in the thigh with a syringe.

Mark backed up against the wall, aiming the gun at the door. "Okay, now who are you?"

"I'm the cavalry come to save you lab rats." The armored soldier lifted his mirrored faceplate, stood and offered a cocky smile. "Sergeant Axel Von Radach, Tactical Assault Group, TMD, North American Command."

Oh, crap. An adrenalin junkie. Mark nodded to the man on the floor. "Is he going to be okay? And what's happening out there? I've been locked in here since the alarms went off. Where's our security?"

"His suit will seal a wound, but in case it's internal, we need to get him out of here—soon. Some terrorists are trying to blow your house down."

Mark nodded.

"And kill you."

Mark heard voices coming from the corridor. They grew louder.

Von Radach pressed a finger to his lips, cradled his rifle, and peeked around the door. "Stay here. Take care of Scarlotti," he whispered, closing his faceplate, and sliding into the hallway.

Mark grabbed a strap on the wounded soldier's vest, and pulled him into the furthermost corner. Blackened scorch marks on the armor indicated a possibly lethal injury. Mark peeled back a glove, checked for a pulse. *Good. Still alive.* A rapid burst of fire startled him. He seized the gun, and faced the door.

Presently, a voice said, "Don't shoot, Captain. I'm coming in." The sergeant gingerly eased through the doorway, carrying an unconscious middle-aged woman in a bloody lab coat.

"That's Dr. Coulter—my lab partner." Mark rushed over to help the sergeant lay the short, pudgy woman on top of the metal workspace island in the middle of the room. "She's Canadian— she's teaching me how to speak French." He checked her carotid. She had a pulse, but he couldn't find any wounds. "I don't know where this blood is coming from."

"Shot a big guy. He fell on top of her. It's his blood. He was a bear, so she's probably got one hell of a concussion." The sergeant removed his helmet, revealing dark eyes in an olive complexion, with close-cropped black hair, and beard stubble. The remnants of a new scar pierced his left cheek. Not a clean-cut military recruitment poster specimen. Mark also got the distinct impression he was the one *nobody* messed with in school, in a bar, or anywhere.

Von Radach turned, stepped away and engaged in a terse conversation on his comm. He spun around to face Mark. "You have any hazardous biomaterials in here?"

They stood eye to eye. Mark judged they were about the same age, but the armor looked intimidating.

"Nope," Mark said, a little too quickly.

"Now that's a bald-faced prevarication, Captain. What are you cooking up in here?"

"It's classified."

The sergeant patted the rifle nestled against his chest plate. "I'm positive this gives me all the clearance I need."

"The XB on the door stands for Xenobiology—synthetic biology."

"And that's the study of...?"

"Creating synthetic life."

"Is it dangerous?"

"Could be."

"How?"

Mark blurted out his stock explanation. "DNA is vulnerable to viruses, ultraviolet light, nuclear radiation, chemicals and a host of other agents. XNA-based organisms aren't."

"Synthetic life, huh? Like...AIs and cyborgs—with military applications?"

"Hmm." Mark shrugged.

"Supersoldiers?" The sergeant scoffed. "Well, hell, Captain, I *am* a supersoldier." He burst out laughing.

The lights stopped flashing red. A steady green light filled the room. The PA system crackled with static, then blared, "All clear! This is an all-clear announcement. The threat has passed. All clear!"

"Yes!" Mark's fight-or-flight feeling ebbed, replaced by a euphoric giddiness.

"All right, Captain." The sergeant donned his helmet. "Let's get these injured out of here." He squatted in front of Scarlotti, and in one fluid movement lifted the armored soldier and slung him around his shoulders, fireman-style. "You get her."

Mark gazed at the plump middle-aged doctor lying on the workstation and didn't know which part to grab first. He picked her up and carried her in his arms as the sergeant had done.

"Follow me," Von Radach ordered from the hall, hurrying toward the stairwell.

"Wait, the lift is the other way."

"It's out of commission."

Mark turned the corner, stopped in his tracks. "Holy…what happened here?" Several feet away, three masked terrorists were splayed out in the hall. No armor covered these bodies. Copious amounts of blood and tissue lay splattered and smeared on the walls, the floor, and even the ceiling.

"We ordered them to surrender. They refused."

Trying not to disturb the scene, Mark clutched Dr. Coulter tighter, rushing to catch up with the sergeant as he entered the stairwell. The door hung askew. Scorch marks emanated from a central blast point inside the landing. Two more masked bodies littered the floor. Mark stood still, paralyzed at the sight. These were missing some limbs. This was a bloodbath, with bone fragments everywhere. He remembered hearing the explosions. Now it was real. Everything. Terrorists had attacked his workplace. He was wading through blood and death. Sweat oozed from every pore on his skin. Mark braced himself and swallowed past a wave of nausea.

"Captain…one step at a time…careful with your Dr. Coulter…"

Mark shook his head. He spotted the sergeant looking up at him from the middle landing.

"Wha—Right. I'm good." Slowly, he maneuvered around the carnage, descending one footfall at a time, regaining his composure as he went. At the bottom, an armored soldier with a rifle stood guard inside the ground floor door. He kept an eye on them as they descended the last half flight of stairs. Mark followed the sergeant through the hall into the lobby where a medical triage area was already in place.

Two Terran military medics rushed toward the sergeant. Their uniforms were pale gray full-length ballistic-proof bodysuits bearing chest insignias of a red caduceus surrounded by a circle of gold stars. After lifting Scarlotti from Von Radach's shoulders, they laid him on a hover gurney, removed his helmet, and attached a medical halo to his skull.

Another medic, an older, white-haired man, approached Mark with his arms outstretched. "I can take her, Captain," he said.

Mark gazed at the poor little pudgy doctor in his arms and tightened his grip. He tried to swallow, but couldn't. He didn't even know if she was still alive. What was he going to do if she died in his arms? He hugged her against his chest as if she were a child. He couldn't let go. A firm hand touched Mark's shoulder, a familiar gesture, something much like his brother would have done. He turned his head. The sergeant was there instead.

"Captain, this is Major Torance," he said. "He's our best combat doctor, and he's going to take your friend now." The sergeant helped ease the woman's body out of Mark's grasp and into the doctor's waiting arms. "Okay, now come with me. We need to get you checked out."

Von Radach escorted him into a small conference room off the lobby, where Mark recognized numerous colleagues, also being treated by medics. They placed a medical halo over his forehead, gave him injections to counteract dehydration, and a stimulant for mental clarity. While this happened, he was debriefed—interrogated—and his vital signs no doubt recorded. The momentary confusion he'd experienced earlier evaporated. Mark recounted the day's events, step by step, in vivid detail, since the alarms had sounded. Death and destruction had shattered his nice quiet corner of the Canadian backcountry.

When he finished, Mark's head throbbed with anger and the overwhelming urge to break something.

***

"How goes it, Ohashi?" Von Radach stood beside his squad's cyber corps Intel specialist. She sat on an overturned box in the middle of the facility's server room. Unlike other female soldiers, Ohashi wore a bobbed haircut, shorter in the back, angled toward the front, with bangs framing her Asian features. Her fingers danced across the keypad, eyes glued to the lines of code streaming down the screen. She had accessed the CAMRI installation's mainframe, focusing on analyzing, deciphering, and searching for anomalies.

"Well, Sergeant, they've definitely been hacked. Oooh, and sneaky, too. A targeted attack from the outside got past the firewalls. That's what shut them down, however, it seems they were also hit with a passive attack from the inside. It's going to take a while to figure out who, or where it originated, but I'm working on it." She rubbed her hands together, wiggled her half-gloved fingers above the keypad, and began again in earnest.

"You keep this to yourself, Ohashi. I'll be back with the lieutenant."

Axel returned to the lobby, mulling over the last bit of news. Espionage wasn't new to him. If a corporation or a foreign government used an electronic device to steal data, it was deemed an act of cyberwarfare. Period. Always quicker and easier to pirate the tech, only this time, they were stealing classified military secrets. The right technology would be worth lots of money. Money equaled power. The mega power belonged to the Terran Space Command. They controlled almost everything from the ionosphere up: the giant space station, the military space dock, the shipyard. In addition, the military had colonized

Mars—with a domed city, underground bases—and a spaceport. What tech in this small, obscure facility could be so important people would kill and die for it? Who did they have on the inside? *Spying? Sabotaging?* Now that was *treason.* And a whole different ball game.

Axel spotted the doctor. "Sir, any news on Scarlotti?"

"Internal injuries. Don't worry. He's already on a shuttle back to base, along with one of Sgt. Russo's men.

"Any hostiles captured alive?"

"All dead, except one, and he might not make it."

"How many?"

"About a dozen—so far."

"Any site personnel casualties?"

"No, but a few injuries."

"I'll let the lieutenant know." Axel speculated the spy on the inside must still be alive. That person hadn't expected any resistance, either. Maybe he or she was still there.

Axel found the blond captain sitting against the wall in the conference room. He seemed angry. "Want to stretch your legs?"

Warren jumped up. "Where are we going?"

"I want you to show me around upstairs."

They retraced their steps back up to the second floor. All the bodies had been removed. Still, Axel watched as the captain looked away from the bloodshed.

"I'm hoping you can shed some light on a few things for me."

"If I can."

"An explosion and a firefight happened right around the corner from your lab here." They passed the open XB door, continued down the corridor, stopping in front of an undamaged open door labeled MNT. "What lab is this?"

"Molecular nanotechnology."

"And—"

"Nano. Little bitty things. Put a bunch together and you can make lots of stuff. However, since this is primarily an astrophysics research facility, the application probably has something to do with," Warren pointed skyward, "up there."

"Look, Captain—Mark—we've already played this game. Like what?" Axel leaned against the doorframe, crossed his arms, waited.

"I'm sure they were just kidding. *Terraforming*—you know—changing a moon or planet's atmosphere and surface into something habitual for humans. I heard them joking about terraforming."

"Back there, your door was locked," Axel said. "When I got here, this door was open. It hadn't been breached. I saw a large man in here, with his back toward me, dressed like the other terrorists. I ordered him to surrender. He turned and fired at me. He missed. I didn't. I checked for a pulse. That's when I noticed he'd fallen on a female wearing a lab coat. She turned out to be your Dr. Coulter. Can you offer any explanation as to why she was in here? With a terrorist?" Axel had been watching Mark grow more confused as the story unfolded.

Mark seemed thoughtful for a moment. "Not a clue."

"And why weren't the MNT people in their lab?"

Mark shook his head, baffled. "Don't know."

"Some things to think about. Right, Captain?"

After they had returned to the lobby, Axel located Monroe. "Sir," Axel said in a confidential tone. "You need to come with me. We have an update on their cyberattack."

The lieutenant cocked an eyebrow at Axel and the sergeant mouthed the word, "*Spy*."

"Lead the way, Sergeant."

Chapter 2

With all due expediency, a secure vid uplink had been established connecting the CAMRI office of Colonel Charles Saunier to the TMD Headquarters of General Eli Dimitrios, in Virginia. Every chair around the colonel's conference table held an officer, including both sergeants, who observed in silence.

Dimitrios, a sizable man, graying at the temples, with a salty disposition, addressed them from the vid screen. "Well, gentlemen," he started out slow, gaining speed as he went. "I gather this wasn't some low hanging fruit stand in the middle of town, so will someone tell me the who, what, why, when, and how one of our primo research installations was shot to shit today?"

Major Nathan Torance, an ER doctor and 25-year veteran, unfazed by Dimitrios's ire, began, "General, sir, the Medical Corps has recovered twelve deceased hostiles, plus one borderline. So far, they're all ghosts. We haven't been able to ID any of them, yet. We'll be able to do a more thorough exam back at the lab. On our side, we sent two TMD wounded back to base. No fatalities. The Canadians have three injured civilians. They've been transferred to the nearest trauma one facility. CAMRI's remaining personnel have been checked out medically and are undergoing forensic questioning. As to CAMRI's onsite security forces, they were apparently called into a fictitious meeting and the room was tranq gassed. Tranquilizer rendered them unconscious. Nontoxic. No long-term side effects. They're coming around now."

Monroe rested his clenched hands on the table. "Gen. Dimitrios, I have the unfortunate distinction, sir, of reporting that our cyber unit has conclusive evidence of a spy within the

CAMRI ranks. Very sophisticated passive system hacks from inside have been detected, coupled with the targeted attacks from the outside today, which shut down the entire installation. It's not yet determined whether this was corporate or enemy nation sponsored, but cyber has barely scratched the surface.

"Fortunate for us, they seemed unaware that attacking the server would trigger an alert in TMD Headquarters, which enabled us to scramble a tactical assault response within minutes. As yet, it's unknown, but doubtful, if any terrorists escaped. However, without a prisoner to interrogate, we can't determine what they were specifically after, and may not know until the spy—saboteur—is discovered. Then we have a dilemma, General. Do we apprehend immediately, or use surveillance to track them to the source? Only the people in this room have been made aware of this information."

"*Mon Dieu.*" The Canadian colonel looked ashen. "This is a nightmare. A Judas among us."

The lieutenant continued. "First, standard operating procedures mandate no electronics leave this facility. They're already being collected and tagged. Second, cyber needs data on every company doing business with CAMRI. And, third, the same goes for every employee—past and present—including any current personnel not here today. Everyone."

After the meeting, Monroe remained in the colonel's office, huddled in a corner with the doctor. He motioned for Axel to join them. "Sergeant, since this was your lead, you get to accompany the doctor here, to St. Vincent's Hospital in town so he can check on the three injured civilians we had shuttled over there earlier. Rank has its privileges, so the major shouldn't have any problems accessing these patients. Make sure to take a cyber with you to record their statements. And shed the armor; let's not frighten the locals any more than we already have."

***

The shuttle silently hovered above the hospital's rooftop. When its hatch opened, all three TMD figures dressed in gray ballistic-proof uniforms stepped out. Axel and Ricky Gutierrez, a cyber specialist, wore leg holsters with sidearms. Torance followed in a black dress hat with a silver braid detail and an imposing black cape. A cadre of hospital personnel stood shivering in the frigid air, waiting to escort them inside.

Axel accepted that he was the muscle on this mission. He enjoyed playing the heavy, for a chance to find out how this scenario unfolded. Torance had rank; he commanded the lead. Gutierrez was the tech, nothing more.

At the nurse's station, the emergency room's charge nurse greeted them with a tight smile, holding the charts and admitting paperwork.

"You've only given me data for two patients," Torance said, enunciating clearly, in case of a language misunderstanding. "We sent three patients." He held up the same number of fingers, supporting his claim.

"Oh no, sir. We have only two, you see," the nurse replied. "Come, I'll show you."

"Wrong," he insisted. "We sent three patients. You accepted three. Two men and a woman." He held out his tablet, pointing to the screen. "These are their IDs, the time they were delivered today, along with the names of your personnel who accepted them."

"No," she repeated. "We have only two."

The major's face had grown an angry red against his silver white hair. Tossing one side of his cape back, exposing his insignia and rank, he leaned toward the nurse. "Get the admitting ER doctor up here in the next thirty seconds, or I'll see to it your license is marked invalid and tomorrow you'll be reporting to work with the janitorial staff."

Axel and Gutierrez exchanged looks. They simultaneously moved up to flank the doctor, thereby enlarging their presence, blocking all movement.

The nurse rushed to the adjacent wall comm and pressed a button. "Dr. Bouchard, second-floor nurses' station, STAT!"

Axel had never seen the major act badass before. He liked it. Just for fun, he counted to twenty-nine before the ER doctor came running in, with the hospital administrator arriving on his heels.

"Your hospital has lost one of our patients," the major snapped, giving the newly arrived doctor no time to catch his breath. "Get the personnel in here who accepted our three patients earlier today."

"Please, *messieurs*, let us discuss this in my office." The administrator motioned with an outstretched arm. The entourage followed him into a richly furnished corner office. The staff seated themselves, now visibly nervous.

As the muscle, Axel assumed guard duty at the door.

Gutierrez stood shoulder to shoulder with the major as he glared at the civilians.

Three orderlies in blue scrubs scurried in, squeezing past Axel.

Again, Torance seized command of the questioning. "We offloaded three accident patients today." He pointed to a male image on his tablet. "Who accepted this one?"

The tall female raised her hand. "I did."

Torance thumbed up another male image. "And this one?"

"I got that one, sir," said the wiry older man next to her.

"And this woman?" Torance asked.

"I did, sir." The last man nodded.

The major turned to Gutierrez. "Record his statement."

"Does this hospital have a video or drone surveillance system?"

The administrator stood. *"Oui, monsieur*, both."

The doctor clamped a hand on his shoulder. "Since we've established you have indeed lost a patient, let's see where she went. *Cherchez la femme.* You may show Sgt. Von Radach to your security office now."

Axel laughed so hard on the inside, he could barely follow behind the administrator. Later, he would congratulate Torance on his performance. Now he concentrated on evaluating the administrator's body language. When he heard footsteps, he glanced back. Gutierrez was double-timing to catch up.

The small room housed a surplus of equipment, and numerous vid screens. Gutierrez shoved the hospital employee out of his chair and took over at the screen. Within moments, the cyber specialist had accessed the vid scene beginning with the patients being offloaded and taken into the hospital. The woman, Dr. Coulter, was placed on a hover gurney, and delivered to the ER. A swarm of activity ensued. Her gurney was next seen without a patient on it. Empty. She had disappeared.

The hospital administrator gasped. The security employee shook his head.

"Gutierrez, download every frame," Axel ordered. "Continue searching all the vids for anyone remotely similar leaving this hospital until you're current. *Cherchez la femme*—literally."

"And you two—" Axel pointed at the hospital staff. "Remain here as witnesses. Your statements will be needed."

Axel stepped outside and commed Monroe. "Sir, Dr. Coulter has disappeared. We're searching for when and how right now. In the event you decide to put out a warrant, you'll need to assign a cyber to do a full background data search, gather any personal items she might've left behind, including a vehicle. She's a civilian, so I don't think she lived in the housing on the grounds."

***

Mark Warren craved a drink—maybe two, more like three—and a nice quiet place to process all the shit that had happened today. After receiving clearance to leave the building, he jogged the chilly quarter mile to his quarters, laughingly referred to as *condos*. They served as housing for all the Terran military personnel stationed on the compound.

"Home sweet home," he said aloud. Once inside his small apartment, he headed straight for a special bottle of Canadian whiskey in the kitchen. He had two bad habits: he drank and he gambled. Right now he focused on the drink. He poured himself two fingers in a coffee mug and downed it. He bolted the door and wedged a chair against it, because now he was officially paranoid.

He wanted to contact his family, but decided to do it later. He took a quick shower, got out, then had a second drink. After pulling on jeans, a sweatshirt, boots too—just in case he had to escape another unforeseen catastrophe—he stretched out on the couch and began to unwind. The third drink smothered some of the raw nerves still lingering in his mind. Mark felt the effects of the jog, whiskey, hot shower. Normally, he'd have the vid on, or music, or he'd be on his tablet checking the stock market. Now he needed to think. In silence.

Dr. Beth Coulter. What an everyday, harmless name.

In hindsight, she'd been the shadow of a real person since day one. Jung called it, "owning your own shadow." Mark never had a point of reference for that phrase—until now. About a year ago, she'd walked into the XB Lab, right after Mark's previous partner, Dr. Suresh, whose specialty was organic electronics, left to work in the private sector. In research and development, many different scientific disciplines produced the finished product. CAMRI's directors believed it was time to combine Mark's work in Xenobiology with neuroscience; Dr. Coulter's specialty. The easiest way to create genetically enhanced humans or artificial intelligence was to start with biological intelligences and modify them, using artificially enhanced biological cells.

As a rule, Mark usually reserved an opinion about people, trying not to label anyone until he got to know them. Admittedly, he'd done a net search for her, and found she had stellar credentials. Plus he learned she spoke three languages, had an irreverent kind of humor, and drank coffee by the bucketful. They worked in the lab together, day after day, and little by little, they'd established a harmonious working relationship, as well as a personal friendship. When she had learned Mark was smitten with a woman he'd met in Paris, she started teaching him to speak French. Alas, Juliette was not meant for long distance relationships, and it had ended. Still, Beth had endeared herself to him and he'd grown to genuinely like her. The truth of the matter was, she'd hustled him. She'd deluded, mislead, sucker punched, and she'd scammed him. *Damn. Damn. Damn.* The question was... *Why?*

Sgt. Von Radach had been correct with his assumption of military applications for synthetic life. Except Mark was actually working on *upgrades*. The program had begun with interfacing applications for the replacement of lost limbs, restoration of sight, and other senses on injured soldiers. It quickly progressed. At last count, there were about 100 Terran military augmented human soldiers, or cyborgs, currently in existence. Half had been stationed on the orbital spacedock for the last six months. Another three squads had been discreetly intergraded through the auspices of the new Mars Military Command. Although not a secret, the military preferred to keep the introduction of these troops as low key as possible.

However, Mark didn't know if Dr. Coulter had compromised the XB lab's work. Or, maybe working in the XB Lab had been a way to get close to the Molecular Nanotechnology lab, since that's where the sergeant found her. Mark understood what his question had implied, but he wasn't sure if the sergeant had branded him guilty by association.

There was a knock at the door. "Captain Warren?"

Mark nearly fell off the couch. "Who is it?" He stood up, feeling light headed.

"Captain Eva Jackson, from the Nano lab."

Mark removed the chair from the door and opened it to greet the scientist; perky, pretty, bronze-skinned, wearing a pink anorak over her uniform.

"They finally released me." She kept glancing over her shoulder, as if worried someone was following her. "And by the time I got back here…well, could you come take a look…please, Mark? I knocked on every door. You're the first one that answered."

"I've had a hell of a day, Eva," Mark said. "Why don't you come in? Tell me what happened."

She spotted the bottle of whiskey.

"Sit down. I'll fix you a drink."

Eva sank into a chair, elbows on knees, cupping her head. "I think someone's been in my apartment."

"This will warm you up." He held out a mug and handed her a fuzzy blanket from the couch. "Now start from the beginning."

"We were all in the Breakroom for Walter's birthday when the sirens went off, and the doors were locked." She took a sip and made a face.

"It's medicinal. Drink it."

"I thought…anyway, I was really scared and just kept praying until it was over. I was so glad when the soldiers showed up and took us downstairs. They separated us. I swear they gave me SP-27, they put a halo on me, and I was interrogated. Interrogated! They asked me questions about Dr. Coulter—who I hardly know. I haven't eaten all day, except for a piece of cake. When they finally let me go, I got home, and it looked like somebody had been in my place. Now I'm scared to go back there alone." She put the cup to her lips, taking a big gulp.

"Isn't SP-27 experimental?"

"Yeah, and they experimented on *me!*"

"How did you feel?"

"I remember feeling like I wanted to choke somebody. And that's not like me."

"Well, shit. I probably got a dose, too."

"Really? Still, that doesn't make me feel any better."

"Okay, let's get back to why you think someone's been in your place."

She had a sheepish look on her face. "You're going to think I'm silly."

"I have a sister. Her middle name is silly. I've heard it all, believe me." He nodded, smiling, trying to put her at ease.

"I'm pretty sure I saw fresh nicks around the edges of the keyhole…for real."

He cocked his head, studying her, and sensed this was important.

"I'm single, five-foot-two, probably weigh only half of what you do. When I got transferred up here, my brother made me promise I would always 'be aware' of my surroundings."

"All right." He stood to put on his jacket. "Wait a sec…I might need something." He rummaged through the coat closet, grabbing a hockey stick. "Now we can go."

"It's around the corner, the last one on the left." Eva let Mark lead but stayed only a step behind.

Mark slowed his approach, peering around the corner. A figure in a dark coat walked away from them. Something about him seemed out of place. Mark sprinted toward her quarters. The door stood ajar a few inches. He called after the man. "Hey! Wait up!" Then in French, "Hey! *Attendez-vous!*"

The man bolted. The race was on.

Mark sprinted after him with long, powerful strides. Within seconds, they both cleared the building. They ran on frozen ground, heading toward the dumpsters and the woods beyond. A couple more seconds at full speed, and Mark finally got close enough to lash out with the hockey stick. He hooked him around the neck with the blade.

The man fell.

Mark dove headfirst, arms outstretched, like heading for home base. He landed on top of him and they rolled with the impact. Mark swung a solid blow to the man's solar plexus. A gut of granite. It didn't faze him. That's when Mark glanced up.

A ski mask.

He snatched it off with his left hand and threw a blazing right cross to his opponent's bare face. *What the hell?* The second blow didn't faze him either. That last rush of adrenalin blinded Mark to the gun pointed at him.

A glint of black metal. A flash of red energy. Pain. Mark was hit. Pure white-hot pain. He rolled off his opponent toward the dumpsters and grabbed his side.

The man sprang to his feet and sprinted away into the woods.

Eva Jackson came running up from behind him, hollering, "Are you all right? Oh, my god...you're bleeding."

Chapter 3

Mark opened his eyes. Things were fuzzy for a moment. He became aware of a medical halo on his forehead. *Again? And where is my shirt?* The image of a silver-haired man with faded blue eyes and a ruddy complexion came into focus.

"Ah, Sergeant," the doctor said. "Your hockey player is coming around."

The face of Sgt. Von Radach floated into view. "Captain, congratulations! You scored a goal. Got a little banged up doing it, but it still counts. Who knows, you might even get a battlefield promotion out of it." The sergeant burst into laughter, flashing a mouthful of white teeth.

"Having nightmare...need to wake up." Mark tried to move. Pain shot through every nerve ending in his body. It hurt to breathe. He opened first one eye then the other. "Where am I?"

Maj. Torance, the same doctor from CAMRI, now dressed in blue scrubs, responded, "You and Capt. Jackson were taken into protective custody. We shuttled you back to our combat support hospital on the Terran Military Command Base in North Dakota."

"Is she—"

"Yes, she's fine, and worried about you."

"Can I—"

"Yes, you can see her, as soon as we're finished here."

"Everything hurts...my hand—"

"We'll get to your hand later, Captain. Right now we're dealing with your left shoulder. It's dislocated, and you have a grazing wound on your ribcage, around number seven, also left side. Second-degree burns. We'll take care of it in a minute. First I have to do this." Torance snapped his fingers and Sgt. Von

Radach body-slammed Mark, pinning him to the gurney. In an instant, the doctor had rotated his left shoulder blade, performing a spontaneous relocation.

"Oh, shit! That hurts!"

"Just a little scapular manipulation." The doctor chuckled. "Now we're going to do a couple of these." He injected Mark with a cocktail of medical nanites, pain meds.

"That better not be more SP-27. I've already had my dose for the day."

"Check your contract, Captain. It's all legal." The doctor smirked as he moved to the other side. "This is where you were shot. You were lucky. A little closer and it would have done a lot more damage." He sprayed the flesh wound with antiseptic, applied a dressing. He nodded at the sergeant, who helped Mark sit up on the gurney so the doctor could adjust a sling around his left side.

"My hand?" Mark raised his right hand, focusing on the translucent cast from fingertip to forearm. "What's wrong with my hand?"

The doctor studied Mark's face intently. "You hit your opponent. Fractured the fourth and fifth metacarpal bones."

"I saw his face!"

"We were waiting for that, Captain." The sergeant smiled. "Deering, you can come in now."

A young cyber unit specialist, dressed in fatigues, with black, spiky, green-tipped hair, drifted into the room. She carried a vid tablet, a handful of wires, and electrodes.

Mark felt woozy. He couldn't help staring at her emerald-colored hair. "Is that regulation hair color?"

"For me it is," she murmured, approaching him. "And is this regulation body art?" She traced her index finger over the intricate tribal tattoo encircling his right bicep.

"My brother and I got them before he went to Europa."

Everyone knew there were no survivors of the Europa mission, so she changed the subject. "I'm sorry, Mark...I can call you Mark, can't I? My name is Petra. Now, hold still while I attach these little beauties to your medical halo...and each one of these to your chest." She backed up about three feet. "Then I'll hook these pins into my screen...now you and I are going to create a 3-D holographic image of your attacker, and I'm going to record it on my screen."

"Is this safe?" Mark felt queasy. "I mean they've just shot me full of drugs and nanites?"

"I promise I'll be gentle." She winked at him. "Now lay back, close your eyes and visualize the first image that comes to mind."

***

Axel and the doctor watched the empty space between Petra and Mark. Within seconds, a hazy cloud coalesced, suspending in midair, it fused into a foot tall rear view of a man wearing a dark knee-length coat, with the collar turned up.

"Very nice, Mark. Now...let's get a little closer."

The image shimmered like desert heat while it grew life-sized.

"Good, Mark. Now...the contact."

A black and yellow hockey stick jutted into the image from the right side, its blade caught the man around his neck.

"And what do you see next...?"

The scene continued to play out as it had in real life, until exactly one nanosecond past the point when Mark grabbed the ski mask off the man's face.

"Stop!" the doctor ordered.

Petra's fingers moved over her vid screen as she enlarged the image, and manipulated it 360 degrees. The hologram gelled into the head of a bald man with Asian features. Mark remained dead still on the gurney, eyes closed, as if in a trance.

"Continue," the doctor ordered.

The incident resumed, showing the body blow, the right cross, and the ending moments after the shots were fired when Mark had lost consciousness.

"Slow–motion replay, with a close up of the assailant. Magnify five times." The doctor watched intently. "Again, with a close up of the assailant. Magnify ten times." Once more, the major scrutinized the hologram. "Thank you, we're finished here. And please send a copy of that footage to me. I'll need to forward it to HQ with my report."

Petra nodded at the major and the sergeant. She patted Mark on the shoulder. "Excellent, Mark. Thank you." She tucked the vid screen under her arm, unhooked all the wires, then left the room.

The doctor removed the medical halo, and helped Mark sit upright.

"I feel dizzy." Mark blinked, stared at the translucent cast. "I broke my hand."

"You hit a cyborg, Captain." Axel and the doctor carefully watched Mark's reaction.

"What?" Mark instantly became alert.

"And it's not one of ours," the doctor admitted.

"He was a…cyborg?"

"Yes, except we didn't know it until we processed the DNA from your hand and discovered it was synthetic skin. Not human. That's why we had you recall the event. To get up close and personal with your assailant. A lifelike combat model cyborg. He didn't breathe. He wasn't human. You've discovered the existence of a new enemy combatant, Captain. Since you saw him—he saw you. "

***

In a hospital room at the far end of the hall, with an armed guard outside his door, Mark finally found some peace and quiet. The sparse, pale green room housed two beds, but only one patient. Mark was hooked up to several machines; the most important one monitoring the progress of his nanites. The prevailing antiseptic hospital aroma floated about nose level. He couldn't find a comfortable spot on the bed. The sheets felt like sandpaper. Mark thumbed the remote to dim the overhead lights, pressed another to self-administer enough pain medication to take the edge off so he could relax and fall asleep. His head hurt, his hand, his side, his shoulder. Come to think of it, there wasn't anything not hurting. He needed sleep, and when he awoke in the morning, everything would be normal again. *No. It would not.* That was wishful thinking.

One day—that's all it had taken for his life to be turned upside down, again. The last time had been the day his family had received the news of his brother, Eric's, death on the Terran Space Command's mission to Europa. The distinction, this time, went to Dr. Beth Coulter. He began to cringe every time her name darted into his mind. Had she been a part of the puzzle, or was she the linchpin of the entire plot? To which, there was now the alarming addition of an Asian non-human cyborg. Could it be a prototype—an exemplar—or were there more? And how many? Did all of them have Asian features—that would certainly be indicative of their origin—or were they multiracial? Too much brain function—he had to shut down for a bit.

The cyber specialist cruised into his room. "Hey, Mark, remember me, Petra Deering? Just came to check on you. See how you're doing. Sometimes there's a delayed reaction to the neural interface. How do you feel?"

"I'm going to feel a little blitzed in about a minute." Mark smiled for the first time since this morning.

"Well, maybe—maybe not. Anyway, you've got company coming. Three nurses are on their way here. I accidentally let it slip that I worked on a real live Viking. Big, good-looking blond with Old World body art. I said the poor guy had a broken hand and a bad shoulder." She giggled. "From their reaction, I don't think they get to see many like you. So I doubt you'll get to feed yourself for the next couple of days. They'll probably want to hook you up to a catheter, too." She snickered. "Think I'll stay and watch."

"No, no. No catheter. I'd have to be unconscious. I'm feeling better already."

"Okay, but I'm not the one you have to convince. Besides, I brought you something." She moved closer, held up a small tablet with an earpiece, lightly placed them on his bare chest. "Thought you might like to listen to some sounds, not music, but waves and wind, outdoorsy stuff. You seem like the type. It might help you relax. Those neural interfaces can be a bitch. I've seen people jacked up for forty-eight hours or more after a session."

"Thanks a lot, Petra. Very sweet of you." Mark's cast caused him to fumble with the small device, but he managed. Soon the sounds of nature were floating through his mind. He closed his eyes. "Sounds like home."

"I thought so." She nodded, smiling. She glanced at the neural readout patterns on the screen next to his bed. "If you can't sleep, at least you can chill." She skimmed her finger over his tattoo. "I'll be back in the morning."

Deering passed the guard outside Mark's door. "Don't let any nurses in there. I don't care what they try to bribe you with."

***

The sergeant had wrestled with a gnawing, gut feeling all day. He kept trying to ignore it, but it wouldn't go away. He needed

27

to head for his quarters and finish his reports; instead he went looking for the doctor. Axel found him, alone at a table in the deserted mess hall, slumped over a cup of coffee. Axel brought a fresh one over, sitting opposite him. "Been a train wreck today, huh, sir?"

"Yes…and it's not over quite yet, Sergeant." The doctor looked up, pale blue eyes, now bloodshot, the day's aftermath a heavy weight on his shoulders. He reached over, and put a hand on Axel's arm. "I need to tell you Scarlotti didn't make it. There's no way to sugarcoat it. The blast impact was lethal. They tried like hell, but his injuries were too extensive; ruptured spleen, punctured lung, too much internal damage to repair. We can do so much more now. But we still can't bring them back from the dead. I'm truly sorry, son."

Axel's shoulders sagged under the shared burden of the news. A searing rush of anger grew in his chest. He wanted to jump up, grab the table, and throw it across the room. Anything except sitting here feeling lousy. However, they sat for a while without speaking, both staring at nothing. Axel stewed in a toxic combination of remorse and revenge, while the doctor clearly had despair and melancholy etched in the lines on his face.

"Both Scarlotti and I were from Phoenix," Axel said. "It's a big place. We didn't meet until he transferred into my squad last year. He wanted to be a soldier. And he was a damn good one. He could tell a joke. He loved country music. I feel like I let him down because I didn't do more to save him."

"Stop right there." The doctor slammed his hand on the table. "I understand all about survivor's guilt, but none of this was your fault—the terrorists did this. Everyone who wears armor acts like they're invincible. But no one is. We had him on a transport within minutes. They took him into surgery the moment he landed. His injuries were severe. He didn't survive. We're all headed in that direction. Some of us sooner rather than later."

"I hear you, Major. I understand, and I'll deal with it." Axel scraped his fingers back and forth though his short hair for a moment. "Here's the thing, sir, my enlistment ends in thirty-seven days. I was almost ready to re-up. I want—need—to be part of this operation. I heard Cyber's already calling it Black Hat, an old earth term for a bad hacker. I've been in law enforcement for eight years. Four here in the Tactical Assault Unit. Four in the Phoenix Police Force."

Axel paused, rubbed the stubble on his jaw and continued. "I have a friend who was in the NSA. He's been after me to join his company, a private investigation firm, sometimes bounty hunters, sometimes undercover corporate work. It didn't appeal to me, until now. If there's any way I could transfer, even if it's lateral, to another unit in the TMD, to work on this operation, I'd re-up in a second. I'd be in your debt, Maj. Torance, if you could speak to Colonel Harben on my behalf." Axel stood, as did Torance. They shook hands.

"I understand your motivation, Sergeant. I'll see what I can do."

"Thank you, Major." Axel saluted, waited for the doctor's nod. He left for his quarters.

***

Torance had been in an early, albeit lengthy meeting with the Base Commander, Colonel Wayne Harben. The major respected the colonel's rank, although he did not care for his heavy-handed style, believing it showed a lack of skill.

Two carafes of coffee, and a tray of blueberry muffins sat in the middle of their conference table. Also present were Monroe, the ranking officer of the previous day's Tactical Assault Group, plus his superior, Major Sydney Buchanan. Joining the officers were two support staff cyber specialists, Ohashi and Deering.

They supplied copies of all the pertinent vids, and statements, including the holographic images from Warren's encounter.

Harben elected to begin with facts; direct, clear, concise. Next, they dissected the personal histories, employment backgrounds of the three scientists, plus their own Tactical Assault NCO. The two cyber specialists were dismissed. Things got interesting when theories, hypotheticals, conjectures came into play. Torance offered candid medical opinions and perhaps a little practical psychology on the people in question.

After a rather contentious discussion, an agreement had been reached. Monroe got the short end of the stick on several counts; a suspected spy had disappeared, an officer had been attacked, and a member of his platoon had been killed. He was peeved at being overruled and outranked. A vid link was established with Dimitrios at TMD Headquarters. He was briefed. The general's rancor of yesterday settled into a smoldering rage now that the scope of this operation had widened to encompass three strategic theaters of operations: Combat, Scientific, and Cyber. He approved their decisions, promised to advise General Yates, Lunar Military Defense Command, of the situation. Furthermore, he would coordinate with all respective agencies, procure whatever resources were necessary to apprehend Beth Coulter and locate the as yet unidentified non-human combatant.

Torance and Harben left for the hospital to give the two scientists their new orders, while Monroe and Buchanan headed back to her office.

***

Mark felt embarrassed by all the attention the two nurses were showing him when Torance and a stocky, balding colonel breezed into his room.

"Ladies," the doctor said. "Will you give us the room, please?

And have Capt. Eva Jackson join us in here ASAP." He checked Mark's readouts. "And how do you feel this morning?"

Mark smiled. "My shoulder and side are much better than I expected. This is the first time I've experienced nanites. It's amazing." He raised his encased right hand. "Just can't tell what's going on in here."

"Well, I'm glad to hear it. Another day or so in the cast and you'll be better than new."

Eva Jackson rushed in. She stopped in her tracks at seeing two officers in uniform standing next to Mark's bed.

"Ah, Capt. Jackson, now that you're here we can begin. Please take a seat. I am Colonel Wayne Harben, Base Commander. I have a lot on my plate today, so I'll get right to it. In regards to the situation which unfolded yesterday at CAMRI, this is the sitrep. You both have new orders. These come straight from Gen. Eli Dimitrios at TMD Headquarters. As of this morning, for your own safety, both of you are being transferred out of the CAMRI facility. You will not be returning. All your personal items have been collected and are in storage. Before leaving here, you will requalify with sidearms and H2H combat training. You will also each be fitted with an ultra-high tech geolocator chip. It is classified Top Secret and you'll be monitored for your personal safety."

"And may I ask, General," Mark said, "are we being sent to Aberdeen or San Diego?"

"You're being transferred to Lunar Base 3."

"The *moon?*" Mark stared at him in total disbelief.

"Yes, Captain. Some people still call it that."

"But, sir, I have leave coming next week. My family is expecting me in Portland."

"All leaves have been canceled. This has officially been labeled Operation Pandora. We have a missing spy, dead terrorists, a dead Terran soldier, and non-human cyborg

31

combatants. Luna is the safest place for you both. Most of your time here will be spent in training and being debriefed before you're cleared for your new location. We own you, Warren, brain, body, and soul for the next five months and twenty-four days. If you're not careful, we can always add a stop on Mars to your itinerary. And when your tour is up you can get in the back of the line, waiting for a ride home. I hope that's clear enough for you." Harben turned smartly, breezed out of the room, leaving Mark and Eva in stunned silence, under the watchful gaze of the doctor.

"Oh, I'm so sorry, Mark. Please, please forgive me. I didn't mean for any of this to happen. It's all my fault…but aren't you excited about going to Luna?"

Chapter 4

The instant Axel received a commlink message to report to Buchanan's office, he became anxious, though he gave no indication of this on the outside. While he double-timed it to her building, he prepared himself for a denial of his request—but still hoped for the best.

Buchanan sat at her desk, looking busy with something on her vid screen. The walls of her small office held dozens of citations, awards and personal pictures of her with other officers. A small bookcase with antique looking, leather bound editions occupied the corner.

"Good morning, ma'am, Sgt. Von Radach, reporting as ordered." Axel held the salute.

Buchanan returned it.

"Well, Sergeant, it seems you have a Dutch uncle, who wears scrubs." She smiled, her eyes crinkled. "I don't know if this is what you wanted, but this is what you get." She stood, a tall, fit, green-eyed brunette. "Sgt. Axel Von Radach, as of this date you have new orders per Operation Pandora, whereas you will function as a security attaché to Capt. Mark Warren, for the remainder of his tour, which will be on Lunar Base 3. As a soldier of the TMD, you will be acting as an agent under the command of Gen. Yates, Lunar Military Defense. You will provide personal security detail safeguards with two primary missions: physical protection of the designated protectee, and reporting any evidence of crimes related to the CAMRI incident."

Axel fell speechless. Unaware he had been holding his breath, he exhaled and came to grips with the realization he would soon become one of the elite. A tour on Luna. More importantly, if it meant payback for Scarlotti, he'd follow this scientist all the way to Mars. "Thank you, ma'am." Axel gave her a genuine smile.

"Take a seat, please, Sergeant." She pointed to the only other chair. "Warren is recovering rapidly due to the nanite protocol. It is now your duty to see he requalifies with weapons and in hand-to-hand combat. We want him off Terra ASAP.

"Plus, we have an additional detail to work out regarding these security issues. A female, Capt. Eva Jackson, is another scientist from CAMRI also being transferred to Luna. She will need a female attaché. Is there anyone you know of who possesses the skill-set required to be your counterpart?"

"Yes, ma'am, I do," Axel responded. "Sergeant Kamryn Fleming, another one of. Monroe's people."

A deep, guttural sound erupted from behind Axel. He spun around to see Monroe standing in the background with a sour look on his face.

"Oh, good morning, Lieutenant…sir," Axel remarked, hoping it sounded sincere.

"Sergeant," the major said, dismissing the intrusion with a wave of her hand. "How long have you known her?"

"A little over three years, ma'am. I believe she started out as DEA in Vancouver, then transferred to an undercover unit. I can personally attest to the fact she's proficient in weapons and self-defense."

"Aha. And your relationship with her would be…strictly professional?"

"Absolutely, ma'am. You need to meet her."

***

Axel found Mark, sitting in a timeworn overstuffed chair in the hospital's institutional green Dayroom, looking miserable. There were no nurses anywhere. *Must be a shift change.* First time seeing him without any women hovering around, Axel had to admit he felt a bit envious. Because Mark was muscular without working at it. That and blond. The guy must exude the pheromones that acted as an aphrodisiac on women. The nurses must have been hiding his shirt because he wasn't even wearing it—or the sling; only drawstring olive scrub pants.

"Captain, I'm glad to see you're up and around."

Mark looked up. "Why aren't there any windows in this place?"

"We're underground."

"The whole base?"

"Most of it."

"Why?"

"That's classified."

"Touché."

Axel tried getting back on point. "Guess you've gotten your orders, right?"

"Um-hmm."

"Well, I'm going to make your day."

"How's that?"

"I'm going with you."

"Oh. Hell. No." Mark looked incredulous.

"Oh, hell, yes. I'm your wingman, Captain, till your tour ends."

"Same nightmare—different episode." Mark sprawled more out of the chair than in and stared up at the ceiling, dejected.

"And guess what? I'm in charge of making sure you qualify in close quarter combat and weapons. Training starts tomorrow. Zero seven hundred hours. When you went through basic, they should have given you a sidearm."

"No. I went through a basic officer leadership course. I'm a scientist. They didn't issue a gun to me."

"Well, you're getting one now. Can you shoot?"

"Yes. I grew up in the Pacific Northwest. I hunted."

"Deer?"

"No. Pheasants and ducks. *Not Bambi.*"

"Weapons?"

"Winchester and Remington, 12-guage."

"Old school."

"They require a greater degree of precision."

"Can you field strip a sidearm?"

"Will there be a test?"

"Yes."

"No. You don't understand. I can't go to the moon—*Luna.*"

Axel detected a tone in the captain's voice indicating a real problem. He'd heard that tone—dread—in soldier's voices before.

"All right, let's find a quieter place to talk." He helped Mark up, escorting him back to his hospital room. Mark slumped on the bed, while Axel took the chair. "For right now, how about we're not Captain and Sergeant? Just Axel and Mark having a conversation."

With his left hand, Mark picked at the crease in his scrub pants. The base laundry pressed creases in everything except underwear. Mark's words came out slow. "My brother, Eric, was a couple of years older than me. And fearless. Never afraid of anything. He enlisted in the Terran Space Command. An astro engineer. He volunteered for the Europa mission." Mark paused. "They didn't make it there. And they didn't make it home. Mom took it hard. Very hard. I'm not fearless. What if I go to Luna, and I don't make it home, either? Too many ifs."

"Okay," Axel said, nodding. "You told me why you don't want to go. Well, this is why I *have* to go. You remember the soldier I dragged into your lab? His name was Scarlotti. Well, he didn't make it. He died. Those terrorists blew up your facility, tried to kill you, and did kill him. So, you and Capt. Jackson are being sent to Luna to keep you safe. If they come for you again, Mark. I've got your back. I owe them."

Axel stood. "Wait a second...after everything you experienced yesterday, Mark, you didn't think twice about helping your coworker. You saw a guy and ran after him. Tackled him. And fought him. In hindsight, it doesn't seem like you thought about it much. I've seen soldiers who trained hard for combat—and then froze when it came time to step up. You didn't freeze. So, I'm pretty sure Capt. Jackson thinks *you're fearless.*"

Axel placed a firm hand on Mark's right shoulder. "Consider that why don't you?"

***

In a corner of the base's cavernous, impressively outfitted fitness center, Buchanan stood flanked by her two sergeants dressed in black running togs, newly appointed as trainers. They faced the two captains, identically outfitted, and newly downgraded to trainees.

"We're under a time constraint here, Captains. Beginning this morning, if you are not sleeping, eating, or in the latrine, you will be engaged in physical activity, or one-on-one personal training, all designed to make you proficient in defending yourselves. For weapons training, you'll begin practice on a holo simulator. Hopefully, you'll almost be an expert by the time you reach the live fire exercises at our indoor shooting range. Because of the nature of this operation, you will dispense with addressing each other by rank. Might as well get comfortable with each other on a first name basis. You'll be eating and sleeping in close quarters soon enough." Buchanan paused, listening to a comm message. "Carry on." She spun, jogged off toward the nearest exit.

Mark stared at the pair of sergeants in front of him. They looked like bookends. Standing side by side, Sgt. Kamryn

Fleming was tall, exotic looking, almost Sgt. Von Radach's female twin, except with unmistakable curves under her body-hugging togs. Both had dark, piercing eyes. She had chocolate brown hair, in what he surmised was the latest style popular with most female combat troops; buzz cut sides, spiky on top. Von Radach maintained his scruffy look with close-cropped hair and a short stubble beard. Apparently, male tactical assault NCOs couldn't spare the time to shave.

Their trainers started Mark and Eva out with stretches, then one full rotation through the circuit training course, followed by a timed one-mile jog around the inside track. Eva didn't say a word, so Mark didn't either. He would not be trumped by a woman half his size, regardless of his dislocated arm, broken hand, and a flesh wound. Although at the end, he was gasping and dripping with sweat.

There were at least a hundred other people working out, however, no one acknowledged their presence. Leaving him to wonder if they had been marked with a 'do not disturb' sign. Maybe this was normal, or not. Either way, it felt disconcerting.

Next came an hour in the holo simulator for weapons training. Mark used his left hand, privately vowing to become ambidextrous.

When they broke for lunch, Mark and Eva felt too exhausted to eat, while their trainers, the *Evil Twins*, polished off the caloric intake of two starving teenagers.

Back in the gym, Fleming took the lead. "The next facet of your training is comprised of moves that are down and dirty. They are do or die moves. These are the dirtiest and most effective H2H combat moves that will save your lives." Their afternoon was spent with instructions in elbow strikes, eye gouging, knee strikes, groin stomps, throat punches, collar grab choke holds, back kicks to wherever, and lastly—the fingers in the mouth, while not being bitten.

The end of their first day came none too soon. Fleming addressed them both. "Today was to get you limbered up. Your real training starts tomorrow. Here. Zero seven hundred hours. I suggest you eat a hearty meal and hydrate sufficiently. If not—tomorrow will not go well for you—and you will not be excused from class because you didn't follow these instructions. Warren, please report to Maj. Torance on your way out. If your cast is removed this evening, I'm told he will be clearing you for full H2H combat training in the morning."

Von Radach had a devious gleam in his eyes, and a smug grin on his face. Axel had allowed the new sergeant to take the lead, while he'd been helpful, even encouraging to Eva today. Mark decided they were playing the "Good sergeant/Bad sergeant" routine. Tomorrow they would probably reverse roles.

"I feel ready to drop—except energized, too! You know what I mean?" Eva's big smile lit up her pretty, bronze face. "I'm going to grab a quick shower and head to the dining hall. Do you want to meet me there?"

"You go ahead, Eva. I need to see about my cast." Exhausted, Mark wandered the maze of corridors. He had to ask for directions twice. He eventually found Torance's office. The doctor wasn't there, but his schedule was posted outside on the wall. Mark set out again, and ran smack into him a few minutes later.

"Well, Captain, it's good to see you up and around. I hear you started PT today. Follow me. Let's take a scan of your hand. See how it's doing." The doctor led him into a small, industrial, green exam room smelling of cleaning agents. He spent several moments passing a small, handheld scanner around Mark's translucent cast, pronounced him healed, and removed it. Mark flexed his fingers, testing the nanite's work.

"I have a few more things for you, too. First, where do you want this?" The doctor held an injector.

"What is it?"

"Vaccinations for almost everything. Can't have you spreading Terran germs up in space."

"Well, I sure don't want it in my butt."

"Actually, that's the best place. Don't be a baby."

Mark groaned, hooked his thumbs in the back of his pants, and bared his bottom.

The doctor injected Mark with a cocktail of biomeds, one shot in each gluteus maximus.

"Okay, now for your geolocator. These were specifically designed for you and Capt. Jackson. Your DNA has been incorporated in them, so they can't be copied or duplicated—again for your protection." He popped the tiny silver device out of its blister pack, loaded it into the injector, and shot it directly through the skin behind Mark's right ear lobe.

It stung like hell. Mark rubbed it gingerly. "I wish I hadn't found you."

The doctor grinned. "We have an excellent cyber unit here. They'll be monitoring you twenty-four/seven while you're off-world. Don't feel like you're being singled out. It's standard operating procedure. Terran military's done this many times before with high-value protectees—and operatives."

"Does this happen often?" Mark resented being 'chipped' and watched like a prisoner while he was forcibly remanded to a big rock 240,000 miles above the planet of his birth.

"Well, we don't yet have world peace," the doctor lamented, "or universal justice, so we do what we can to move toward the betterment of humankind."

"So, yes. It happens often." Mark shook his head. "Have you ever been to Luna, Major?"

"Yes, a couple of years ago. I did a six-month rotation."

"Your impression?"

"I've lived on this planet far too long to be comfortable off-world."

"I hoped for a more objective opinion."

"It wouldn't be fair to influence your perceptions."

"You just did."

The doctor shrugged, turned away.

Mark switched to a different topic. "Does anyone know why the cyborg was in Capt. Jackson's apartment? It must have been searching for something. It has to be connected to what happened earlier at CAMRI and Dr. Coulter, right? Have they found her? Have they found—it?"

"That part of the operation is still being investigated. It's coming together. We don't have all the pieces. My involvement is mainly related to the injuries and fatalities. You'll both be briefed before you leave for Luna." The doctor passed the scanner over Mark's hand again, his shoulder, and side wound. He nodded, admiring the nanite's recuperative properties.

"You're better than new. One hundred and ten percent. I'll forward your release for H2H combat to Maj. Buchanan." The doctor's pale blue eyes shone as he added, "Say, I heard Sgt. Fleming's part of the team now. She's a peach, isn't she?"

"Yes, a real 'class A' peach."

***

Mark heaped his plate with protein, carbs, a milk, a juice, plus two large glasses of water. He went back for seconds. Flushing the meds and nanites out of his system, getting back to feeling healthy again became his number one priority. He tried, but couldn't remember if he'd ever been ordered to do something he didn't want to do. Maybe that's why he was having such a hard time now. He was intelligent, resourceful, and clever. He'd find a way to get through this the best way possible.

Eva spotted him in the dining hall. "Oh, Mark, I'm glad I

found you. We have new quarters. They're not far from the fitness center. Real convenient. Not as nice as CAMRI, but not too bad. Are you ready? Do you want to go see them?"

He followed her to the new room, agreeing it was no-frills acceptable. A single bed that housed storage compartments underneath, vid screen built into the opposite wall over a fold-out desktop with an integrated keypad, a double-wide locker with bottom storage, plus a small private bath. It would do for a few days. The clothes were a nice touch. Neat piles of olive drab underwear, black running togs lay on his bed, with the correct size boots, three uniforms in the locker. No name or rank on the uniforms—he must be going incognito. Were Eva's the same?

Mark showered, then decided to hit the sack early. He fell asleep thinking of his family. He needed to let them know his leave had been canceled. Aside from getting up to pee twice, he slept like he was in a coma. The best night's sleep he'd had in a while.

His alarm went off at zero six hundred. Mark showered again, dressed in black running togs. He finished a healthy breakfast of six eggs on wheat toast, a bowl of oatmeal, milk, and a glass of juice with ten minutes to spare by the time he arrived at the fitness center. Eva zipped in right after him.

The sergeants appeared in tandem, perfect physical specimens reeking of superiority. As Mark suspected, Axel assumed the lead. Their day began with stretches, a cycle through the Circuit Training course, and a one-mile jog around the inside track. Eva seemed slower her second day. Mark felt lighter and faster. It might be the endorphins, so he didn't overdo it. He worked up a sweat to flush any remaining toxins from his body.

Weapons training in the holo simulator came next. Mark's score increased, even splitting the time between his right and left hands, continuing to work on becoming ambidextrous with the weapons. His sidearm field strip session went much better without the cast. Mark smiled to himself, feeling this morning had improved over yesterday.

They broke for lunch. Mark focused on protein and carbs with plenty of liquids. He remained quiet, preferring to observe Eva and the sergeants. More than once he caught Axel studying him. For exactly what, he didn't know, although he had a feeling it wouldn't be good.

After lunch, Mark and Eva were directed to an area in the gym with mats on the floor. Mark felt the end coming—this was it.

Axel began, "This particular style of H2H combat is designed to keep you alive. It's not a sport. It's an art. If you're attacked, assume they mean to kill you. You need to learn how to survive and control dangerous situations. The primary purpose of these aggressive moves is to deliver a maximum amount of damage, fast. We will show you offensive and defensive techniques. They do not require long-term training. Are easily recalled under stress. And extremely effective in life-threatening encounters when a weapon or reinforcements are not available. They will become reflexive. You will create conditioned reflexes and you will act and react without thinking. We can teach you the skill set and the mindset. The most important part is—you have to be willing to use them." He tried grinning. It came out as a smirk. "Besides, if you 'accidentally' clock somebody, don't worry. We'll take care of it."

Mark and Axel faced each other, an arm's length apart. They were both over six feet tall with muscular builds. Mark averaged around 185 pounds.

Okay, maybe one ninety after pizza and beer.

He estimated the sergeant weighed a good twenty pounds more due to his muscle mass. He glanced over at Eva. She was David to Kamryn's Goliath; shorter by eight inches, lighter by 60 pounds.

"Protect yourself," Axel warned.

Mark quickly adopted a classic boxer's stance, leading with his left. He didn't know what was coming, but the look in Axel's eyes meant he wasn't going to like it.

Axel sank to a crouch with his feet apart, lunged with arms wide. He grabbed Mark slightly above the knees, lifting him a couple of inches, scooped his left leg around Mark's right leg, throwing him off balance, pushing him backward to the ground. Axel landed on top of him like a hungry lion, with his left arm over Mark's throat—all in two seconds flat.

"Well, that was fun," Mark grunted. "You've been waiting to do that all day?"

Axel offered Mark a hand getting up. "I warned you. This is not a game. This is serious as hell—to keep you alive if there's another attempt on your life, or hers." He jerked his thumb toward Eva.

"I'll show you how to do what I just did." Axel dissected his move. They reversed roles. That's how the training went for the rest of the day. A new move. Break it down. Reverse rolls. Point—and counterpoint. After spending five hours working on five, simple moves, they called it quits.

The next three days became a blur of exhaustive physical repetition. Building muscle, speed, stamina, self-confidence, and conditioning reflexes to prepare for the unexpected.

Chapter 5

On his seventh day of living underground, without breathing fresh air or seeing the sky, Mark arose, showered, and dressed for another grueling round of combat training. He opened the door, to find Axel leaning against the frame.

"Follow me, Sleeping Beauty."

"Where are we going?"

"To Col. Harben's office. We got new orders—we're leaving today."

"*Today?*" Mark's self-confidence evaporated in the blink of an eye. He started to break out in a sweat. He'd gotten sidetracked in the physical aspect of training to go off-world, and had neglected the psychological preparation. He had known this day was coming. He needed more time. "I'm not ready."

"Doesn't matter. It's an order. You don't have a choice. Don't think about it. Just do it. You're good at that."

Mark should have had something to eat first. No—maybe not. Could make him nauseous.

Kamryn and Eva were waiting for them as they rounded a corner. Eva was practically bouncing up and down. "I'm so glad to be leaving here. I can't wait to get back to work. I wonder what kind of labs we'll have up on Luna."

"Don't ask questions, or you'll regret it," Axel warned.

"Yeah, I learned that one the hard way. The colonel makes one hell of a first impression," Mark said. He remained pensive for the remainder of their trek to the far side of the underground base to the commander's office.

Harben sat behind his desk with his fingers steepled. The only other two chairs in his office were positioned at forty-five degree angles at each corner of his desk. Buchanan and Torance occupied them. The captains were ushered in to stand side by side between the majors. The two sergeants stood flanking them.

"Well, now that everyone is finally here," Harben snapped. "We can begin." He produced a small tablet with an earpiece and a data chip and placed it on his desk in plain view. "Capt. Jackson, can you tell me what this is?"

"My music—Sir." Eva grinned.

"No. It is not."

Her face fell. "But—"

"This data chip had massive amounts of Classified Terraforming research from your Nano lab on it. As well as Classified Advanced Cybernetics research from the Xenobiology lab. Not music, by any means. Do you know how this happened?"

"No, sir," she gasped.

"Lucky for you, the DNA found on this data chip belongs to the fraudulent Beth Coulter. The CAMRI servers were indeed hacked. It was likely a ploy to detract from the real reason she was in the Nano Lab with this chip and a terrorist. She must have been in a hurry to hide this. The cyborg was probably looking for it in your quarters. If we had any evidence you were guilty of participating in this crime, you'd be spending the next twenty years in a military penitentiary."

Eva shriveled under the weight of Harben's allegations.

"Since all the terrorists died, interrogation wasn't an option. None of their prints were on file—anywhere. Their DNA is multiracial. All over the globe. TMD uses the planet's most sophisticated facial recognition, so a few have been identified as mercenaries. Others may have originated from remote areas and were never intentionally scanned by biometrics. Apparently, all were expendable. Maybe a distraction so the woman known as Beth Coulter could access data not stored on the servers. She didn't get it; that's the important thing."

Mark felt overjoyed at this news. He needed to brainstorm

with Eva to see where their research might have converged. Maybe they could figure out what she'd been after.

"We now have conclusive proof through the medical data and images we've been able to access that the woman at CAMRI was not the same Beth Coulter who graduated college. The change took place about ten years ago. We don't yet know who this imposter is. We also don't know where the real Beth Coulter is, whether dead or alive. She was an only child, born in London, never married, never had children. Both her parents are deceased, and they had no siblings. It seems a lot of effort went into locating the type of person who would be easiest to impersonate."

The profound sense of foolishness Mark had felt at being scammed by the imposter a.k.a. Beth Coulter faded. CAMRI had hired her, brought her into the facility, so they'd been hustled, first.

"The non-human cyborg is a different story. His facial features were duplicated. The original features are identical to David Wu, a popular Asian model." Harben paused, to roll his eyes. "His image is everywhere. He was on a photo shoot in Shanghai for a solid week while all this happened. If there are more of these machines, we can presume they, too, have duplicated features of real people.

"If we get any new information which directly impacts you or your research, you'll be briefed by Lunar Military Defense Commander, Gen. Yates," Harben concluded. "He's up to date on all the particulars."

Buchanan spoke up, turning the discussion to her jurisdiction. "I've monitored your physical H2H and weapons training—which will continue on Luna. Your deployment has been approved. You four will be on a shuttle for Virginia this morning. From there you'll board a Terran warship bound non-stop, straight for Lunar Base 3. This is where Capt. Warren and Capt. Jackson will complete their military service."

She took four small boxes off the edge of Harben's desk, handed one of each to Mark and Eva. "These are your new comm devices and tablets. You are not cleared to use them until you reach Luna. All your net use, and personal communications will be rerouted through military geosats, so if anyone's looking, it will seem as if your service is still originating in Canada. Do not let these out of your sight. Also, your lunar location is classified. All information pertaining to CAMRI, everything that has happened to you for the past week, is classified. You are not cleared to divulge it to anyone. Whoever these people are— they're not playing games. This is the reason we've kept you sequestered—for your protection. If Operation Pandora is resolved here on Terra, we'll let you know. In the meantime— stay safe."

Torance stood and smiled. "Everyone's passed their physicals. All four of your geolocators have been activated—and will be monitored for the duration of your time off-world. So you're good to go. *Bon Voyage.*"

***

Axel warned, "We'll be back to get you two in an hour. Don't eat a heavy breakfast, in case you puke. Make sure you go to the Latrine before we board. And don't sneeze after we're on board, either." The two sergeants walked off chuckling.

Mark could see from her forlorn expression Eva hadn't recovered from Harben's accusations. "Look, I'm sorry he gave you such a hard time. You didn't deserve it. I'm going to pack, then whip by the dining hall to grab a few energy bars. I'll get some for you, too. Meet me back here in an hour." He gave her a hug, and they parted.

He wasted no time in changing to a uniform and boots. After packing his meager possessions in a small duffle, he went in search of Torance. He hoped to persuade the doctor to give him something for acrophobia, claustrophobia, or for anxiety, afraid of having a severe stress-induced panic attack in full view of the whole universe.

He found the doctor in the first place he looked—the dining hall. Mark swung by the cafeteria line, snatched all six bars, plus two apples, and stuffed them in his duffle bag as he threaded his way over to where the doctor sat.

Torance was enjoying a breakfast of champions; pancakes swimming in syrup with heaps of bacon and fried hash brown potatoes.

"Good morning again, Major."

The doctor looked up from his plate, his white brows pinched together. He held a piece of bacon between the fingers of one hand and a forkful of dripping pancakes in the other. "Captain, to what do I owe the honor of your presence?"

"I need to ask a favor, sir."

The doctor devoured the food with both hands. He made a show of using his napkin. "What kind of favor?"

"I need something for anxiety, an SSRI or benzodiazepine."

The doctor stared up at Mark for an interminable moment.

Finally, Mark felt compelled to admit the reason he needed the medication. "It's not fear of flying. It's leaving the planet that's kicking my ass."

"If this stems from your brother's death off-world, you've waited a little too long to speak with a mental health professional, however, I could try to find a Chaplin."

Mark stiffened. "I don't need sanctimonious rhetoric, doctor. If this goes against your Hippocratic Oath, fine, I'll self-medicate." Mark spun around, aiming for the exit.

"Captain Warren."

Mark stopped, and looked back.

"Carry this." The doctor pointed to his plate. "Grab a tray and follow me." In silence, he strode through the dining hall, around corners, down deserted corridors, finally arriving at a small exam room. He unlocked it and Mark joined him inside. The doctor pressed his thumbprint onto the panel of a glass cabinet, opened it, removed a bottle, and shook out four tablets. He pulled open a drawer, took out a leather-encased flask, handing it and the pills to Mark.

"Take one now. If Jackson needs something, break one in half."

Grateful, Mark followed the doctor's instructions. The liquid in the flask tasted like brandy. He took another drink, handed it back.

"And deal with your problem, Captain. You'll find the doctors on Luna aren't nearly as obliging as I am. Now go catch your shuttle. Leave me to clog my arteries in peace." He picked up a piece of bacon and resumed eating.

"Thank you, Major." Mark checked his watch. He had ten minutes to make it back. He ran like his life depended on it.

***

Mark and Eva followed the two sergeants to an elevator, boarded it, and descended one level. They exited, turned right a few paces, then got on a moving walkway.

Mark tapped Eva on the arm, holding out a couple of energy bars, and an apple. "In case you get hungry," he whispered.

Eva stashed them in her pockets. She still looked like she'd been flogged.

After several minutes, they arrived at an enormous indoor hangar. It had floor sections marked off for a dozen vessels. Four spaces were empty. Their shuttle was one of the six remaining. They were identical. All the black transport-class shuttles displayed a red TMD insignia of eagle's wings surrounded by a circle of stars. They walked toward one bearing the tail number: N913. It was shaped like a boxcar with a slanted front, twin side nacelles, two torpedo tubes, and a side hatch. Imposing, but unattractive.

Eight other soldiers were already inside when they boarded, strapping themselves into the harness stations. Kamryn and Eva took seats on one side, Axel and Mark sitting opposite them.

Axel leaned close. "Don't worry, these things are pretty safe."

"Wiseass." Mark closed his eyes, practicing deep-breathing meditation. He remembered his first trip in a shuttle when he'd transferred from Virginia to CAMRI in Canada. No problems whatsoever. During the second trip, he'd been unconscious from Canada to North Dakota.

Without a sound, the shuttle maneuvered forward, swung left, floating out of the hangar. Moments later they cleared the tarmac, rose straight up, becoming airborne. The interior lights switched to dark blue, as did the twin glow strips on the floor. There was no sensation of ascending or speed. Smooth as glass. They cruised at 10,000 feet. In less than twenty minutes, they descended onto the tarmac of TMD Headquarters in Virginia.

Everyone filed out. The instant Mark's feet hit the ground, he took a deep breath. He did not smell the salty ocean, or any hint of nature; only ozone, trioxygen, and a sharp whiff of chlorine. Plus, he hadn't seen the sky in a week. This would be his last opportunity to experience the outdoors on Terra for the next six months—just his luck today was overcast. No blue skies. Gray as far as he could see. Mark felt gypped. To compensate, at least the first leg of the trip had been uneventful.

Axel led them toward two armed soldiers standing guard on either side of a door leading into an immense hangar. Their IDs were scanned and they were allowed to enter. Inside, all four of them paused to gaze at the impressive sight. Two rows of sleek, liquid silver spacecraft parked on pylons, tails to the wall, noses pointing toward the middle aisle. Mark estimated close to a couple of hundred maintenance crew milling about back in the hanger. All incoming personnel entered a metal barricaded walkway to a checkpoint manned by six, beefy-looking soldiers. Beyond them, two parallel rows, with the females directed down one side, males to the other. IDs were scanned again; they were fingerprinted and their DNA taken.

A few steps farther, they passed through a security system rivaling Fort Knox, with sensors that could detect bio, mech, and tech. Duffel bags were emptied, every item inspected, then locked in a clear bin. People were instructed to pass through an opaque decontamination chamber—in case you were ordered to disrobe for some unknown reason.

Behind them, a security violation set off a flurry of beeps. Everything stopped. Dead still. Mark almost stopped breathing. He felt paranoid—with good reason. The beeping ended. Laughter broke out. Mark started breathing. Things resumed.

The four joined up again after exiting the chamber and ushered to a holding area to await their flight. About forty-five others also waited. Some officers, mostly enlisted, with twice as many men as women. The sergeants stayed together, laughing, and joking.

Mark and Eva, not so much. She still wore a lost puppy expression. Mark began to think Harben might have done irreparable harm.

Damn, that pompous ass. Maslow's concept came to mind: *"When you're a hammer, everything else looks like a nail."* It indeed applied to the colonel. Eva had been so excited about going to Luna. Now look at her. He had to try to cheer her up, even if he regretted it later.

"Eva, once we land, and get processed, do you want to walk around the Base, get acclimated, maybe grab some dinner?"

"Really?" She looked up at him, a glimmer of a smile in her big eyes. "You would do that—with me?"

"Sure. We're partners. We have to stick together." Mark nodded toward Axel and Kamryn. "They are. So should we."

The PA system in their waiting area crackled with static. "Attention all TMD personnel traveling to Lunar Base 3. Boarding will begin in five minutes. Thank you."

Mark hardly had time to get nervous before eight soldiers appeared at the door, instructing the passengers to file into two rows. He and Eva paired off and were escorted onto a hover bus. It carried them to the far end of the hangar.

They got off in front of a spacecraft. A frighteningly beautiful warship. Arrowhead shaped, with a burnished silver hull, a sloped nose, and stub winged nacelles. Designed for a frontal assault, it bristled with six weapons to the fore, two in the aft section. Functional, yet aesthetically pleasing. It displayed sapphire blue Terran Space Command lettering, insignia, with the tail number: SS-N64.

Soldiers ushered everyone onboard. The officers were directed to seating in a forward cabin. The enlisted to the rear. Since the captains wore uniforms devoid of any rank or name tags, they were seated alongside the sergeants.

Flight crew members bolted the airlock hatch closed. Their uniforms were similar to the medics; pale gray full-length ballistic-proof bodysuits, bearing sapphire blue chest insignias of eagle's wings surrounded by a circle of stars. The same Terran Space Command uniforms like the one his brother, Eric, had worn.

A voice over the ship's comm announced, "Attention all TMD personnel. Harness up. One minute to liftoff." Again, all interior lighting dimmed to a soft blue.

The vessel moved without a sound, only a slight vibration. He realized he felt relaxed, not anxious or nervous. Maybe the doctor's medication had started to work. Good. He searched for the pills in his pocket. Found them, settled back, and tried to stay relaxed.

"You really do have a sister, Mark?" Eva asked in a small voice.

"Oh, yes. Her name's Gina. We grew up outside Portland, Oregon. My backyard was the Pacific Ocean, Columbia River, mountains, trees—lots of nature. Mom is a dentist. Dad is a child psychologist. So growing up, I was a well-adjusted kid with perfect teeth." He shook his head and chuckled.

"My brother, Eric, was two years older. My sister, Gina, is five years younger. I remember Grandma Hilde saying, 'That Gina, she's a real pistol.' The night before my senior prom Gina snuck into my room while I slept. She colored my fingernails and toenails with a red permanent marker. When I woke up, saw what she'd done, I tore through the house threatening to kill her. She ran outside, laughing, and screaming like a banshee. I was right behind her cussing like a sailor. Mom jumped in her car. Chased us down. Got between us, made Gina get in the car. She took Gina to grandma's for the weekend. When Mom came home, it took her hours to get that stuff off my nails. She never heard me cuss before. She didn't say a word. I don't think she ever told Dad.

"Anyway, Gina never wanted to go to college, like Eric and I did. She wanted to dance. Ballet. And she did—until she hurt her knee. That's when she went downhill. Sunk right into a black hole. Wallowed in it for a while. Then she went to rehab. When she came out, she opened a yoga studio. She loves it. She's happy again." Mark made a face, adding, "She's still a pistol." Mark had prettied up the story for Eva. The horrifying parts would remain forever untold.

"Oh, that sounds like so much fun—except for the sad part about your sister."

"Yeah, well, I could talk all day about the stunts Gina used to pull. What about you, Eva?"

"Me? My story's not anything like yours." Eva drew in a deep breath and began unraveling the different layers of her life. "My parents were born in what used to be called the Dominican Republic. Now it's The United Caribbean. They were killed in Harlem when I was fourteen, and my brother, Dion, was seventeen. He quit school. Kept us together so I could finish. He never told me how he paid the bills. I didn't ask. When I got a scholarship to MIT, he sent me pocket money so I could do things. After I graduated, I enlisted. Now I send him money. Last year he opened a small restaurant in Brooklyn. You could say we're successful, despite what we've been through, except sometimes down deep, I don't feel it. I miss him."

Mark patted her small hand. "I miss my brother, too."

Chapter 6

The captains sat in silence for a while, munching on energy bars until Mark broached the subject that had bothered him for days. "We need to collaborate on figuring out what Beth Coulter wanted with our research."

"Agreed." It seemed Eva had been waiting for him to bring it up. "With one provision. I can't refer to her by name. I just can't. So if it's all the same to you, let's refer to her as 'BC', unless you have something better, okay?"

"Agreed." They exchanged conspiratorial smiles. Mark watched the woebegone expression fade from her face. "Col. Harben said the recovered data chip had megabytes of your Nano lab's Classified Terraforming research on it."

"Plus, classified advanced cybernetics research from your XB lab." Eva lowered her voice to a whisper. "Do you design the biotech to create cyborgs? Like the one you fought with?"

"No. That was a metal bot. It only looked human. The Terran military program began way before my time, with augmented replacement limbs on injured soldiers. It progressed to eyesight, hearing, and neural implants to repair certain kinds of brain damage. It's simply a matter of modifying human biology with artificially enhanced biological cells. My work focuses on *upgrades*. Our military has almost one hundred augmented humans—cyborgs—if you want to call them that, split between the orbital Spacedock and Mars."

"Have you ever seen one?

"Yes."

"In action?"

"Yes."

"How do they compare?"

"They're human. They look like you and me. They're intelligent, have free will, know right from wrong, they're cognizant, sentient beings with *exceptional* abilities."

"What would happen if you put them on a dwarf planet or a moon that has been terraformed?"

"That concept occurred to me the minute Harben said it. Wait, Eva. Take a step back. We're thinking about this in the wrong order. Distance is the biggest obstacle. First: you must get to the astronomical body, moon, planet— whatever. And something with gravity as close to Terra's as possible would be optimal."

"Do you think we have that kind of long-range capability?"

"I don't know. The Europa mission didn't make it." A chill always washed over him when he thought about Eric. "The cause is still unknown. Or so they say."

"We can work around it. Maybe network to find others we know who might have gone into the propulsion field or aerospace engineering. Old classmates. Friends or somebody we dated." Eva took a breath. "Okay, what's next?"

"Second: manning the vessels—with non-human metal cyborgs to mitigate risks, for the long trips. No need for food or sleep, and immune to radiation and health hazards. With human cyborgs in cryopods."

"Oooh, I've always wondered what it would be like…sorry— go ahead."

"Third: using human cyborgs to do the terraforming. They'd have to be aware, perceptive, intelligent enough to design the habitats, plus physically capable of helping to manufacture the structures." Mark stared straight into her eyes. "Reduced to its prime concept, Eva, it's world-building."

Eva scrunched up her face. "This is one diabolically malicious plan."

"Like spying on your fellow scientists and stealing their

work? Like killing people and blowing up a military research installation? That kind of diabolically malicious plan?"

"Absolutely."

***

The sergeants were ordered to keep their principals, the captains, under surveillance and protect them. The theory being—if a spy or terrorists could infiltrate a classified military installation on Terra—there was a possibility—slim, but still—the same could happen on Luna. So the brass weren't taking any chances.

While they were on TMD bases and transports, the sergeants remained vigilant. Kamryn's background in undercover work helped them devise a plan to tag team their principals. During the trip, they played leapfrog; the one leading, switching with the one in the rear. Although, on the longest flight from Terra to the Spacedock, Axel watched the captains getting downright chummy, which had never happened before. He mentioned it to Kamryn.

"Didn't you say he had a problem with going to Luna?"

Axel nodded.

"Well, maybe she knows it too, and is trying to keep him talking to take his mind off it?"

They flew into the orbital Spacedock. Crew members opened the airlock hatch. All passengers filed out through a tube, exiting into a holding area. Ten minutes later they boarded a shuttle through a tube on the opposite side of the room, which would transfer them to Lunar Base 3.

"Shuttle passengers please standby for liftoff."

Everyone harnessed themselves in again. The interior lights switched to a dusky blue. In a few minutes, they arrived at their destination, Lunar Base 3.

Axel's party disembarked. They passed through a security barrier and received instructions to take the elevator down one level. As the doors opened, two soldiers stood waiting. They were escorted into a side room and issued full wraparound vests to wear, plus leg holsters, and sidearms.

"Lunar Base 3 is divided into quadrants," said the taller soldier.

"Your new IDs are encoded with the location of your quarters, your work areas, plus restrictions to certain classified sections," said the shorter one.

They were released to a hover bus that dropped them near their quarters. An annoying persistent low frequency humming background noise seemed to be everywhere.

"You two stay out here with Kamryn, while I check the room." Axel unlocked the door, and stepped inside. It smelled stale, with a whiff of furniture polish. It reminded him of a cheap hotel room. Axel didn't like this arrangement. Neither would Mark. They were both used to separate, nicer quarters. Nevertheless, he carefully searched their new rooms. Once satisfied, he brought the two captains in while Kamryn checked the quarters she would share with Eva across the hall.

"We're living underground again?" Mark tossed his duffle on a bed. "And bunking together? I'm going to develop a terminal case of claustrophobia."

"Well, this is larger than our last barracks." Eva walked around, touching everything. "But not as nice as the ones in Canada. Listen, when Kamryn gets back, let's go explore the base. We need to get our bearings. Maybe get something to eat. I'm starving."

"Hold on," Axel ordered. "No one's going anywhere until these vests and weapons are strapped on. And your new commlinks, and tablets are synchronized."

The captains retrieved the devices from their duffels,

activating them in no time. Axel removed his shirt so he could instruct both in the correct sequence of strapping the vest on, also how to adjust the holster, sidearms. They followed suit.

Finally, Eva asked, "What's taking Kamryn so long?"

Axel commed Kamryn. He waited. She didn't respond. He sent a message from his tablet to their home base for them to check her geolocator interface. He waited. The base didn't respond. Not good. Axel was beginning to get an eerie feeling in his gut.

Eva moved toward the door. "Let's go find her."

"No. It's not protocol. If she's been compromised, it's stupid to follow her into a trap."

Mark shook his head in disbelief. "So we abandon her?"

"That's not what I said." Axel moved over to the desktop keypad, tried to establish a link on the vid screen. No luck there, either. They'd been here less than an hour, and already one of them was MIA. Not good at all.

Without warning, Axel's tablet vibrated in his pocket. Messages flooded into all their tablets, alerting them of disrupted transmissions caused by CMEs, Coronal Mass Ejections, or solar flares.

The door abruptly swung open. Kamryn stood there with her gun drawn, and a fierce look on her face like she could rip somebody's heart out with her teeth.

Axel laughed. The captains started laughing—in between explanations of the solar flares and a communications blackout. Once Kamryn understood, she even started laughing.

Recovering, Eva said, "Let's go eat."

***

Directional arrows posted on the corridor walls pointed to all the major areas: Gym, Dining, Chapel, Emergency Services,

Medical, Security, Transport, Flight Deck. A separate sign pointed toward the Plaza.

Eva stopped the first person she saw. "Excuse me, what's the Plaza?

"Restaurants and shopping. Like a mall," they were told.

"Forget the dining hall. I'm going to the Plaza." Eva took off, the petite, shy, reserved Nanoscientist was shedding that persona, transforming before their eyes. Everyone scrambled to catch up.

The north side of the underground base housed about a dozen different food restaurants, plus a couple dozen retail businesses. Lots of people milled about. If not in uniform, most everyone wore rich jewel toned leather clothing; women in trendy knee-high boots being the current Lunar fashion. According to Mark, this could be a mall in Anytown on Terra.

Eva approached a woman in a honey-colored leather outfit. She asked where to purchase clothes. The woman pointed to a shop in the northeast corner. Eva asked her about food. The woman pointed to a nearby Oriental restaurant next door to a Mexican one.

"I'm up for cashew chicken." Not waiting for approval, Eva rushed off toward the Golden Pagoda, with Kamryn in her wake.

Mark and Axel headed for the colorful eatery next door. The Cancún Cantina. It displayed a red and yellow striped awning for atmosphere. A few patrons sat at tables out front in a gated area, as if it were a sidewalk café. Canned mariachi music played in the background. The heavy aromas of salsa and tortillas whetted Mark's appetite. He ordered the *Especiale*; tacos, enchiladas, chiles rellenos, rice, beans, guacamole, with chips. Not cheap, but undeniably delicious. Mark enjoyed himself so much that he had three beers. He would have had four, if Axel hadn't given him a disapproving look.

Everyone met outside to explore what their new home had to offer. Many ethnic restaurants were present: Italian, German,

Greek, Seafood, Southern, Heartland—meaning meat and potatoes. As they passed each one, food aromas wafted out like perfume.

Just beyond the eateries, Mark saw a man exiting a nondescript door tucked back into a small alcove. He was shoving a wad of cash into his pocket. Cash was an oddity these days. Walking away, he kept looking over his shoulder as if he expected, or feared, being followed. He disappeared around the first corner. Mark committed the location to memory.

A winding pathway led them to the clothing store indicated by the woman Eva had spoken to earlier.

"We get hazard pay now, so I'm treating myself." Eva acted like a kid in a toy store. She splurged on a crimson red leather tunic, black leather pants, and knee boots.

Mark chose a dark blue jacket featuring rows of detailed stitching, black leather pants, and suede boots. The sergeants opted for black from head to foot.

On the meandering return trip to the barracks, they passed the gym, conveniently located next door to the firing range. Both would be used in the coming days.

Back at his quarters, the first thing Mark did was try to contact his parents. He stood in front of the vid waiting for a connection until Gina's face filled the screen.

"Hi, Buvver." Gina looked happy, fit, clear blue eyes with blonde hair waving around her face, and over her shoulders. She wore a skimpy pink floral yoga top.

"Hi, Ginny. Where's Mom?"

"At the office, like she is every day at this hour."

"Oh, I forgot the time difference. Listen I just wanted to let Mom and Dad know that my leave's been canceled. I'm sorry, but I can't make it home like I'd planned."

"Why not?"

Nosy Gina. "Change of command at the base. Big shake up.

All our leaves are canceled. And just so you know, there's been a lot of solar flare disturbance lately, so if you have any problems contacting me, it's probably because the geosats have been affected."

"Okay." She leaned in closer. "Where are you now? That doesn't look like your apartment."

Nosy Gina—more lies. "Pipes burst. They're remodeling. I'm in temporary quarters."

"Oh, who's that?"

"Who—where?"

"Behind you."

"Uh…my new roommate."

Mark saw Axel lurking at the edge of his peripheral vision. He stepped up beside Mark.

"Axel Von Radach. Pleased to meet you, Miss…"

"Gina Warren." She batted her eyes and tried to look demure. Failed miserably. "What do you do? You're not a Post Hole Digger."

"Excuse me?"

"She means Ph.D. It's a joke." Mark gritted his teeth.

"Well, I guess you could say I have an SGT in Securities."

"Oh my, a real live badass. I like this one, Mark. You can bring him with you the next time you visit."

"No, no, no." He had to end this before things got out of control. Axel and Gina were sizing each other up like hungry wolves. "Not going to happen. Got to go now. Tell them I love 'em. Love you, too, Ginny."

"Love you too, Buvver."

"Bye, Axel. See ya." Gina flashed him a megawatt smile—with dimples.

The screen went black. Mark exhaled audibly, feeling like he'd run a marathon.

"What's a buvver?"

"Gina couldn't say brother as a child. It came out buvver. I hate it—and she knows it."

"You never told me you had a sister. Or that she's...umm, stunning." Axel looked like he'd seen something shiny, and was mesmerized by it.

"I also have a mother who's a dentist and a father who's a child psychologist. Now, you know all you need to about my family. And I'm going to bed."

***

Mark awoke not knowing if it was morning or evening. He'd lost all sense of time. Living in the underground base for a week, now again here on Luna; sleeping, waking, eating—everything was out of sync. He didn't sense the passage of time. His circadian rhythm was nonexistent. Maybe when he got back to work, he could establish a pattern, achieve a normal routine. He didn't want to turn on a light, and wake up Axel, so he fished out his tablet, checked the time. Damn. 3:30 a.m. Sunday morning. Lunar time.

If he couldn't get up and go to work, he could still do research. Remembering his earlier discussion with Eva, he used the tablet to search the Terran military database for a roster of Lunar personnel that might be working on projects like theirs. He'd start with people they could speak with in person. Maybe branch out to friends or classmates back on Terra working in propulsion or aerospace engineering. Mark scanned through the names on the roster, searching for anything familiar. Eva Jackson wasn't listed. Mark Warren wasn't listed either. He tried accessing some classified material, checking to see if he still had clearance. He did. Neither he, nor Eva appeared on the personnel listing at CAMRI. They were missing. Persona non grata. Or, since the military had gone to the extent of relocating them, this could be the only way to keep them hidden. He recalled the CME's. The solar flares probably disrupted the data stream. It was also a weekend. He now had several possibilities, all perfectly logical.

Mark resumed his efforts. After a time, he found a familiar name stationed on Lunar 3. An old acquaintance from Grad school, Captain Zachary Pearson, who specialized in Astro Engineering. Mark sent a message to Zach, suggesting they meet for breakfast. He blind copied the message to Eva with his progress. After this slight bit of success, Mark drifted into a light snooze until Axel made waking noises.

While Axel showered, Mark received a message from Eva. She'd been up early too, with similar results. They'd both made plans to meet with old colleagues for breakfast. Only her friend, Captain Dantrell Shepard, with a background in the propulsion field, seemed to be of the romantic persuasion. Mark smiled. This would be interesting.

After Mark showered, donned his vest, uniform, and sidearm, they all left for the dining hall. The sergeants planned an agenda: breakfast, exploring, H2H and weapons training, with a free afternoon.

Buttercup yellow assaulted Mark the minute he entered the cafeteria. Painters had overcompensated for lack of sun by a factor of ten in this room. Zach Pearson stood, signaling Mark from across the room. Same as always, tall, thin, short spiky hair, bushy brows. "I think I might be meeting an old associate for breakfast." Mark's comment brought evil-eyed looks from both sergeants.

"Me, too." Eva waved at her old friend, a brown-skinned, beefy type, with a shaved head, and a goatee. She motioned for him to join her as she followed Mark through the food line over to Zach's table. The sergeants followed, one sitting alone at a table on either side; bookends.

After the introductions, all four captains sat. Three ate while Zach sipped coffee and talked. "I know why you contacted me."

Mark looked up, pretending to chew so he didn't have to say anything.

"Yeah, man. I'm real sorry about your brother. Everybody in our field knew he was one of the crew on the Europa mission. Eric was a great guy. I know how close you two were. We still don't understand how it happened. Honestly, I don't have any information I can give you."

"Thanks, Zach." Mark shrugged, spreading his hands. "We just arrived yesterday. I'm trying to find some people I know."

Zach sipped his coffee. "So, what are you two working on?"

"Special project." Eva pursed her lips together, shaking her head.

"Okay. Got it. Classified. Well, there's a lot of that going on. So you're in good company. That's why we're all here, right? Research. The military gives us legitimacy. It looks good on a résumé. People respect you more for devoting a part of your life to the greater good. When your tour's finished and you enter the private sector, you have rank, credentials, and a work history. Not to mention, the ladies love an officer in uniform." He waggled his eyebrows. "It's a win-win."

"We explored the Plaza yesterday." Mark switched subjects. "I have no idea what's on Lunar 1 and 2."

"Lunar Base 1 is strictly military. A whole company of hardcore armored badasses. Lunar Base 2 is Space Command." Zach snorted. "Training for Pilots—space aces—more like space asses, flight crews, ground crews. We can't go to either base. But they can come here. Lunar 3 is us, which includes military and civilians. Hell, there are even children here, so there's a school, too. Mostly for the brass. Besides, there's a moratorium. No pregnancies. No children born on Luna. Period. Besides, there's a six-month rotation, so we're all back on Terra in no time, and home free."

Zach stood. "Listen, it was nice meeting you guys. I've got to go. Contact me, Mark, if you want to do anything. I know where all the best stuff is." He waggled his eyebrows again, smiled, left.

Capt. Dantrell "Danny" Shepard was soft-spoken, bright, and still obviously attracted to Eva. She'd been discreet about steering their conversation around to propulsion. "Is there any news about the Europa mission? Have you heard anything?"

Danny looked from Eva to Mark. "Well…maybe."

Chapter 7

Mark assessed Shepard's demeanor, waiting for a 'tell' of some kind, indicating where this conversation was going.

Danny pulled a slip of paper out of his pocket, and began folding it origami style, while he spoke. "Plasma engines are used on tugs for repositioning the orbiting space station, the spacedock, and orbital shipyard. These tugs also repair and service satellites, retrieve space junk, deflect asteroids, capture and reposition space rocks for mining, and resource recovery. The crowning achievement is that plasma engines are reusable, economical, super powered, and have no problems traveling to Mars, or the outer reaches of the solar system. I'm telling you they're safe. There were no inherent problems with the Europa Mission's propulsion system."

"Thank you, Danny. That was enlightening. Now, what about the "maybe" you alluded to?"

"The NV-300 rocket core design is capable of operating in a thermally stable mode in the vacuum of space indefinitely, even with a three million-degree plasma exhaust. Again, I'm trying to convey a message here. Propulsion was *not* the cause of failure." He squirmed a bit. "For a definitive answer, you might need to speak with someone in neuroscience."

"*Really?*" Eva kicked Mark under the table. "Umm…just how far are the outer reaches?

"Neptune. Maybe even farther out." He pushed the origami bird he'd fashioned while talking across the table to Eva. "Let's get together sometime." He winked at her, said his goodbyes, and left.

Mark turned to look at Eva. Both startled expressions.

"Neuroscience." Mark spit out the word as if it tasted bad.

"B.C." Eva covered her mouth as if she'd just cursed

"I don't want to say it—but I have to. In your wildest dreams, Eva, do you, for one minute, think that the Europa mission could be related to what happened at CAMRI?" Mark shut his eyes tightly, shaking his head. "No, damn it—don't tell me. We have to postulate this separately, independently of one another. Given what we know, or think we know. You work it from your angle. I'll work it from mine. I need to give this some time. Tomorrow, maybe. Okay?"

Eva nodded.

Mark could almost see the synapses firing in her brain.

He wasn't ready to digest this now. He couldn't think about this new information until he was alone, without any distractions, so he compartmentalized his thoughts and feelings, continuing as if this day were any other. Mark was good at that.

***

After another exploratory stroll around the military perimeter of the base, they returned, changed into black exercise togs, set off for the gym. At this point in the H2H training, Mark and Axel had reached a style facetiously called roughhousing, or horseplay, where both men actually laughed, at times, while being thrown or choked. Mark and Eric had engaged in this kind of wrestling since childhood, although Axel wasn't near as fair, or forgiving, as Eric had been.

They were all about to leave for the firing range when Mark spotted a familiar face. The guy with the wad of cash. The same man he'd seen yesterday wearing civilian clothes in the Plaza. Today he wore the requisite black togs while working out in the gym, so he had to be military, but no visible name or rank. He walked toward the exit.

Mark signaled Axel it was time for a bio break and followed him. He caught up with him in the Latrine.

"Say, didn't I see you yesterday in the Plaza?" Mark splashed water on his face, busily washed his hands.

"Yeah, mate. I was there." The man had a slight Australian accent. He was shorter, sandy-haired, wiry.

"I'm Mark Warren. Just got here yesterday. I'm looking for a good place to get a drink, maybe pick up a little action."

"The Starr Bar is a good place to meet the ladies. There's live music on the weekends, too."

"Thanks, man. I was thinking more like—sports betting, or a nice friendly card game. I'll go crazy up here for six months if I don't have more than the ladies for recreation, know what I mean?"

The guy took one step closer to Mark. He glanced back over each shoulder, scanning the empty latrine, and remarked, "Well, mate, there's a lively little game most every night. First, you need to check in with Tiny at the Starr Bar. Five hundred cash buy-in."

"Thanks a lot, mate." Mark clapped him on the back, and walked out to join his group on their way to the firing range.

Mark Warren hadn't drunk or gambled for the past week. He'd begun to feel like a monk. With luck, that was about to change. Early on, Mark learned he had a gift for numbers. While playing poker with his brother, he figured out how to count cards. Eric accused him of cheating. Mark thought of it more as a Divine Gift. Later, in college, Mark discovered he enjoyed gambling. And why not? He was good at it. Sometimes it was relaxing. Sometimes exhilarating. He invested his winnings in the stock market. Then he played the market, too. That's how he'd put himself through Grad School. He was successful. Not to any degree that would cause notice. He kept it under the radar. He had enough—but not too much. The drinking began in high school. Sneaking out. Doing things he wasn't supposed to.

Normal teenage behavior. Except, when he gambled—he drank more. Since Eric's death—it had even increased.

He still didn't want to think about the conversations from breakfast. He needed to clear his mind first. To get away from it all; the doctors, majors, colonels, sergeants, combat training, geolocator, not to mention being forced off the planet. Tonight he had a plan. Mark went to bed wearing his vest underneath his exercise togs, with everything else he needed stuffed under the bed. He'd waited until Axel rolled over, heard his shallow breathing, signifying REM sleep. He got up, pushed the pillow under his covers, grabbed the clothes, and snuck out the door. *Easy peasy.* Just like sneaking out of his parents' house.

Now, to find the Starr Bar. He went straight to the gym's locker room, changed clothing, stored his exercise togs in a locker. The gun went into the small of his back, under his t-shirt, and new jacket. Weaving through the corridors toward the Plaza, he reasoned that if people had to be "vetted" to get into the game, where cash was necessary, someone there had to convert credits into cash. They probably charged a hefty vig, or fee, for doing it, too. Plus, if they were the House, supplying the location and the dealers, they'd be taking a cut of the games as well.

Within minutes, Mark heard loud noises. They seemed to come from around the next corner. He turned. Yep, the Starr Bar. His clandestine plan was working. He eased through the swinging doors and blended into the crowd. It smelled boozy. He watched for a while, to get a general feel for the place. A tavern bathed in dim red light, with a heavy beat coming from loud music. Lots of ladies mingling, dancing, drinking. The sound of a bottle cracking, and a fight breaking out in the far corner. This could be a bar in Anytown on Terra.

Mark zeroed in on a huge, long-haired bodybuilder type, who broke up the fight, then walked behind the bar. This had to be "Tiny." He watched for a few more minutes before approaching him.

"How's it goin'? I was told to ask for Tiny."

"That'd be me. What can I do you for?"

"I was hoping to catch a little action."

"We got plenty of that out there tonight." He motioned toward the dance floor.

"I was hoping for a different kind." Mark showed Tiny the card in his left hand. He picked it up with two fingers of this right hand, flipped it over, and placed it on the bar as if he were dealing cards.

"You got ID?"

Mark nodded, and placed his ID on the bar in the same fashion.

Tiny leaned his elbows on the bar, hunkered down for a good look at Mark's ID, compared it to his face. "It's $500 to buy-in, with $100 for the foreign exchange fee." He smiled. One upper-left canine tooth was missing.

"Ready, willing, and able." Mark nodded. "You have any Canadian whiskey?"

Tiny walked away, returning with money and a bottle. He pushed five one hundred dollar bills in front of Mark, set a shot glass in front of him, filled it almost to the rim with a decent brand of whiskey, and rapped his knuckles on the bar twice—meaning the drink was free.

A tug at his left sleeve caused Mark to look down. A child, no, upon closer inspection in the dim light, a small woman stood by his side. She had long, black hair and wore black clothing, so he had difficulty noticing anything but her face. Oriental.

"Follow me, please." She walked in silence through the bar toward the rear, turned left, went down a long hall, with another left into the gaming room. "Change currency for chips at the tables. Each one has signs for minimum and maximum bets. See the cashier's booth for converting chips to cash before you leave.

Good luck."

Mark turned to view his surroundings. Hanging lanterns with tassels, painted dragons and bamboo trees on the walls. There were three tables, Blackjack, Lowball and Texas Hold 'Em. The game runner, the guy in charge, another Oriental. The bouncer, a black belt ninja looking character. When he glanced back, the small woman had disappeared.

He sauntered over to the Blackjack table, took the last seat, and pushed one bill toward the dealer. He played for about thirty minutes, carefully winning several hundred. Not everyone drank while they played, but Mark did. He began to relax and enjoy himself.

Next, he moved to the Lowball table. Most players don't have the experience or discipline to win consistently. To be profitable, it's a grind. He'd come on a good night. Late on a Sunday, last day of the weekend, when people were making bad bets trying to break even. He stayed until he won twice the amount as he had on Blackjack.

Mark had been eyeing the last table, Texas Hold 'Em, since he'd walked into the room. When a player left, Mark moved over to take his place. This was his favorite game. He could play it in his sleep. He continued drinking, though not too much, just enough to unwind. Poker is about playing your opponent, not your cards. He watched the other players, cataloging their "tells," betting accordingly. When he held a Kings Full hand, three Kings plus a pair of Queens, he doubled down. He won, felt elated, and decided to quit. Mark casually walked to the cashier's booth, to exchange his chips for $8,600 cash. The scary ninja character escorted him out a different way than he had entered. On the outside, he stood in the same alcove he'd seen the night before.

***

Axel was pissed. He just hadn't thought it would be so soon. He commed Kamryn. "My captain's MIA."

"Wow," she whispered. "He lasted a whole day and a half. Amazing. Well, that means an ass-kicking for Blue-Eyes. *Just don't kill him*—they'll write you up for that." She chuckled. "I'd like to go out, have a few, raise a little hell, too, you know. But *nooo*, I'm stuck over here with Miss Goody-Goody. Shit, Axel, you get to have all the fun."

"I'll comm you after I've put him to bed."

"You'd better. I want to hear all the gory details."

He donned the vest, black leathers and stuffed the gun behind his back. Axel could contact Petra back on Terra. Have her track Mark's geolocator, tag the coordinates and send him the data. He could do it almost as fast by himself.

Axel knew Mark drank. His blood alcohol level had indicated as much the afternoon he tackled the cyborg. He decided on a quick trip to the Plaza to check the bars. Wouldn't be many open at this hour. Axel jogged in silence, passing few people as he maneuvered through the passageways. Sound carried in an enclosed area. Axel heard the music before he reached the mall, dimly lit now because the retail stores were closed. He slowed to a normal pace, cut across the mid-section, and veered toward the noise.

Before he entered, someone snagged his attention about a hundred feet farther down; tall, blond, dark blue jacket.

Gotcha!

This was almost too easy. Axel backed up to the wall, watching Mark walk away, then turn right. He started after him.

Three more men filed out of a nearby doorway, following the same path.

Uh-oh. Axel charged after them. He slid to a halt, peering around the corner. About ten yards down, those same three men held stun batons and had Mark surrounded. They were ready to have a party. With Mark as the prize.

Axel snuck up as close as possible before they noticed. "Oh, there you are, Sweetcakes. I can't leave you alone for a minute." He strolled over to Mark, flung his left arm over his shoulders, and murmured, "Did you miss me, honey?"

The leader, a scary-looking guy, moved forward swinging his baton. "Oh boy, twofers."

His short friend to the left said, "We just want Blondie's money."

The third guy made a rude gesture with his baton. "Well, I might want some of that lily-white ass."

"Oh, no, gentlemen. His ass belongs to me." Axel gave them his best cocky smile. He took a half step forward, winked at the leader, beckoning with his index finger.

Scary came at Axel with the baton. As if dancing to choreographed moves, Axel grabbed it with his right hand, and turned it inward shocking his opponent.

Scary yelped, bending forward.

Axel grabbed his collar, pushing Scary's head down so he could deliver a powerful knee to his nose. Axel heard nasal cartilage disintegrate. He let go.

Scary fell. One down.

Axel wheeled around to see Mark fending off the others.

He chose the nearest one, pulling Shorty away.

He and Mark were fighting in tandem now, back to back. Conditioned reflexes took over.

Axel nabbed Shorty's sleeve, yanked him forward then down. The guy tried to retreat. Axel used his leg to trip him while pushing on the chest, and pulling on the arm.

Shorty lost his balance. Axel lashed out with a swift kick to the torso and sent him flying into the wall.

Shorty screamed.

Oops. Axel might have cracked some ribs. Two down.

Choking sounds came from behind Axel. He swung around to watch Mark straddling number three; death grip on the guy's neck with one hand while he pounded him with the other. It was getting messy. Evidence of blood spatter, and an eyeball that didn't look normal.

He swatted Mark on the shoulder to get his attention. "Stop playing. Finish it."

"Well, he wanted some of me. So I'm giving it to him." Mark delivered a knockout blow. He wiped his hands on the man's shirt, stood, adjusting his clothes.

"Is any of that blood yours? We don't want to leave any evidence."

Mark inspected his hands. "No broken skin."

They gazed down at the trio of would-be thieves sprawled out like demolished bowling pins.

Mark waved a vague salute. "Good night, boys. Sweet dreams."

They left the scene, and walked without speaking until Axel broke the silence. "Blondie's money?"

"I won a little gambling."

Axel shook his head in disgust. "You're not up for this, Warren."

"Look, I'm sorry. I just needed a little space."

"No. You're not sorry. Not. One. Damned. Bit. You'll do it again the first chance you get. You're just a self-destructive, rich dick. I'm not going to let you take me down with you. You're not going to be the reason I lose my stripes, or get sent back to Terra, or get kicked out of the military. You have orders. I have orders. We are going to follow our orders. When you don't, I'm going to beat the crap out of you. Maybe that's the only way you'll learn." The more Axel talked, the angrier he became. He had to let his anger go. He was teaching a lesson. He had to be in the right mindset to accomplish the desired results.

They approached the intersection leading to the Gym. Mark started past it. Axel reached out, put a hand on his shoulder. "Oh, hell, no. We're taking a little detour—this way."

A few more steps and Axel herded Mark into the deserted gym, steering him over to the mats where he peeled off his jacket, t-shirt, vest, and gun. Axel could tell Mark had been drinking, so he wouldn't kill him. He'd just make Mark wish he were dead. Trying not to enjoy this would be a wasted effort. He could hardly keep from grinning now.

Mark followed suit. "We're really going to do this?"

"Hell, yes. You're an egotistical, condescending, arrogant bastard. I'm going to beat your ass with extreme pleasure." Axel focused on provoking and intimidating him. He adopted a boxing stance, something he'd never done with Mark before.

Mark grinned and did likewise.

"Lesson number two. No hitting in the face. The bruises are too hard to explain."

That seemed to throw Mark off-guard for a second. "What's lesson number one?"

"Disregard Lesson number two." Axel hit him in the jaw with a powerful left hook that sent him sprawling on the mat. "Merry Christmas, dumbass."

Total shock spread across Mark's face. He scrambled to get up.

Before he had a chance to square off, Axel hit him with a right cross to the opposite side of the jaw. "Happy Birthday, dickhead."

Mark didn't go down that time. Instead, he came back with a lucky punch to Axel's face. "That's for calling me a bastard."

A slugfest ensued. Both men threw blows to the ribcage, torso, abdomen, and kidneys.

Mark went down multiple times, but kept getting up, until he couldn't. He'd lasted longer than Axel had expected. Not only could Mark take a punch, he knew how to deliver one, too. He was persistent. And he had heart. All admirable qualities.

Maybe Axel could make a soldier out of him, yet. "Get up, damn it. I'm not carrying you back to the barracks." He stood over Mark. Fists clenched, breathing heavy, hair plastered to his head, and rivers of sweat running down his body.

Mark lay beaten, spread-eagled, defeated. "I can't."

"You want respect; you earn it."

Chapter 8

Axel commed Kamryn. "You still awake?"

"Yeah," she whispered. "How'd it go?"

"There was foreplay. Three dirtbags ambushed him in the mall. I showed up in time to help him out of that little skirmish first."

"Two fights?"

"Yes. But the second one was *epic*." Axel paused, feeling for a sore spot near his left kidney. "Listen, this is Monday. If we're called into the colonel's office this morning for a briefing, Mark's going to need something to cover bruises, fix a split lip, and pain meds—plenty of those."

"No problem. I can do that. Be there in a flash." She giggled. "I gotta see this."

Mark came out of the shower. "Thought I heard voices."

"Put on some pants. A nurse is coming by."

Axel took a five minute shower, dressed in exercise togs.

Mark was stretched out on the bed when a knock sounded at the door.

Axel opened it. Kamryn and Axel exchanged glances, as she prodded Eva inside and pointed to a chair. Eva sat quietly, watching.

Axel leaned against the wall beside her, arms crossed, trying not to show any amusement.

Kamryn approached Mark, and motioned for him to stand. He groaned, but obliged.

"Hold up your arms and turn around."

Though visibly humiliated, Mark did as instructed.

"You have more bruises than a rotten banana." Kamryn touched him with experienced hands, asking many times, "Does this hurt?"

Mark kept grunting and shaking his head, then he flinched. "Ouch."

"Another accident—there—and you'll need to see a medic. Now, sit down so I can fix your face." She produced a MedKit plus a small blue pouch. Mark winced as she applied salves, medical grade super glue, and makeup over his eye and jaw line. She finished with a spray fixative to set everything so it wouldn't rub off. She handed him four yellow pills. "Take two now. One tonight. One tomorrow."

He managed a small smile. "Thank you, Kamryn." He stood, dry swallowed two.

"This makes twice now that you've gotten your ass kicked in a week. Are you learning anything?"

"Yeah, not to fight with cyborgs or sergeants."

Kamryn laughed. A hearty, robust laugh. It seemed to clear the air.

Mark gave her a sheepish grin.

Suddenly, all four comms received a message to report to Gen. Yates's office at zero eight hundred hours.

"Perfect timing." Axel opened the door for them. "We'll meet you in the dining hall for breakfast in a few minutes, then go report in.

***

Yates's office had about every amenity imaginable, plus an impressive Italian mural scene in greens and ivory, an ornate wooden desk, a leather couch, and a conference table with a dozen chairs. After formalities, the general closed the door, and invited them over to his table. A steaming carafe of coffee with mugs, and cookies loaded with large bits of chocolate sat on a tray in the middle. He seemed to be the polar opposite of Harben;

friendly, tall, lean, with the weathered face of an old American cowboy.

Without assistance from a cyber, he had no trouble establishing a link from tablet to vid screen to record the meeting. "I hope your trip to Lunar was uneventful, and you're finding everything you need here." He poured himself a coffee before passing the carafe around. "Please help yourselves to the cookies. My wife made them."

Mark liked him already.

"I've received several updates to the original briefing concerning Operation Pandora. The most recent being a notice just this morning. The good news is a non-human cyborg combatant was taken down while attempting to steal classified data from an obscure research facility in Washington State. Both captains should consider themselves lucky. The bad news is several of our armored personnel suffered life-threatening casualties before subduing this one. We don't know if there were more. I'm told it was pure happenstance our people were at that location. It wasn't scheduled. If they hadn't been, we can't speculate what might have transpired.

"Also, evidence has surfaced that a woman—one suspiciously similar in appearance to the missing Dr. Beth Coulter—was responsible for recruiting several of the dead terrorists which attacked your CAMRI installation. There's an All Points System Bulletin out for her arrest. That includes Terra, Luna, Mars, and all the Orbitals."

Eva kicked Mark under the table, twice.

"You're our guests here." He almost sounded as if Lunar Base 3 was an upscale vacation mecca. "Your safety is our responsibility, and we take it seriously. To lessen any threat ratio, you two will be working together in a secured, stand-alone lab in a restricted section. This means the sergeants won't be spread out in two different locations. It's fortuitous that we've just completed a system-wide security update to include a retinal scanning entry to every lab. I believe we have all the avenues covered." He stood, gesturing toward the door. "Lieutenant Scarlett McDonnell is waiting outside to take you there now. Let her know if you need anything."

McDonnell was an auburn-haired beauty. Tall, curvy, with unusually long hair piled on top of her head in some intricate fashion, strands of loose hair framing her face. And she smelled good. Axel was looking at her, too.

She escorted them to a small hover vehicle.

Eva elbowed him. "We *really* need to talk."

"As soon as we're alone."

McDonnell drove for a good fifteen minutes, talking nonstop, acting as a tour guide, until they approached a checkpoint labeled Restricted Access Section 9. Two security guards verified their IDs and fingerprints, before allowing them to pass. Within minutes they stopped at a room with a door simply labeled Classified. They all entered. Two vid screens large enough to be windows were mounted on opposite walls; one showing New York street scenes, the other Canadian ski slopes. He and Eva inspected every shelf, drawer, and cabinet, taking inventory of each piece of equipment. Someone had even thought to bring in an air freshener, which made him wonder what had previously been in the lab.

Mark started asking questions. "What if we need a piece of equipment?"

"We have an extensive geodatabase of research equipment. Depending on location, it could be here in twenty-four to forty-eight hours."

"Where are our files?"

"I'm told all your files are stored on data chips, in a safe, in our security office until you sign for them. Also, these systems are SAPS; stand-alone power supply not connected to any outside net so they cannot be hacked."

Are we monitored in here?

"Twenty-four/seven."

"Are we monitored out there?"

"Twenty-four/seven."

"Living underground, spied on constantly, chipped, no privacy, no sunshine or fresh air. I feel like a bug in a petri dish."

"I know, Captain Warren. It takes some getting used to. By the time you do, your rotation is over, and it's time to go back to Terra."

"How are we supposed to get over here to work every day?"

"We're looking for closer accommodations for you. On our way back, we'll stop to get all your retinal scanning done and pick up your files from the security office."

***

Mark chose a table for two in the dining hall, forcing the sergeants to eat apart from them. He deliberately positioned himself so he could see them, and Eva, at the same time.

Eva couldn't contain herself. "I want to know what happened to you last night. First, we need to talk about what Gen. Yates said this morning."

His jaw ached. Chewing hurt, so he picked at his food, then pushed his plate away. "Your friend, Danny, implied the Europa mission's failure had something to do with neuroscience—"

"No, Mark. He didn't imply anything. You don't know him. I do. He was spelling it out. Neuroscience. Plain and simple."

"Don't you think I know that? I just didn't want it to be true." Mark looked squarely at Eva. "Here's my epiphany: I helped save the woman's life who was instrumental in my brother's death." He hung his head, fighting back a lump in his throat. His eyes stung. If Mark ever got near that woman again, he vowed to rip her heart out. "It wouldn't surprise me if she masterminded the whole damned thing. Kidnapping the real Beth Coulter. Engineering the metal cyborgs. Recruiting terrorists. Stealing research. Sabotaging Eric's mission and killing 152 people. All while she's hell-bent on her way to world-building and terraforming the outer reaches before anybody else gets there." He wanted to tell her the rest of it. He just didn't have the strength. "Does that about sum it up?"

Eva stared at him. The color ebbed from her face. "I need a drink."

Mark spotted McDonnell with her empty lunch tray. He flagged her over. "My colleague isn't feeling well. Is there anywhere we can get a bottle of medicinal brandy."

The lieutenant studied Eva, before glancing back toward the sergeants. "Might your guardians object?" Her hazel eyes sparkled with mirth.

"We outrank them." Mark almost choked at the word "guardians."

"Yes, sir. I understand. Be back in a moment."

"What are we going to do?" Eva leaned in, whispering, "Should we tell someone? Except, we don't have proof. So would anyone believe us?"

Mark tried to calm her. "It only took us a week to figure out who, how and why with just bits—pieces of information. Now we concentrate on putting the rest of the puzzle together before we share it. Right? Besides, Eva, we're the scientists she was stealing *from*. We're smarter. We can do this."

The lieutenant returned with a towel and a cup. She stood blocking the sergeant's view. After emptying mints from the cup onto the table, she handed it to Eva, then showed Mark the concealed bottle underneath the towel.

He poured a single shot in Eva's cup, and a double in his glass. He drank it, as he slipped the bottle inside his shirt.

Eva downed hers in two gulps, made a face, and popped several mints in her mouth.

Mark patted her hand for moral support.

"Thank you, Lieutenant," Eva said. "I seem to be having a bad day. I've had several of them lately."

"Well, maybe this will cheer you up. We've located living accommodations not far from your new lab. Shall we go take a look?"

They all trouped out, boarded the little vehicle and sped over to the new location.

Eva elbowed him in the ribs.

He flinched. "You're beginning to act like my sister."

She grinned, as if it were a compliment. "What about last night?"

"I went out alone. Being under surveillance twenty-four hours a day is nerve-racking, it's restrictive, it's not normal. I'm almost thirty years old. I haven't had a keeper since elementary school. And I've had a few weird days myself, recently. I needed to unwind. Axel disapproved. I was penalized."

Eva's eyes widened. "He's dangerous."

"Who? Axel? He's a soldier. They're trained to be lethal."

"I know things. I've seen things—growing up. My minor was in psychology. You be careful. Trust me."

The pretty lieutenant pressed an item into his hand as he exited the hover vehicle. He opened his palm and glanced at it. A small key, maybe to a safety deposit box, or a jewelry chest. Or, a liquor cabinet. Mark quickly surveyed his new quarters, noting they were even better than the ones at CAMRI. All four of them, now had separate lodgings, complete with a bath. Mark's had sandy colored walls, white ceilings, comfy furniture, a large vid screen over a desktop, with a cabinet underneath.

The key fit the lock. It was truly a well-stocked liquor cabinet. *Hallelujah.*

McDonnell had just endeared herself to him. Big time.

He could hear Eva squeal from across the hall. Good for her. She deserved a little happiness, too. She and Mark seemed to be riding one hell of a roller coaster. Thrills and spills. No sign of a level playing field, yet, but he was working on it.

***

That afternoon Mark and Eva spent a few hours in the new lab downloading all their data, and making sure everything interfaced. They kept their voices low, so as not to be picked up by any audio recording devices.

He whispered, "Have you devised a theory, yet?"

She nodded.

"If I were to say neural implants..."

"Oh, my god," she hissed. "Yes, exactly. Do you want to hear my unabridged synopsis?"

"Go for it."

"Did the crew of the Europa flight have neural implants? If so, did B.C. have access to programming any of those neural chips? In order to sabotage the mission, she'd only have to hack into just one—the weakest link—then send a signal, or a little virus into the brain, straight to the implant—from there to the whole network. They'd all be vulnerable to a few lines of code."

A shard of ice pierced Mark's heart. Those same thoughts had floated through his mind; however, this was the first time he'd heard them voiced aloud. He also didn't know if Eric had a neural implant. Wouldn't that information have been classified? If he had been fitted with one, would he have told Mark? Eric had become much less talkative about the mission the closer they got to departure.

His head ached again. Mark stoked his jaw, not sure whether thoughts of his brother or the aftermath of his fight with Axel was the cause. He swallowed another of Kamryn's pills. He had to focus on what was important now; stopping Beth Coulter.

Mark made a concerted effort to keep his voice to a whisper, but it wasn't easy. "If she could do it to one of *them*—then she could do it to someone *here*. Lunar Base 1 is armored personnel. Some of them have neural implants. The Spacedock and Mars have augmented human cyborg soldiers with neural implants. Hack into one, distribute a behavior-altering code or virus. Use them to blow up one of these bases on Luna. Maybe start a chain reaction. How horrific would that be? All three Lunar Bases? Why stop there? The Orbitals? Mars? She'd decimate our colonization capabilities. We'd come back, of course, rebuild, maybe take us ten to twenty years. By that time, she'd already have a foothold, on the entire outer reaches. Terraforming. World-building."

Immediately, Eva's demeanor plunged. "I'm scared."

"You've every right to be. This is scary shit. If I weren't so damned angry…wait—I have one more idea. We need to find out what kind of classified data that cyborg was trying to steal in Washington. I've never heard of that research facility? Have you?"

"No, but I could ask Danny."

"I was thinking of asking someone, too. Maj. Torance, back at the base. He seemed to wield some kind of power—influence. Only if you agree, though. We know they can hack, so we'd have to figure out how to send and receive encrypted messages. People have been hurt and *killed* over what we know. We must be ultra-careful from now on. With what we say. Where we say it. And whom we say it to."

"That's your call. I personally liked him. He struck me as trustworthy."

They locked the lab. He escorted Eva back to her quarters to change for dinner in the Plaza.

Mark noticed Axel's open door and strolled in to see him doing one-armed push-ups. "How long have you known Torance?"

"Four years. Why?" Axel stood.

"What kind of relationship do you have with him?"

"He's saved my life—twice."

Mark lowered his voice. "Back on Terra, did you or any of your armored personnel have neural implants?"

"None of us did. Why?"

"Would Torance know how to find out what that cyborg tried to take from the Washington facility?"

"He's been in the military for over twenty-five years. He knows people everywhere, so he probably could. Now tell me why, or forget about asking me any more questions."

"If I do," Mark whispered. "It will put you in eminent danger, Axel. Life or death. You can put me in touch with Torance without my explanation, and maybe you'll be safe. Or, I can tell you about the kind of pit Eva and I are digging for ourselves, and you'll be right in here with us. Each person who knows what we're doing, reduces our chances of survival exponentially."

Without hesitation, Axel held up his right hand with two fingers crossed. "You and Eva." He held up the other hand with two fingers crossed. "Kamryn and me."

"It's your funeral."

Chapter 9

The Plaza was busy when they entered. Not wanting to be overheard, they maintained a safe distance from everyone else in the mall, while deliberately moving in a slow window shopping circuit.

"Eva and I are working on a theory about this whole Beth Coulter-cyborg scenario. We need more information. There can't be any record of it being passed to us." Mark and Eva took turns explaining all the information they'd pieced together, along with their current theories on the worst case scenario.

The sergeants listened; exchanging looks, nodding to each other.

Axel spoke first. "I know why Mark wants to do this—because of his brother. He asked us if we wanted in. We both said yes. Kamryn and I are soldiers. We protect our country, our people, our planet. We chose this life because we like delivering justice to bad guys. Why do you want in on this, Eva?"

"If that woman hadn't left her DNA on my data chip, I'd be in a military penitentiary. As if that's not enough reason. She was trying to steal my work. Nine long years I spent getting my degree to do this research—so she could steal it? No way. I'm not strong on the outside like you. But I'm strong in here." She tapped her temple. "And I need to know why, so I can help figure out how to stop her." She added with an impish little smile, "Maybe I like catching bad guys, too."

Kamryn reached out to shake Eva's hand. In a surprising show of affection, she yanked her into a big bear hug. Kamryn told them about her background in undercover work. "Since we're being surveilled here constantly, it would be wise to adopt code words and hand signals to minimize detection. We'll teach you ours."

The door to a restaurant called Caesar's Little Italy opened, spilling people out along with the aroma of garlic bread and meatballs. Eva pointed toward the door, and grabbed Mark's arm, pulling him along. They entered just as a table was being cleared. An hour later they left filled with pasta, wine, tiramisu, plus a plan for contacting Torance.

On the return route to their new quarters, Mark spied a candy shop. He went in, picked out his sister's favorite kind of chocolates, and requested they be sent, "To Lt. Scarlett McDonnell, please."

"The general's daughter?" The woman behind the counter, added, "Well, actually his step-daughter."

"Tall, auburn hair?"

"Yes. Very pretty."

"Does she like these?" He pointed to the box of truffles he'd chosen.

"Yes. I assumed you knew."

"May I add a card?"

She handed him a small card, an envelope, and an antique writing instrument.

He wrote "*Merci,*" stuffed it in the envelope, sealed it.

***

Axel sent an encoded message to Ohashi, the cyber unit specialist on Terra, with instructions to hand deliver it to Deering. Everyone lounged around his quarters waiting for a reply. Axel leaned back on the couch, laced his fingers behind his head. He watched the others, sensing the invisible walls melting away, and a genuine bond starting to grow. Leave it to a good old-fashioned ass kicking and some sharing of secrets to pull the four of them into a real team. It was all about respect. It had to be earned on both sides.

He needed to tread carefully, though. These scientists ate, slept, and bled the same as he did. But they thought differently. The same things mattered to them. But they handled it differently, because they were different. Except, now they all had a common enemy—Beth Coulter. Axel hoped like hell that the worst-case scenario they'd cooked up wasn't anywhere near becoming a reality. His gut told him just the opposite. They wouldn't have voiced their fears, if they hadn't believed it was about to happen.

An image of Deering flashed on Axel's vid screen. The tips of her hair had changed from emerald to violet. She established a two-way uplink with Torance, who appeared in pajamas, hair combed, eyes bright, holding a steaming cup.

"I'm told we're bouncing this connection around the system. It's being timed, so we don't have long. I'll go down the list as it was sent. Yes, you were right about the Washington data being implants. The thief was not the same one. It's being dissected as we speak. We will research files for images and DNA to check for anyone we know who might have worked on implants for personnel currently stationed on all Lunar Bases. We'll start there first. Data on the Europa crew will take longer. Good work people. Watch your butts. I'd hate to lose any of you. Torance out."

Deering's violet-haired image remained onscreen. "Ohashi and I will devise totally unhackable passwords with keys so each of you can encrypt and decrypt our messages using rotating quantum transmissions. We will send an alarm to one of your tablets. Do exactly the opposite." She winked at Mark. "Petra out."

Silence enveloped the room. Axel waited for someone to say something—anything.

"I knew it." Mark laughed grimly. "Don't get me wrong. I'm

not happy about this—at all. I just needed to know we were on the right track. Now we try to get in front of this, instead of playing catch up."

Axel nodded. "In the morning, after breakfast, we'll all go to the lab. Put everything on the table. See what kind of a plan we can build."

***

Mark shed his leather clothing, pulled on black exercise pants and settled in with a well-deserved glass of wine. He needed to unwind.

There was a knock at his door.

What now?

He opened it, expecting to see Eva or Axel.

"Thought I'd stop by to see how you liked your new quarters. And to thank you for the truffles." The lieutenant stood in his doorway looking gorgeous. Her long auburn hair down, almost hiding one eye, tumbling over her shoulders. She wore sharkskin-colored leather pants trimmed on the sides with dark red stitching and a matching jacket. "How'd you know they were my favorites?"

"Lucky guess." Mark smiled, leaning forward a few inches. She smelled delicious, and she was the perfect height.

"Oh, what happened to you?"

Mark glanced down at the bruises on his bare abdomen. "Roughhousing. Horseplay."

"Looks like some very rough play."

"You should see the other horse." He couldn't take his eyes off her. She hadn't moved, so he gestured for her to enter. "Please, come in."

She walked in slowly.

He watched her every move. "Those are some fancy pants."

She turned, flashing a wicked smile back at him. "Thanks."

"No, thank you."

She arched an eyebrow.

"For these new quarters. Much better than the old ones. The lab's nice, too." He handed her a glass of wine, and sat on the couch, draping his right arm over the top.

"Can't stay long." She sat beside him and sipped the wine. "I'm meeting the family for dinner."

"With the General?"

"Yes." She arched her eyebrow again. "And my mother."

"You normally eat this late?"

"Only when it's obligatory." She sipped more wine. "Are you getting acclimated to Lunar 3?"

"Been busy exploring the Plaza, restaurants, gym, the new lab. Especially my new liquor cabinet. It's the little amenities that make a place feel like home." He smiled and hoped he wasn't leering.

"I'm glad you're settling in." She stood and moved toward the door.

He followed, watching her body move in the figure-hugging leather pants. "Oh, give your mother my compliments. Her chocolate chip cookies were mouthwatering." He opened the door. "Drop by anytime…Scarlett."

"Goodnight…Mark." She batted her hazel eyes and turned, her intoxicating fragrance fading as she walked away.

Mark lingered in the doorway, absolutely certain he was leering now, watching her disappear. *Hot damn.*

Axel opened his door. "That's a no-no…*a big no-no.*"

"What?"

"She's the general's daughter."

"You knew?"

"I make it my business to know things. I saw the way you looked at her."

"You looked, too."

"Yeah, but I wasn't going to make a move."

"Well, I didn't."

"Keep it in your pants—and put a shirt on."

"You suck the fun out of everything."

* * *

Danny Sheppard waited for Eva at a table in the far corner of the dining hall. His cleanly shaved brown-skinned head glowed against the buttercup yellow walls. Eva joined him alone, while Mark, and the others sat one table away, though still within earshot.

They sipped coffee and talked for almost half an hour. When Danny left, Eva moved over to their table. "He said numerous people, mostly family members of the crew, some coworkers too, noticed small things prior to departure. Not enough to raise suspicions before, just enough so that people remembered afterward. Families got together, began comparing notes, so to speak, until it became clear to everyone in their small group that something had been wrong. Especially since there still hasn't been any conclusive reason given for the mission's failure."

Everyone looked at Mark.

He smoothed the stubble on his face. He'd skipped shaving to cover the bruise. "Eric and I were always close. Except I don't know if he had a neural implant. If he did, he didn't tell me. I do remember that we talked less as the departure date grew closer. I don't know if that was normal or abnormal for the other crew members. If he had acted, or looked different in some way, I'd like to think I would have noticed. We need to find out who the mission operations manager was." Mark rubbed the back of his neck, as if he'd sensed someone staring at him from behind. He looked back over his shoulder. Didn't see an Asian cyborg, or

Beth Coulter. He reached down, checking for the gun strapped to his thigh. He relaxed—a bit.

"I need a change of scenery. How about having breakfast in the Plaza?"

Eva jumped up. "I saw a place where they had chocolate covered éclairs, crullers, and cream horns."

Everyone laughed except Eva.

Mark pulled Axel back, walking in step with him. "Can I get another gun? A small one? With a shoulder holster?"

Axel narrowed his eyes. "Yes. You can carry a concealed handgun. Want to tell me why?"

"Do you trust your gut feelings?"

"Hell, yes."

"I'm going to start trusting mine."

Axel made a quick trip to the quartermasters. Both registered for new weapons—lethal ones this time. Their current sidearms were stun only. They chose shoulder holsters, plus new short-waisted Recon jackets roomy enough through the chest to accommodate concealed weapons.

"If Eva's anything like my sister, we'd better go find that donut shop, before she starts acting like a three-year-old on a sugar rush."

Axel commed Kamryn. She and Eva were already on their way to the lab. He and Mark stopped for breakfast then went straight to the firing range for the first time since they'd landed on Luna. After checking magazines, they "test drove" the deadly new weapons for about an hour before Axel was satisfied.

***

The box of pastries Eva had purchased was half empty on the counter by the time Mark and Axel entered the lab.

"Oh, Mark, come take a look" Eva scurried over, and grabbed

his sleeve, pulling him to the microscope. "I've been thinking about something for a week. It came to me this morning. I may have found the perfect protein particle for terraforming. It might just be what B.C. was hoping to steal."

He peered dutifully into the electron microscope at a 3-D image of an individual protein particle. Mark knew that finding what you were looking for was one thing. Figuring out how to make it work was the kicker—and much more difficult. "Congratulations. What shall we call it? The Eva Particle?"

She playfully elbowed him and continued with her explanation of how it would function. "Combined with CFCs, it could help us raise surface temps, atmospheric pressure and produce a greenhouse effect on the surface of a moon or planet. It would help vaporize carbon dioxide at the poles, which would rise, feeding the warming cycle and increasing the temps." Eva tried to subdue her enthusiasm. "First we'll do a full spectrum analysis on it. Of course, if it looks promising, we'll have to test this hypothesis on Mars."

Mark could see the sergeants were bored. "Why don't you to go to the gym. We're in a Restricted Area. We're being monitored. It takes retinal scans to get in the door. I won't leave Eva alone. We'll be fine."

After they left, he commed McDonnell, requesting a large mobile double sided whiteboard with a box of markers.

Within minutes, the buzzer sounded at the lab's door. He opened it for the lieutenant and unloaded a large box from her hover vehicle. She carried in a small bag. All three of them worked setting up the whiteboard on its rolled frame.

In a hushed tone, Mark asked her, "Do you know where the video and audio monitoring devices are in this room? We're working on proprietary information here. A lot of trouble has been taken to make sure it doesn't leak out."

She pointed to her eye and covertly indicated several areas in the ceiling. She tugged on her ear and did the same.

He positioned the whiteboard so as to hide the side that would be used. Then rearranged lab equipment to indicate the location of audio devices.

"Are you sure this is necessary?"

"Murphy's Law: Whatever can go wrong, will go wrong."

Chapter 10

Mark suffered another fitful night's sleep. He kept waking to the illusion of a shadowy figure reaching out for him. Twice, he got up, and walked around before going back to bed. The third time, he went straight to the liquor cabinet, got a drink, grabbed his tablet, and settled on the couch. He drank, while jotting down ways to eliminate risks until he finally dozed off again, only to dream of impending doom.

At zero six hundred, his tablet pinged. He checked it. Read a cryptic message: "Meet me in the dining hall for breakfast. Your Pet."

Okay, Petra. I'll stay put.

After a quick shower, Mark pulled on exercise pants and commed everyone, alerting them that a meeting in his quarters was forthcoming.

Axel arrived just as the vid screen blinked on with a notice saying the caller was Leslie Warren, Mark's mother.

Mark signaled for Axel to move out of sight, before he opened the channel. His mom appeared in mauve colored dental scrubs; a mature but no less beautiful version of his sister.

"Hi, honey. We missed your last call, so it's our turn now. How are you? Are you growing a beard?" She tilted her head and leaned closer to the screen. "You look a little pale."

"I'm great, Mom. Been busy. Did Gina bring you up to date?"

"Yes, dear. Sorry to hear your leave's been canceled. We were so looking forward to seeing you. Gina says you have a roommate now?"

Mark hung his head in resignation, as Axel moved into view.

"Good morning, Mrs. Warren. I'm Axel Von Radach, pleased to meet you." Axel flashed his most charming pearly white smile.

"My pleasure, Axel. And please, call me Leslie." Again, she tilted her head, moved closer to the screen, studying Axel. "Gina was right." Her manner grew serious. "I don't know where you're at, or why. You will keep my son safe, won't you, Sgt. Von Radach?" Leslie Warren hadn't asked a question; it had been a statement of fact.

"Yes, ma'am. I'm his wingman."

His response brought a slight smile to her face. "Well, I have an early patient scheduled for an emergency extraction, so I need to leave. Your dad already left. He's due in court today. You know how he hates that. One of his patients was abused by a family member. He has to testify this morning. We love you, Mark. Be careful. Take care, boys." She blew them a kiss. Her image blinked out.

"Your mom's nice. Pretty, too, just like your sister. How did she know you weren't at CAMRI?"

"I don't know. She's always been like that. It's why I still try not to lie to her. You can't imagine growing up in a family where your dad's a child psychologist, and your mom's a human lie detector. We were all in trouble, constantly."

The vid screen blinked on with a TMD insignia, followed by an image of Deering sitting in a cramped office with the major.

In the meantime, Axel opened the door for Eva and Kamryn, who took seats, waiting for the vid stream to begin.

Deering began. "We've devised passwords for each of you, ones easily remembered. If you can't, write it down somewhere nobody will see it, like on the bottom of your foot," she joked. "They will appear in a ribbon at the bottom of your screen for this communication only, so be quick."

The doctor was dressed in wrinkled blue scrubs, his silver hair mussed, a surgical mask draped around his neck. "Again, I have good news, and bad news. First, TMD traced some of the parts of that now dissected cyborg to a factory in Malaysia. They were using slave labor. We were able to exert enough leverage to shut down the plant, freeze all their assets, plus arrest the owners for crimes against humanity. To avoid an international incident, the principals were turned over to us and are on Terran soil, about to undergo questioning, momentarily."

He closed his eyes, shook his head, before continuing. "There's no way to soft-pedal the next part. A person fitting Beth Coulter's description worked in a Houston facility designing neural implants up to just about the time of the Europa mission's failure. All video and DNA traces of this person were eradicated from their system. Her image has been positively identified by current employees. Some of the implants produced by that facility have been traced to twenty-eight current military personnel stationed in all three of the Lunar Bases. These people are quietly being collected. They'll be sent to a classified military hospital here on Terra for newly constructed replacements as we speak. All this information has been sent to Dimitrios at Headquarters in Virginia, as well as Yates on Lunar 3. Extremely good work people."

"Major, a moment, please. I, for one, would like to know who vetted Beth Coulter for hiring in Houston and CAMRI. Have you searched for connections between any of the people involved, financial or otherwise?"

"On that point," he chuckled, "all I can tell you is that a bunch of butts are in the frying pan, and it's being held by Dimitrios, himself."

"Sir, may I have copies of all the military and medical reports compiled on the CAMRI assault.

"For what reason?"

"Bedtime reading. I have one of those elusive feelings that I know something, just can't zero in on it yet. Maybe perusing the report will help jog it loose."

The major nodded to Deering.

"Oh, by the way, were you aware that she spoke three languages. English, French, and German?"

"German?"

"Yes, I overheard her speaking it several times—on her comm."

"Watch your butts. I'd hate to lose any of you. Torance out."

***

Axel approached Mark. "You been drinking?"

"I couldn't sleep. Woke up three times. Just trying to quiet my thoughts."

"Grab a shirt. We're going to the gym. Maybe if you work out enough, you won't have that problem."

Mark didn't argue.

They jogged to the gym, completed a full circuit, followed by a trip to the mats for a friendly little wrestling match. After peeling off their shirts and shoes, Axel let Mark make the first move. It was all out war. They hadn't spared since Axel's teachable moment—or Mark's attitude adjustment—depending depending on your point of view. It surprised him Mark didn't seem to harbor a grudge or any resentment. Although Mark outranked him, the captain had still disobeyed orders. Technically, Axel had saved his butt first, then delivered punishment for the offense. The whole episode was a gray area.

Today they engaged in Freestyle, or standup wrestling, which allowed using their legs in offense and defense, merging several different techniques. Trying to escape a hammerlock, Axel twisted, rolled back, immobilizing Mark in a head scissors arm hold. "Did you and your brother wrestle?"

"Yeah," Mark grunted, trying to squirm out of Axel's grasp. "And skied, fished, climbed boulders, scuba-dived, played pool, chess." He slapped the mat twice to signal submission. Axel released the hold. They both stood.

"I'm sorry…about your brother. I think I would have liked him."

"I think he would have liked you, too…sweetcakes."

Axel saw the glint in Mark's eyes—too late.

Mark lunged, grabbing Axel's knees. He swept his left leg out, knocking Axel off balance, pushing him down. Mark pounced on top, holding Axel's arms down with his knees and a forearm across his throat—all in just seconds.

"Well, that was fun," Axel grunted, remembering when he'd performed the exact move on Mark.

"Did you think I wasn't paying attention?" Mark rolled off Axel onto the mat and broke out in unreserved laughter.

Axel chuckled, stood, extended a hand to Mark. Both were breathing heavy, muscles pumped, glistening with sweat. Axel realized he missed combat. This was how it felt. Two gladiators walking off the field of battle. Victorious, adrenalin flowing, comradery.

They heard hands clapping, turned in unison to see a smiling McDonnell in exercise togs. "An amazing display. You two should make a vid and sell it. You looked like two wild animals going at each other, a fight to the death, then finished by collapsing in laughter. I'm impressed."

In less than a heartbeat, Mark replied, "I'm glad we were able to provide you with some entertainment while you worked out."

Axel gritted his teeth and tossed Mark's shirt at him.

"If you're done here, I can give you a ride back to your quarters."

Axel watched the two officers play a cat and mouse game, while his gut was telling him somebody would burn in hell before this was all over. When Axel had asked for this assignment, he had no idea how hard it would be to keep Capt. Mark Warren out of trouble. Women, booze, and gambling. Damn if it didn't look like he was addicted to all three. Regardless of his IQ, he just didn't have his shit together.

When they arrived, Mark waved Axel away. "See you back at the lab."

Axel vigorously shook his head and drew a finger across his throat.

Mark opened the door to his quarters for the lieutenant and followed her in.

Axel rarely, if ever, felt as helpless as he did at this moment.

***

Mark checked his tablet. He found files waiting for him from Petra. He fought the urge to open them.

Scarlett's tablet pinged. "I have to go. There's a meeting."

He moved to the door, leaned back on it and crossed his arms. "I want you to have dinner with me this evening. Your choice. Anytime. Anywhere."

The auburn-haired beauty studied him long enough to make a normal man squirm. But Mark held his ground.

"All right. I'll comm you later. Let you know when."

He moved to open the door. She walked out ever so slowly. Their attraction hung in the air, making it almost impossible to breathe. He watched her drive away, humming to himself.

Afterward, Mark showered, dressed, stretched out on the couch, and started reading the files Petra had sent. Page after page, he encountered a few interesting facts, but nothing illuminating. On page fifty-two of an AAR, After Action Report, he ran across an entry citing the reason CAMRIs security forces hadn't responded. They'd been notified of a fictitious meeting, and the room had been tranq gassed. He stopped. In the lab, he'd made puny attempts at misdirecting the audio and video devices for the purposes of thwarting a spy. What he hadn't considered was a more overt avenue of interference—the air supply.

He checked the report. CAMRIs personnel had been unconscious for an hour. Using the same gas would give the assailants plenty of time to download, copy or directly transmit all Eva's data, including her new formula. There would be an investigation, with the possibility someone might be caught. All the previous terrorists had been expendable. Maybe the same rule would apply here.

Neural implants. A few lines of code—sent to an implant in an engineering technician, ordering them to pop a tube of tranquilizer gas into an air supply hose and then forget about it.

He commed Eva. Got no answer. Commed Axel and Kamryn. Still no answer. He checked for a warning of CMEs. There was none.

Mark strapped on his sidearm, grabbed his new gun, slipped it into his shoulder holster, snatched his jacket, and tablet before sprinting out the door. He kept trying to reach Eva. Poor little Eva. If anything happened to her, he'd never forgive himself. He poured on the speed and slid up to the retinal scanner. The door opened. The lab looked empty. He ran around to the far side of the center island workstation.

Oh, Shit.

All three of them were lying on the floor.

Lifeless.

He dropped to his knees. Checked Eva's carotid. A pulse. But faint. His worst fears were coming true. He slipped and fell on the floor. He reached up to grab the counter, trying to pull himself up. It was almost impossible.

Gassed. He felt the walls closing in.

He sent a message to Petra: HELP LAB GAS

He sank to the floor. Fought to stay awake. Images floated in and out of his mind. Bad ones. Nightmares. No, memories.

Mark banged his head against the cabinet. Pain. Again. More

pain. It helped.

Must stay lucid.

He pulled out both guns. One in each hand. Protect Eva.

No. Protect Gina. He was looking for Gina. In a rundown house on the seedy side of Portland. She was using drugs. First prescription pills for her knee. Then street drugs. Now he didn't even want to know what she was using. Just wanted to find her. Alive. And bring her home.

Mark heard a noise. Peered around the island's corner.

Two men were coming for Gina.

He banged his head against the cabinet again. Time stood still. He saw two men walk to the data center and begin taking things. In a superhuman effort, Mark stood. He tried to make a noise. Hatred or fear strangled him. He banged a gun on the counter. Both men turned toward him. He looked straight at them, then shot them both.

One dropped to the floor. The other came at Mark.

A vivid shade of red was all Mark saw as he attacked the man who had come for Gina. He picked him up and slammed him into the wall, then with both hands around his neck he squeezed until he could hear his own voice screaming, "Leave. Gina. Alone."

His body was on fire. Death by electrocution.

At least he had saved Gina.

He fell into a deep, deep well of darkness.

***

"Capt. Warren, can you hear me?"

"Gina?"

"No, I'm Dr. Illingsworth. Do you know where you are, Capt. Warren?"

After a long silence, Mark answered, "Moon." He tried to open his eyes. He couldn't.

"Yes. And you've been injured."

"I can't see—why can't I see?" Mark tried to lift his arm. He couldn't do that either.

"You had to be subdued."

"Subdued—what do you mean subdued? You're not answering my questions. Why. Can't. I. See?"

"You were attacking someone in your lab. You refused to stop and had to be stunned into submission. As an unintended consequence, it seems to have affected your sight. We believe it's only temporary."

"Your bedside manner sucks. What kind of a quack are you?" He kept pulling on his arms, trying to free them. It dawned on Mark he was being held down with restraints. Now he felt afraid.

"That's uncalled for, Cap—"

"Where are my colleagues?" He heaved with all his strength to free his right arm from whatever held it down.

"They're being held."

"Held? What the hell is wrong with you people?" Mark exerted every ounce of rage he could muster, and ripped his arm free from its restraint. He reached for his face, pulled the bandages away from his eyes. Fuzzy. He saw fuzzy figures. *Oh, thank god.* He wasn't totally blind. He lashed out, grabbing the first thing he touched, and flung it away. He heard a tremendous crash.

"Release my friends. Now. Before I tear this place apart." He grabbed a handful of the electrodes connected to his body and wrenched them off. "And get me a real doctor, or I'll wrap these around your neck and strangle you with them." He kept grasping at everything within reach, flinging it in any direction. He heard screams and yelling in the background, while he worked to free his left arm from its restraint, then his legs. He rolled out of bed and stumbled around, scattering equipment, picking up anything that wasn't nailed down and pitching it away from him. His chest felt tight. He found the door. It was open. He felt dizzy, steadied himself by grasping both sides of the frame. Sounds faded away. Silence.

"Mark." Eva's soft small voice carried like a stage whisper.

"Eva?"

"I'm here."

Mark felt close to tears. "Are you all right?"

"We're all okay."

Mark had used up his adrenalin. Any moment, he knew his knees would buckle. Still, he reached out, only able to see vague shapes.

Eva took his hand, patted it, then came closer, lifting his heavy arm, and draping it around her shoulders. She whispered, "You're naked."

"Oh. Sorry. I can't see."

"Let me help you back to bed." Eva led him into the room, nudged him into bed and pulled up the sheet. She leaned over, wiping away the blood oozing from the open wound on his forehead, as she murmured words of comfort.

"Axel?"

"I'm here." The voice belonged to Axel.

Mark reached toward Axel, who firmly grasped his forearm. "And Kamryn?"

"They're still taking her statement."

"Gas in the air vent," Mark said. "I thought you were all dead."

"Down. But not dead."

"Who did it?"

"We can't tell you."

Mark couldn't make sense of anything. "Am I under arrest?"

"Well, it looked like it for a while." Axel chuckled. "Not anymore."

"Explain."

"We had no warning. It was odorless and invisible. We all went down within seconds of each other. We were out for about an hour. We demanded to see the vids. If you hadn't sent Petra that message—"

"And kicked ass," Eva interjected.

"Yeah, that's what almost got you into trouble."

"Why?"

"Can't say." Axel sounded cryptic.

"Why not?"

"Because we're under orders—from Gen. Dimitrios—at TMD Headquarters."

"Not Yates?"

"He's under orders, too."

Chapter 11

Torance and Buchanan sat in Harben's office facing his vid screen. They watched, without audio, the recorded scene of the Lunar Base lab, showing three uniformed personnel drop to the floor. Warren entered, located the bodies, and became disoriented. He fell, sent a message from his tablet, drew his guns, purposely beat his head against a workstation multiple times, until he was bloody. He detected someone entering the lab. Watched as two people began downloading data, struggled to stand, and fired at them. One fell. He attacked the other, almost killing that one with his bare hands before lunar security forces invaded the room. Four soldiers used stun batons on him before he became unconscious. They watched it, twice.

A few minutes later, the vid screen displayed a 2-way image of Dimitrios and Yates.

Never known for his patience, Dimitrios began. "Gen. Yates has confirmed the two perpetrators were indeed the same security guards stationed at the Restricted Access Section 9 Checkpoint into the classified lab area. It was only after they were taken to the hospital and scanned that their neural implants were found. Up to that point, the men hadn't been on the list of personnel with neural implants to be transferred off any Lunar Base. Their records were searched. No indication of this procedure for either one was in their files. How could this happen?"

"Those men were transferred up here from Terra. That procedure was done on your soil, not mine, just like all the others. I want your people off my base. Tomorrow." Yates wore a cantankerous scowl while drumming his fingers slightly off screen.

"Well, Forest, if we pulled all Terran military off that base, you'd be left with nothing but a few children and some shopkeepers. I'm going to let you keep that poor excuse of a doctor Illingsworth. If he ever comes any closer to Terra than a communication satellite, I'll have him transferred in perpetuity to Anchorage's Bertrand facility. They only work on cadavers up there. He misdiagnosed and mistreated the very person who apprehended the sabotaging thieves that were stealing proprietary scientific data. From a Lunar lab. On a Lunar base." By now Dimitrios's temples had started throbbing, and his face went florid.

"Your security held the other three victims for two hours, interrogated them without representation, even after my people sent you confirmation of the request for help. Plus, you had all the videos to back up their accounts. Hell, Forest, it's the Wild West up there. You've failed to keep my people safe, so you'd better have them on a ship back here just as soon as Warren's ready to travel, or I'm on the first warship leaving orbit in the next twenty minutes to get them myself. Now I want those two sabotaging thieves drugged unconscious, stuffed in cryopods, put under armored guard, on the next ship leaving Luna straight to Headquarters. You hear me, Forest?" Dimitrios manually terminated Yates's connection. He loosened the top two buttons of his uniform, took a big gulp from a mug on his desk, steepled his fingers, and resumed in a much calmer tone.

"Maj. Torance, can you explain Warren's reaction to the tranquilizer gas?

"No, sir. In his altered state of mind, he might have tried self-inducing pain to ward off unconsciousness. Otherwise, it's an anomaly. Not everybody reacts the same way."

"Are you sure he's one of ours?"

"Yes, sir. I've personally scanned him numerous times. No neural implants. No augmentation. Totally human."

"And he's a scientist? The same one who caught that first

cyborg after the attack on CAMRI a couple of weeks ago?"

"Hard to believe, but, yes, sir."

"Well, hell. We should put him in armor. Turn him loose on the battlefield. I like this boy. He gets a Silver Star. Bring him and his team back to your base. We're certain they'll be safe there, right, Col. Harben?"

"Yes, sir. Over my cold dead carcass."

"Let's hope it doesn't come to that, Wayne. Now...I will have these two saboteurs interrogated until they're reduced to nothing more than puddles of shit. We will find out who gave them the orders and when. As we speak, I'm implementing a Universal Order, mandatory scanning at every TMD facility including all research and development installations. If it breathes, bleeds, or farts, it gets scanned. No exemptions. I'm due for mine in five minutes. Next, we need to draw up a strategy for dealing with civilians running around out in public that might be a potential threat. Finally, are we any closer to locating this damned Beth Coulter?"

***

Twenty-four hours after the incident, the hospital released Mark into Axel's protective care. A small strip of micro tape covered his head wound. He was more than ready to leave that facility. They were sitting in the back of a hover vehicle, driven by a burly sergeant. On the way to their quarters, both their tablets pinged with a message.

"Coming home to ND 08:00 Pet."

Mark and Axel exchanged looks. Axel nodded and shrugged. Mark had anticipated this. Wreck a Lab. Damn near kill two men. What did he expect? Never mind that it wasn't all his fault.

Mark commed Eva while Axel commed Kamryn, making sure everyone had received the message.

"Eva, we need to go to the lab and retrieve all our data."

"No. Not to worry, though. Just come to my quarters."

The sergeant dropped them off in front of their doors. "You four are restricted to your quarters. Indefinitely. Access to all other areas has been cordoned off. Your meals will be delivered. Do you have any questions?"

"Nope. Thanks for the ride, Sergeant." Mark wouldn't fight it. He didn't have the strength. He had visions of emptying his liquor cabinet this evening. Might as well enjoy his last night on Luna.

Eva opened her door when she heard the voices and motioned them inside. "I've already taken care of the data."

"When?'

"When Kamryn and I were released. We returned to the lab. Double-checked the data to make sure it was all there. I downloaded it, scrubbed the drives, then we took it to the security office and put it in the safe."

"Great, Eva. Now we can sit back. Wait for our ride home."

"There's a hitch. I don't know if the lab was breached between the time we were removed, and the time Kamryn and I returned. I've asked to see the vids of that time period. So far, there's been no response."

"Let me try. I need to take a shower. Change clothes first. I'll comm you in a little while."

He walked out. Axel followed him. Mark stepped across the hall and unlocked his door. It swung open. *Hot damn.*

An auburn-haired vixen, wearing nothing except very skimpy black lacy things—hardly worth putting on—but a whole lot of fun taking off—stood just inside his doorway. He smiled, probably leered, secretly thanking the gods his last night on Luna wasn't going to be spent hugging a bottle of scotch. Scarlett looked intoxicatingly…delicious.

"Thought I'd drop by to see if you needed anything after

being released from the hospital." She sounded sultry.

"As a matter of fact, you look exactly like what I need." He reached for her. She twisted away. He reached again. This time, she let him catch her. He kissed her, soft and playfully while they melted together. He picked her up and she straddled him, wrapping her legs around his waist. He didn't know yet if those stun batons had scrambled his brains. The important parts of his body had recovered perfectly. When her playful mood turned inviting, he lifted her over his shoulder. She giggled and squealed as Mark slammed the door shut with his heel, followed by peals of laughter that rang down the hall.

***

Two hours later, Mark was alone. His tablet pinged with official orders direct from TMD Headquarters to return to Terra. Mark commed the store where he'd purchased his leather clothing and spoke to the owner. He described what he wanted, saying he would pay in cash. The owner assured him she had everything. He explained where they were to be delivered. Next, he commed the Golden Pagoda, then the Cancún Cantina, ordering meals to be delivered with the payment in cash. Lastly, Mark sent a message to Petra stating Eva's concerns about the unviewed video which needed to be examined ASAP.

He took a shower, dressed in his captain's uniform, gathered his gambling winnings, and headed to the closest checkpoint to the Plaza area. He approached the two soldiers guarding the entrance. They engaged in small talk until an older woman, dressed head to toe in burgundy leather, arrived carrying three shopping bags. She approached Mark.

"May I see the green one?"

She opened the smallest bag.

He peered inside. "Excellent. You'll wrap that one and

deliver it?"

"With pleasure." Her eyes sparkled with their secret.

Mark slipped her the agreed upon payment. She handed him the other bags, bowed, and walked away.

Two waiters, one from each restaurant, appeared with bags of food. Mark paid, took the boxes and commed everyone that the last supper on Lunar was being served in his quarters. He was met by three salivating ravenous friends. After their initial pangs of hunger had been satisfied, Eva spotted the shopping bags.

"When did you have time to shop?"

"I ordered in, just like the food."

She pointed to the nearest bag and gave him a questioning look.

Mark nodded, not wasting time talking. He hadn't eaten any of the hospital food. After the extremely pleasurable workout with Scarlett, he was starving.

"Oooh…" Eva pulled out crimson red leather pants. Her face puckered up, eyes brimming with tears that spilled down her cheeks. She came over and threw both arms around his neck. "You're my best friend."

Mark held up his index finger, pointed at the bag.

Eva went back, pulled out a pair of black leather long coats.

"Those are for Axel and Kamryn. I thought they'd be good for concealing weapons. Hell, you could carry a whole arsenal under there without being detected."

Kamryn jumped up and tried one on. She smiled and in an uncharacteristic expression of gratitude, hugged him.

At last, Eva drew out an edgy looking black jacket decorated with jewel toned metal studs, decorative stitching, and pockets.

"For Petra. I couldn't send a request for help to anyone here, without knowing who was compromised, so I contacted Petra. If she hadn't acted so fast, I might be in the stockade awaiting trial."

Mark adopted a serious tone, looking at each one as he spoke. "I want you all to know how sorry I am for not getting to the lab sooner. I never knew CAMRIs security had been gassed until I read the report that morning. Then I raced over there. I was too late. If I had gotten there sooner..."

"You would have been on the floor with us. I knew about the tranq gas. It didn't occur to me that it could happen here, too. Kamryn and I both wish it had been one of us that took down those two. It wasn't. You came at the right time and neutralized the threat. A little unorthodox, but that seems to be your style. You are a soldier, Mark Warren. You may not see it, but we do. Soldiers learn they can't stop all the bad shit from happening. We can only minimize the damage. You did exactly that. Take it as a win."

Eva's tablet pinged. "They're sending us the vid I asked for. Petra says they've verified it's authentic. It's all original. Nothing's been edited."

They all watched the entire vid—without audio. From before they succumbed to the gas until all four of them were removed from the lab. Then two armored guards were posted at the door. No one entered until Eva and Kamryn returned to retrieve the data.

Axel stood, moving toward the door. "We need to pack. Turn in early. I don't know yet when they'll be coming to get us so we should be ready."

* * *

After retrieving the data chips from the Security Office, procedures for leaving Lunar Base 3 were a reversal of how they'd entered. However, the lunar security barrier personnel failed to request the return of any of their weapons or vests. He made eye contact with Kamryn. She nodded in agreement. They stood by in the docking bay to board a shuttle bound for the

Spacedock where they would catch a ship back to Terra. He hadn't realized how eager he was to return to his home base until now.

The instant he stepped through the airlock, he spotted the cryopods in the rear of the shuttle. Axel raised his hand, halting the procession. "Who's in charge here?"

A vertically challenged portly officer with a prissy attitude stepped forward. "I'm Lieutenant Jennings."

"Sir, do those two cryopods hold the criminals bound for Terra?"

"Affirmative."

"Our people cannot board this shuttle, lieutenant. Standard operating procedures mandate that protectees and detainees cannot travel on the same conveyance." Axel's hand cradled the butt of his sidearm. Kamryn eased up, taking a place at his side. Both towered over the lieutenant. Shoulder to shoulder, immobile, they blocked the airlock tube pathway.

"I have orders to transport you four to the spacedock. On this flight. So don't give me any trouble. Sit down and harness up."

"And I have my orders. Straight from Gen. Dimitrios of TMD Headquarters in Virginia."

One of the armored personnel guarding the cryopods clanked up the metal aisle, stopping behind the lieutenant. "Problem, sir?"

He waved the guard away. "My orders are from Gen. Yates. He's in charge of Luna. We're on Luna. So you'll follow his orders about leaving Luna."

Kamryn held up her tablet. "Jennings, if you'd be so kind as to read aloud the TMD Article 9-65.140, I believe it will corroborate Sgt. Von Radach's statement."

The lieutenant craned his neck to look at it. As if the data on her tablet had been corrupted, he keyed it up on his own device. His pinched face expression was all the proof Kamryn needed.

"Thank you. Have a nice trip." She and Axel executed a

perfect about-face, escorting their protectees back through the airlock, out onto the docking bay.

While Axel searched for the person in charge of Flight Operations, the shuttle they were scheduled to be on departed. The sergeant in charge of the docking bay assured him another flight would be leaving in fifty minutes.

A loud commotion back at the last checkpoint caught their attention. Within seconds, Scarlett came racing down the ramp wearing emerald green leathers, waving, her auburn hair flowing around her face.

All docking personnel watched as Mark dropped his duffle, spread his arms, and she rushed into them. Their embrace was the kind women loved to watch in old Earth movies. Even Axel appreciated the view. Eva and Kamryn elbowed each other, captivated by the spectacle. Then he realized news of this would spread all over the base faster than an airborne virus in a wind storm. He needed to get them out of sight before Mark was arrested for sexually assaulting the general's daughter. In public.

"Capt. Warren." Axel jabbed him in the ribs. "You're already on Yates's shit list. I believe you might have crossed the line into the stockade this time." He propelled everyone into the small waiting room, off to the side, out of direct view.

Without warning, an emergency siren started blaring from all comm systems in the docking bay. Lights dimmed to a flashing red.

The PA system announced, "There has been an explosion on the shuttle en route to the Spacedock. All future departures are canceled. A security lockdown is in place."

Together, Axel's team drew their weapons, as he kicked the door closed. Mark forced Scarlett down into a back corner. Axel sent a message to HQ with the report of the explosion. Kamryn dashed another off to their commanding officer, Maj. Buchanan. Mark sent his message to Petra, just to cover all their bases. Eva dropped to one knee beside Scarlett, guarding her.

There were never survivors of an explosion in space. If it hadn't been for Axel, all four of them would be dead. There was no doubt now that Beth Coulter meant to kill them all.

Chapter 12

A disturbed flurry of activity enveloped the docking bay on Lunar Base 3. Armored troops marched down the ramp to the waiting room, broke open the door, disarmed everyone, and took all five people into custody. Mark tried to stay close to Scarlett, but the sexes were separated. He managed to get off partial messages about being arrested to Petra, while Axel sent one to HQ. Neither one expected help anytime soon. Fifteen minutes later, they were in the Stockade, including Lt. Scarlett McDonnell, the general's daughter.

The three females were grouped into one large detention cell, with Mark and Axel in a separate cell across from them.

McDonnell, apparently never having been manhandled before, wasn't accepting her current predicament very well. "Touch me again, you draconian metal head, and I'll have you turned into a eunuch. Don't you know who I am?"

"My prisoner." The armored guard walked out of the holding area, metal door clanging behind him.

No sooner had he left than three JAG Corps Officers entered, followed by a tall, stately auburn-haired woman.

"Mother."

The woman pressed a finger to her lips.

Scarlett fell silent.

The woman, Scarlett's mother, otherwise known as Gen. Yates's wife, motioned one JAG Officer to the men's cell, one to the women's cell, with the third solely to speak with her daughter.

Mark noted that getting arrested with the general's daughter was by far the fastest way to receive representation. Tablets pinged, like a doorbell on Halloween, with messages from TMD Headquarters, and their release came minutes later. After all the charges had been dropped, Scarlett introduced everyone to her mother ending with Mark.

"Mrs. Yates, I apologize for all the confusion. We're exceedingly grateful for your assistance. What can we do to make it up to you?"

"Capt. Warren, you can explain why my husband's been acting strangely—erratic the past few days?" Her request caught everyone's attention.

Eva nudged Mark. He glanced at her. She mouthed the words "neural implant."

"Ma'am, did the general give you any indication as to why we were sent here?"

"He mentioned your facility was attacked, and you'd been sent here to continue your research."

"Yes, ma'am. There were extenuating circumstances. Might there be a private place we can talk?"

Six people gathered in, of all places, a small pantry inside the Cafeteria's kitchen. All four of Mark's group took turns divulging only relevant parts of the last couple of weeks to Ms. Yates and Scarlett. The two women stood together, arms around each other's waists, with their demeanors growing more somber with every word.

Mark concluded by saying, "And your comment, ma'am, leads us to believe that the general may have no knowledge that he's carrying an implant, or that it's remotely...manipulated."

Mrs. Yates ventured, "Like the two men who were arrested? The ones on the shuttle that exploded this morning?"

"Yes, ma'am. The same shuttle we were scheduled to be on— if it hadn't been for Sgt. Von Radach's quick thinking and Sgt. Fleming's persistence."

Mrs. Yates turned ashen, sunk until she was sitting on a crate of canned vegetables. "I heard him give orders for all of you to be on that shuttle." She cupped her head, elbows on knees, and began to weep.

Scarlett knelt to comfort her mother. "He wouldn't do anything like that on his own. He's a good man. He knows the regulations. He's third generation military, for God's sake. It's been his whole life."

Mark and Axel huddled for a moment, then agreed to send a priority message to HQ stating that the security of all three Lunar Bases might be compromised by its commanding general. Mark was torn between wanting to help him, or choosing to save the rest of the people under his command. Axel wasn't conflicted at all, so he was the one who technically sent the message.

Mark tried to soften the blow. "Mrs. Yates, several days ago a universal order went out for all military personnel to be scanned for implants. Any unsanctioned devices are being removed. Patients are, in all likelihood, being returned to duty with a clean bill of health. We were all scanned before leaving Terra. It's just a matter of time before all personnel undergoes the procedure."

Axel's tablet pinged. He read the message, scowled, showed it to Mark, Eva, and Kamryn.

Shit, shit, shit. Dimitrios was on the way to Lunar to personally relieve Yates from command, take him into custody, and appoint a new general to the post. Lives had been lost. More were about to be ruined.

It all lead back to Beth Coulter.

***

Unknown to the others, the two sergeants had received covert orders. They were to keep Mrs. Yates and her daughter from communicating with the general and as far away from him as possible. Without knowing his state of mind, or anyone else's on Luna, the sergeants were entrusted with keeping two additional people safe until Dimitrios and his security forces arrived.

They couldn't spend the next three hours in the pantry. It had already become too small for the six of them. Kamryn approached Eva with an idea; all four women would fade into the Plaza, doing lunch, drinks, or beauty spa—hiding in plain sight. Everyone except the two women in uniform, stepped out of the pantry for a moment, allowing them to change into civilian clothing, to blend in better. Kamryn also removed the tablet from Mrs. Yates's bag, thereby alleviating the possibility of any communication—to or from her husband.

The two sergeants agreed upon a code to use for where to meet, plus an emergency code for any dire situations, which they did not want to use. Axel and Mark were too easily identified, so they could not possibly hide in plain sight. They were relegated to the pantry for the duration. Just as well. Axel was tired of Luna. He'd encountered far too many problems here. He sat on a crate, stretched out his legs, and leaned back. "I'm relieved to be going home."

"I just hope we all make it in one piece."

"We should have been on that shuttle."

"Yes. My mother almost lost another son today." A sadness came over Mark as he spoke the words.

"So...you can thank me now, Blondie." Axel delivered a power punch to Mark's bicep and then laughed like hell.

They traded blows for a moment until it seemed as if the air was getting thin in that small room.

"I've had a very unpleasant time here myself." Mark started looking around at the crates of supplies. "Do you suppose there's anything in here to drink?"

"Oh, no. Not happening. Not until we're all standing back on Terra firma."

The two men shared childhood stories, raunchy jokes, and played mental games of one-upmanship to occupy the time until their tablets pinged with the alert Dimitrios had arrived. They abandoned their hiding spot, sought out the rest of their party, then took the most obscure route to the docking bay. The six of them maneuvered through the security barriers again, staying as inconspicuous as possible.

Apparently deceived as to the purpose of Dimitrios's visit, Yates came down the ramp, ready to greet the general, only to be rendered unconscious at once, then carried aboard the shuttle. Mrs. Yates and her daughter broke through the crowd, sprinting into the airlock with seconds to spare before Yates's shuttle departed.

Now reduced to the original four, Axel continued to observe the changing of the guard. Without the usual fanfare of such an auspicious occasion, General Wanda Reynolds became the first female commander of all Lunar Bases. She was bronzed-skinned, Amazonian in stature, with buzz cut hair, and uniform creases so sharp they'd draw blood if anyone dared come too close.

A trio of military doctors, plus the same number of combat majors were a part of her contingent. According to Dimitrios, the medics were to conduct scans of every living human on Luna; the officers were to deal with any unforeseen disagreements regarding the change of command. Since he wasn't in the mood for a leisurely visit, as the next shuttle arrived, his troops ushered him back through the airlock. Axel hurried his party aboard right behind them for the return trip to Terra.

***

Once they were back on Terra, in the cocoon of the underground base, where they felt safe among friends, a euphoria descended upon them.

Mark managed to find a quiet moment with Petra. "I wanted to thank you for everything you've done for me—for us all. When I saw this, I thought of you. It's not a gift. It's a souvenir of our adventures on Luna. You can accept it." He handed the jacket to her.

Petra blushed as she ran her hand over the soft dark leather with the stitching and the metal studs. "It's so…me." She put it on, still caressing the feel of it. "It's like finding a treasure. Thank you." She was still smiling when he left her to join his team in the dining hall.

Life was happily returning to normal. They spent time in the fitness center, firing range, and designing a new lab.

A knock at the door in the middle of the night awoke both Mark and Axel. Two soldiers ordered them to dress, pack duffels, weapons, and vests so they could double-time it to Harben's office. Eleven minutes later, they practically skidded through his door.

"Capt. Warren, you've received an emergency message from your family, routed through the CAMRI facility. Your father was assaulted. He's in ICU. We do not yet have proof, but there may be some indication that it's related to the incident you experienced in Canada—with the cyborg. The hospital is expecting us. They've been notified of the classified nature of this situation. We're sending a team with you to investigate—take statements."

"Sir, any news of my mother and sister?"

"Your father was alone when it happened. I believe they're with him at the hospital." The stocky, balding colonel glared straight at Mark. "You have a track record, Warren. So, I'm giving you a direct order. Do not kill any civilians. Or that stockade on Luna will seem like a dream vacation compared to where you'll end up next time. Your shuttle leaves in fifteen minutes. Now get out of here."

As they raced to the tarmac, Mark commed Eva with the update about his dad. "If they're coming for our families now, tell your brother to run and hide as if the devil himself were after him."

Waiting in the shuttle were: Torance, Fleming, the two cyber specialists, four giant soldiers in black tactical combat armor, weapons, plus some very unorthodox-looking heavy armaments. Mark stared at the armored soldiers while he harnessed himself to the hull. "I thought your armor was gray."

"It transitions. Snow white to pitch black, non-reflective, even changes to camouflage if we need to take a stroll in the woods."

The shuttle lifted off, became airborne, interior lights faded to deep blue, as did the twin glow strips on the floor. Mark hoped his mother and sister were braving this latest catastrophe. Like most humans in moments of great duress, Mark found himself making irrational promises to any deity listening, that he would forego all his bad habits, if only his father would not die.

Mark still harbored the secret he'd carried since his brother's death—that he'd been the one to dare Eric to volunteer for the Europa mission—which had taken his life. He carried the torment of that guilt every day. Now his father was another victim of an attack, orchestrated by Beth Coulter. He could not bear the burden of two ghosts. Rage smoldered inside Mark as he renewed his promise to physically rip her heart out to avenge his father and brother.

"Don't do it."

"Don't do what?" Mark glanced over at Axel, then realized that everyone had been watching him.

"Make promises you can't keep. I know what you're doing. I'm telling you it's a waste of time. Instead, you should be putting all those high-priced brain cells to work figuring out what needs to be done and the best way to do it the minute we get to Portland."

Axel was right. Mark had been through this same scenario. He looked across at Torance, a combat ER doctor imminently qualified to treat his father. Kamryn, Axel's badass female counterpart. Petra, the very same cyber who had helped him create the hologram after his encounter with a cyborg. Ohashi sat next to her, another cyber he'd met once, who was said to be a wizard on anything electronic. Plus, the four armored giants, and their various weaponry. All the military people knew their jobs. What Mark had to do was pull the local constabulary into a cohesive unit to track down his dad's assailant, in Portland, in the middle of the night.

Mark had a plan ready the second they all climbed out of the shuttle onto the hospital's rooftop. He raced to the waiting room outside ICU, hoping to see his mother and sister. He did.

Leslie Warren, sat motionless, staring off into space, a vacant look in her eyes. Gina jumped up. She ran to him, her face pink and puffy, tears streaming down her cheeks. He hugged her until she stopped crying. "I brought some friends, Ginny. We're going to fix this. Dad's going to be okay."

One armored soldier planted himself as a sentry outside Mr. Warren's ICU room. Kamryn secured the waiting room area. Axel gathered all the clothing Mark's father had worn. Petra scanned it for biologicals and trace evidence, then put it in an airtight bag.

The doctor scanned Mrs. Warren, administered an injection, did the same for Gina Warren. Then he entered David Warren's room to scan him, confirming the hospital's diagnosis. Torance consulted with the attending physician before the room was overtaken by the military. After a moment, Torance motioned Mark into the ICU room, followed by Petra with all her equipment, and Ohashi carrying two attachés of electronics.

The doctor had placed a medical halo around David Warren's forehead. "Talk to you father while I monitor his brain activity."

Mark approached the bed. He choked, looking at his father, half his head shaved, battered, bruised, hooked up to tubes, electrodes, surrounded by blinking machines. Mark bent over to whisper in his ear. "Dad, I'm home. Mom and Gina are okay. I love you. I'll be here when you wake up."

"He heard you. This is good." The doctor clapped Mark on the shoulder. "He has one linear skull fracture—no brain swelling—broken clavicle, humerus, femur, with spiral fractures of the radius and ulna. Plus various contusions, abrasions, lacerations. It could have been much worse. I have military grade nanites. Some other enhanced pharmaceuticals I can give him that will aid in a faster recovery. We will help him regain consciousness in a little while. Petra will get a hologram of the incident. Now—" Torance waved him away. "Good hunting."

As Mark entered the waiting room, he spotted two of his high school teachers. Rachael and Iris Lambert were sisters. One taught math, the other history. After retiring, they'd opened a dessert catering business called *The Chocolate Moose.*

"Mark, I shot it." Iris Lambert held up her hand as if she were in class. She hadn't changed one bit; a stocky, large bosomed, gray-haired woman, with petite hands, who had marked all his algebra tests with a big red "A."

"You shot what?"

"There was a big awards dinner at the Willamette Mansion tonight. We always supply the desserts. Rachael pulled the van up to the front, and started unloading. I heard a commotion, grabbed the shotgun—thought it might be a bear or something. Heard a man's voice cry for help. Ran in the direction of the noise. A form was bent over a body on the ground. I fired both barrels. Got it with my trusty old 12-gauge over and under. It should be dead—laying right where I found your dad. Surprised me when it ran off. More like limped. Didn't know it was your dad until I checked for ID while I was calling for EMTs and the Sheriff. So sorry. If you're going after it, we can stay here with your family."

"Who's the sheriff?"

"Harold Blackwell."

"Shit."

"Now, Mark, I don't have a cuss jar anymore. If you keep that up, you'll be spending time at our house chopping wood."

"I'm sorry, Miss Lambert. It won't happen again. We have...history—bad blood. Was he at the crime scene? Did he bring dogs?"

"No, he wasn't there. No dogs either. A deputy I don't know showed up. Here. I have his card."

"Does Cliff Morgensen still have dogs?"

Rachael Lambert stepped forward. "Yes, he and his brother, Stan, both have about a dozen dogs between them. Even uses the dogs to hunt for lost hikers." She took his hand, leaning in toward him, whispering, "I saw it."

He studied her for a couple of seconds.

Rachael nodded, sincerity etched in every crease of her face. She was the taller, thinner sister, not as outgoing or gun-toting as Iris, but just as honest.

"Come with me, please." Mark led her into the ICU room. Introduced her to Petra and Torance. "Eyewitness."

They acted in concert, explaining the hologram process while Petra sat Rachael down, applied the medical halo, electrodes, hooked up the screen, before shooing Mark outside.

Mark stepped back into the waiting room. "Miss Lambert, can you contact both Morgensen's—have them bring all their dogs to the Willamette Mansion right away? Tell them I'll pay double."

Iris nodded, holding up her tablet, pointing to the screen. "I'm on it."

Ohashi approached him "Capt. Warren, I've been monitoring all bands, frequencies, and net traffic since I set up my equipment. There's been no mention of your father being assaulted or any crime committed at the location the EMTs responded to. However, I picked up a small bit of encrypted data being sent to a private satellite just after your father was attacked—from the same location."

"Here's the deputy's card. Can you check him out? Odds are he's a part of this—somehow. Please send the GPS of the Willamette Mansion to the shuttle. When Petra's finished with her hologram—send the image to everyone's tablet."

The doctor joined the group. "Synthetic skin. We're positive."

Mark's heart skipped several beats. Then a rush of adrenalin began burning through his veins like molten lava. Mark felt a contradiction of emotions. Fire on the inside, with death wishes for Beth Coulter struggling for supremacy over the cold logic of a strategy for capturing the wounded cyborg. He switched on his poker face.

Mark turned to his mother and sister, knelt in front of them, taking their hands. "I have to go now. Don't worry. I'll be back soon. I promise."

There was a light in his mother's eyes now; color had returned to her face. They sat united, leaning on one another. Gina's fingers were laced through hers. They both looked better than when he'd arrived. He kissed their foreheads, turned, then sped off to the rooftop with both sergeants and four armored soldiers in his wake.

Heading from the hospital to the Mansion took three minutes. The shuttle began emitting searchlights around the perimeter as it descended. They jumped free the second the hatch slid open.

The grand Mansion was a charming relic of times past. Three stories, with over twenty-five rooms, now used for all sorts of events. It sat in the middle of a cleared circle surrounded by fifteen wooded acres, rose gardens, with some hiking trails. Mark hadn't smelled cold, crisp outdoor air in weeks. He felt invigorated. The familiar aroma of Christmas in the Douglas firs, the rich, heady scents of cedar and maple.

All their tablets pinged. The image from Rachel Lambert's hologram appeared. An exact duplicate of the cyborg from Canada. Maybe the same one? Or were there multiple copies?

Two vehicles had arrived, several men unloaded packs of dogs. Mark ran toward them. He counted a mixture of eleven bloodhounds, beagles, and shepherds. The two Morgensen brothers, plus their father handled the leashed canines, herding them toward the shuttle.

After greetings, Cliff Morgensen, bearded, in a red plaid shirt, stepped up. "Pop came along because he knows these woods better than anybody. All our animals have GPS trackers in their collars so we can see where they're going. Who or what are we looking for? And why is the military involved?"

"Iris Lambert shot at and may have wounded my father's assailant. This is the image Rachael Lambert saw limp away." Mark showed his tablet to the three locals. "According to Terran military records, he's on a wanted list for other crimes."

Axel handed the bag of David Warren's clothing to Mark. "This is what Dad was wearing when he was attacked—right over there in those bushes." He pointed to an area off to the right of the Mansion's front steps. "Dad's scent is all over his attacker. Your dogs can follow it, right?"

"You betcha." Cliff pulled on sterile gloves, to avoid contaminating the scent on the clothing, then led the dogs to the bushes. Two beagles sniffed, moved off, noses down, following a trail away from the scene. Twenty feet away, they pawed at the ground. Stan, their handler, searched the ground with his light, then motioned for Mark to come forward.

Mark ran to the spot, looked down, and dropped to one knee. He was stunned. A foot. The left foot—to be precise. No wonder the cyborg was limping. Mark commed the others. "Iris Lambert shot its foot off."

Both sergeants came running.

Mark pointed to the booted foot on the ground. "Can the shuttle scan metal, or track a metal signature?"

"Yes." Kamryn used leaves from the ground to pick it up, ran it into the shuttle. She commed him, "It's a titanium alloy. We're going airborne to get a fix on a location."

Mark turned to Cliff. "Turn the dogs loose."

Commands to: "Find it," rang in the air.

The pack of dogs took off like they were after a fox. Some howled and barked, others were silent hunters. The shepherds followed an air scent, bloodhounds and beagles sniffed the ground. They were all headed in the same direction. Mark so enjoyed being outside, he ran with the pack as far as he could, until they entered the wooded area.

Mark commed Kamryn. "Alert Ohashi that we're after it. Find out what we're supposed to do with it when we catch it. Tell her it could have a built-in tracking device, or a self-destruct protocol. No doubt we've got enough firepower to blow it up, but that's not going to get us any closer to finding Beth Coulter."

Axel ran past him, along with Cliff and Stan, as they followed their dogs deeper into the forest. The pack began to zigzag, circle and loop. In time, all the dogs became quiet. A spotlight from the shuttle shone down through the trees to an area near a creek. Mark caught sight of Cliff's father, followed him into a tiny clearing, where several trees had been cut down. Dogs gathered, some sat quietly, others growled. Mr. Morgensen pointed to a spot almost hidden in the shadows. Mark could barely make out a human form on the ground, curled up in a fetal position.

Mark commed everyone. "I see it. Kamryn? Orders?"

"Disable it."

Their four armored soldiers moved out of the tree line into the spotlight. Two with pulse rifles, the others holding weapons

Mark had never seen before. In slow motion, they advanced to within about six feet of the form—before it uncurled itself—leaping into the air. The ring of armor jumped backward. The cyborg came down almost on top the nearest soldier. The pair with unknown weapons shot what looked like foam at the cyborg, totally immobilizing it.

"Disabled. Affirmative. Now what?"

Chapter 13

Beth Coulter wasn't her given name. She'd had many different personas and had worn many disguises. She was a chameleon. A chameleon with a goal. To claim what was rightfully hers, leaving all the pretty people with their fancy degrees wondering where they'd gone wrong.

She had recently shed the Beth Coulter image; now she was a dead ringer for Josef Scheinberg. A short, stubby man, with a heavy beard, obscuring his aging face. This humble man's last mistake had been asking a woman he'd just met out to dinner. Today she sat behind his desk on the third floor of the Terran Space Station. Josef's job had been to coordinate water supply to the station, which amounted to more than a million gallons a week. After only half a day of literally walking in his shoes, she was already bored to death with his job.

Using his passwords, she established an encrypted channel to check with an operative—one of the last few with a neural implant in Portland. It would take a few moments to establish the connection.

She waited and thought about being marooned on Terra for weeks after the All Points System Bulletin, plus the Wanted Notice image that went out following the huge CAMRI debacle. She was furious when her well-planned appropriation of data had been so disastrously mismanaged. Since then, a cyborg had been captured, all Terran military were being tested for neural implants, and she'd been identified at the Houston facility. Beyond which, the Malaysian plant had been discovered, ultimately closed with the owners arrested. The Lunar shuttle explosion should have taken care of all the pesky loose ends. Again, things didn't go as planned. The loss of Yates as a key operative on Lunar was another blow.

Her two wayward targets held crucial data that kept slipping through her grasp. Which left her with no recourse. She was forced to redirect her efforts toward the next best thing—their families. Not a fatal accident, yet. If they were dead, she'd have no leverage. The injuries needed to be so damaging it wouldn't be misconstrued. She'd send an unmistakable message to Mark Warren and Eva Jackson. They were brilliant—not geniuses—but borderline. The logic of a fair trade wouldn't be lost on them. Their data for the lives of their precious families.

A trio of musical notes sounded, notifying her to transfer an avatar she used to communicate with this person to the vid screen.

"Mayfield here."

"Report."

"Your orders were carried out successfully. However…"

"Speak."

"Only one casualty. And…it did not return."

"Last known location."

"On the outskirts of the property near a creek."

"*Scheisse.* Retrieve it. Now."

"It's dark—in the middle of the night. Lights out in the woods at this hour will attract attention, maybe even law enforcement. Shouldn't it be given more time to return on its own?"

"Retrieve it. Now. Or suffer a worse fate than its last victim." She manually terminated their connection.

Although she controlled a small army of cyborgs in countries around the globe, the Malaysian plant's closure had blocked the production of additional units. The new plant in India wouldn't be operational for some weeks—or more. She needed to be back on Terra to prevent any oversight issues. Because it had been almost impossible getting off Terra, she wasn't anxious about going back. By the end of the day, she would possess all the clearance codes for arrivals and departures to the space station. Then she would be able to come and go as she pleased. When the time came, those codes would grant her access to the Martian space station with the same ambiguity as well.

She walked into the next office. It was lunchtime and vacant. After moving a chair under the air vent, she climbed up, then squirted three droplets of RX-59, an airborne pathogen, into the air shaft. She put things back the way they were, then went to Josef's quarters to check on the status of his liquefaction. The process was working quicker than expected, so she went to lunch, too.

***

Mark drew the three Morgensen's off to the side of the foam-encased cyborg. "Under penalty of treason and imprisonment in a military penitentiary, you must sign these waivers of non-disclosure, and take an oath never to divulge anything you've seen here tonight. You can say it was a bear. Hell, I don't care if you say it was Big Foot. You just can't say what you really saw."

"Shit, Mark, we're not here, we're all at home watching Westcoast Wrestling Superstars on the vid." Cliff punched him in the arm, good-naturedly. "We'll sign whatever you want us to." They did, then corralled all the dogs, gave them treats, packed them in the vehicles to go home.

Kamryn approached Mark. "Headquarters says they're sending an express shuttle with a special container to transport this—specimen—back to Virginia. In case it sent out a distress signal before we rendered it inoperative, we need to secure the area. Watch for anyone coming to rescue it."

Mark stayed close, fighting the urge to laser through the foam and dissect it himself. Instead, he just waited like the rest of them.

Axel ordered one armored soldier to guard the cyborg,

spreading the rest into hiding places near the Mansion's parking lot, to beyond the tree line. In the interim, their shuttle moved off about 100 feet, as another shuttle silently appeared. It descended, black armored troops jumped down with a large crate. They lifted the foamed mass into the box, locked the lid, and sped away without uttering a sound.

Their shuttle assumed its original position, dispensed an aerosol from vents in its undercarriage, thereby eradicating any evidence of the foam substance. It drifted down, nestling in between the trees, then went dark—into stealth mode.

Faint headlights flashed through the trees, alerting everyone to a vehicle entering the empty parking lot.

Axel commed orders to everyone. "Do not approach."

A shadowy figure left the vehicle carrying a small tablet with a LED light. It made a beeline for the trees.

Mark took out his gun, set it on maximum stun, moved up near the clearing, careful to stay hidden within the trees. He squelched the urge to fire at the moving shadow as it advanced into the forest. It passed just yards from where he stood. The shadow did not waiver, but walked, head down, straight toward the spot last occupied by the cyborg.

A few yards before he stumbled into the shuttle, Kamryn stepped into his light with her gun drawn. "Halt, by order of Terran Military Defense."

He shot her.

She shot him—twice.

They both fell.

In seconds, the injured were loaded into the shuttle, along with everyone else. Kamryn was unconscious, bleeding profusely from the neck. They took off at breakneck speed to the hospital. One armored soldier pulled a packet from a hidden seam on his bicep, handed it to Axel. He tore off the wrapper, dropped to one knee beside Kamryn, jabbed her in the thigh with a syringe. Before long, those closest to her were standing in blood.

Mark looked on, feeling helpless, remembering this scene from his first meeting with Axel. The soldier, Scarlotti, had been injured. He had died. For the first time, Mark was overwhelmed by his mortality. Death and dying. Eric, Scarlotti, his father, now Kamryn. All of it, in his mind, arranged by Beth Coulter. Mark Warren vowed to himself he would end her if it were the last thing he ever did.

The major waited on the rooftop with gurneys and doctors. Medical halos went on at once. "He's just stunned. Restrain him in a private room with two guards. Send in Deering and Ohashi."

The doctor held Kamryn's hand while jogging alongside the gurney as they sped through the halls. She was ushered into an Operating theater. The doctor passed through the adjoining Cleansing anteroom, donned a sterile gown, mask, and gloves. The armored soldiers, including Axel, gathered outside the Operating room, holding vigil.

Mark couldn't. Instead, he went to join his family. In the ICU waiting room, Mark found the Lambert sisters waiting with his mother and sister. He gave them a thumbs up gesture. They broke into beaming grins, moved away so he could have a private moment with his family.

Gina Warren sat composed, holding her mother close, as a parent would comfort a child. Leslie Warren looked totally different than when he'd first landed in Portland. Worry was written on her face. Stress weighed on her shoulders. A hopeful look in her eyes spoke volumes. Mark knelt in front of them. "We got him."

They both breathed sighs of relief.

Axel walked in. Took a chair next to Gina.

Mark's mom began to speak. "We were supposed to go with Dave tonight. He was getting an award after the dinner. Before we left, I got an emergency call from a patient. Carol Ellison was taking her garbage out. She fell—broke a front tooth. Dave didn't want me going to the office alone at night, so he made Gina go with me. It only took a few minutes to make a dental impression. Then I swung by the dental lab—tossed it in the overnight drop box. We were on our way to the Willamette Mansion to join your dad when Iris Lambert called. She said to meet the EMTs here."

***

Beth Coulter, still in the guise of Josef Scheinberg, strolled along the concourse of the Terran Space Station with impunity. She had completed the disposal of Scheinberg's remains.

She'd booked passage on a private starship, scheduled to leave the station in less than an hour for a return trip to Terra. Las Vegas would be her next stop. That gambling cesspit served as a delicatessen of ethnicities. There she would acquire a new persona. Portland was her actual destination. She needed to be closer to her target—and his family—to better execute a plan for acquiring the data she needed. She had the superior position, which meant she must hold on to it at all costs.

The other target's family member resided in Brooklyn, a huge population area compared to Portland, where it had been easy to locate the Warrens. Her New York operative had not yet sent a report on the status of his progress, meaning a stop on the east coast might be necessary as well. From there, she'd continue to India, to oversee the new plant and the titanium shipments required for cyborg production. Once she was in possession of all the data from her targets, she would execute the final phase of her ultimate goal. She intended to write history—and the elimination of anything or anyone that got in her way.

***

Torance joined the small group in the ICU waiting room. He looked drained, with a surgical mask dangling from his neck, but no longer wearing an operating gown or gloves. His hands were clasped together at his chest, as if in prayer. "She's alive."

Mark was jubilant. Axel acted ecstatic. They rushed to shake his hand and clap him on the back.

"Hold on. I didn't say she was in the clear—she's still critical. I've already given her the maximum nanite protocol. Need to wait another twelve hours before I can administer any more. They're going to set her up in the adjoining ICU room next to you father, Mark. I'll have a hover gurney brought in so I can catch a nap in her room. That way I can monitor both my patients."

The doctor walked over to his mother, knelt cupping her hand. "Mrs. Warren, I'm Maj. Nathan Torance. I'll be taking care of your husband. Do not fear, ma'am. He's improving as we speak. You can look in on him now, but make it quick. Then you need to go home—come back after you've had some rest—there's nothing you can do here."

Leslie and Gina both stood to hug the doctor then hurried in to see Dave Warren.

Mark watched the hospital staff guide Kamryn's hover gurney through the hall, with the doctor following behind it into the room next to his dad's. One armored soldier took up sentry duty inside each room, while the other two stood guard outside their doors.

"Axel," Mark said privately, "I'd sure feel better if you'd come with me to take my mom and sister home. If they meant to take out the whole family, I might need some backup at the house."

"I'm your wingman." Axel thumped his chest with a fist. "Where you go—I go. Besides, the major's right. Nothing I can do for Kamryn here. Go check on your dad. I need to find some more firepower." He sprinted down the hall toward the exit leading to the rooftop.

The minute Mark entered the room he saw the armored soldier in the corner, keeping watch over his father. He went straight to his dad's bedside, put his arm around his mother's shoulder, hugging her close. The medical halo had been removed. His dad's whole head was shaved now, not just half as before. His father looked strangely intimidating bald, more than he had with a full head of hair. The creases had faded from his brow, nanites already healing his facial injuries. The machines continued blinking, showing his dad's condition was inching toward improvement. If he'd been a child seeing his father like this, he would have cried. Not now. From somewhere deep inside his memories, he heard his father's voice. "Deal with it—and persevere." So he made a mental promise to his father. Deal later—Persevere now. Mark's priority was to keep his mother and sister safe, and he needed Axel to help him do it.

***

Beth Coulter, still in the persona of Josef Scheinberg, felt effervescent as she disembarked the private starship onto Terra firma. Her seatmate on the flight to Las Vegas would be her ticket to anonymity in Portland. The middle-aged chemical engineer, Tessa Underhill, now returning to Terra after her assignment ended on the Space Station. She'd been so talkative on the flight home, that Beth practically knew the woman's whole life story by the time their ship settled on the tarmac. When Beth offered to buy dinner, Tessa had freely given up her hotel and room number.

Before dinner, she had time to shop for a suitable wig, makeup, clothes and undergarments. At the appointed time, Beth knocked on Tessa's door. When it opened, she used a stun baton to render Tessa unconscious. After opening a body bag on the floor, Beth rolled Tessa onto it, then set the stun on lethal, and terminated her victim. She took off the corpse's jewelry, poured one hundred and twenty-four milliliters of liquefaction solvent to the face and various identifying marks on the epidermis. While that was working, she used Tessa's credit account to book a flight to Portland, leaving in four hours.

She stripped down, eliminating all vestiges of the Josef Scheinberg disguise and began the meticulous work of turning herself into the new persona of Tessa Underhill. She showered, dressed in new undies, clothing, borrowed jewelry, applied makeup, a wig. She felt like a new woman. Beth snorted. She was a new woman. Her reflection in the mirror was a very good likeness of the picture on her new identification card; an inconspicuous female of average height with brown hair and eyes. Then she removed the corpse's fingerprints, using surgical glue to apply them to her own. She admired her handiwork. Handiwork—she was witty, too. Now her prints would match those on the card as well.

Beth emptied Tessa's suitcase, stuffed the body bag with its contents inside, then guided it to the service elevator. There she dumped the body bag out, pushed the button sending the car to the basement, walked out of the elevator with an empty case. Before leaving the room, all evidence of anyone's presence was expunged. Female clothing went into the travel case; men's went into a shopping bag—to be discarded in an appropriately ubiquitous location.

Functioning as Tessa Underhill, she checked out of the hotel early—giving a family emergency as a bona fide reason—and went straight to the spaceport for her flight to Portland.

Chapter 14

Axel stood on the hospital's rooftop. He seethed with anger as guards loaded their prisoner, the man who had shot Kamryn, into a shuttle. It was bound for HQ in Virginia, where the prisoner would undergo extreme interrogation. He wanted to pounce on the man and drive a stake through his heart. But he wouldn't—today.

As that one left, another TMD troop transport carrying a fresh platoon of armored reinforcements descended to the rooftop. Axel commed Mark to bring his family up to board the new shuttle.

A few soldiers jumped out. They would remain at the hospital guarding the two injured. When Kamryn was off the critical list, she would be transferred back to their home base. Now the bulk of the troops would be sent to the Warren's residence to scan, search and secure the grounds, exterior and interior before the women would be allowed to enter.

After the two women had boarded, Axel helped them harness up. Mrs. Warren trembled. Gina tried to console her. They were both anxious and afraid.

"This is like a walk in the park, Mrs. Warren. Nothing to be afraid of. You'll be home in a few minutes. We're just going to make sure everything is safe."

"I don't understand, Sergeant. I hoped...expected...Mark to come home when his father got hurt. I'm confused as to why the military is involved. Especially this much military." She waved her hand, to include the twenty-five black armored soldiers, wearing helmets, with their weapons and gear. "This is unnerving."

Gina nudged her mother. "It's Mark, Mom. It's what he

does."

"He's a scientist. In Canada."

Mark looked like he didn't want any part of this conversation, so Axel answered for him. "Well, not exactly."

"I knew something wasn't right." Leslie Warren's eyes narrowed.

"We'll finish this when we get you inside." Axel used his best sergeant's voice, hoping to discourage any more of her questions.

Leslie Warren didn't seem happy, however, she stayed quiet.

The rambling two-story house sat on a quiet cul-de-sac, with a grove of trees sheltering the backside. In stealth mode, the shuttle descended into the Warren's large backyard. All the armored soldiers exited and made quick work of securing the property, then faded into the shadows to monitor the perimeter. Axel grabbed two duffels from under his seat. He ushered the last three people out of the shuttle and into the house through the back door, while the shuttle returned to the hospital.

Leslie Warren went straight to the liquor cabinet, chose a fine bottle of whiskey, along with three glasses. She set them on the dining room table. She sank into a chair, poured herself a stiff drink, then motioned for everyone to sit.

"I don't know what was in that shot your doctor gave me, but I'm thinking very clearly right now. Somebody better tell me what's going on. Why is the Terran military involved in my husband's assault?"

Everyone filled their glasses half full. Gina abstained. Axel looked at Mark, who shook his head.

Axel turned to watch Leslie Warren, swearing to quit if she showed any signs of stress. "Mrs. Warren, about three weeks ago, Mark's Canadian installation was attacked. My unit suppressed the incursion. That's when I met your son. His lab partner—a woman—had planned it so she could steal classified military data from Mark and another scientist. She escaped. We've been searching for her ever since. In the meantime, Terran military transferred Mark and the other scientist out of Canada so we could keep them secure.

"This woman is hell bent on acquiring their research. Using it for her personal gain. She is clearly pathological. Now she's resorted to using force against the scientist's families to coerce Mark and Eva into giving up their data. I apologize in the name of the Terran Military Defense. I'm sorrier than you'll ever know that harm came to your husband."

"The other injured person they brought in...was that a soldier—a female?"

"Yes."

"What kind of data?" Leslie Warren finished her drink.

Several moments of silence passed.

"Cybernetics and terraforming," Mark whispered, before emptying his glass.

"My god, she wants to terraform moons and inhabit them with cyborgs."

"Yes," Mark said.

"We were leaving for the awards dinner until I got the emergency call. So you're telling me Gina and I would have been attacked, too?"

"Unknown," Axel said. "The most likely outcome? Yes."

"I don't imagine she was the one who assaulted my husband tonight—so she has others doing her dirty work—right?"

"Affirmative."

"That's how your soldier got hurt?"

"Affirmative."

"I'm going to assume not everyone has lived through these attacks. How many have died so far?"

Mark blurted out, "One hundred sixty-eight...that we know of."

"Well, find that bitch and kill her!"

"Yes, ma'am. First chance I get." Axel drained his glass.

***

Upstairs, Axel had been assigned Eric's old room. After tossing his duffel on the bed, he got in the shower. He needed to purge the night's events from his system, cleanse all the raw emotions from his mind. Scarlotti's death still weighed on him. Kamryn was in the ICU—directly because he had recommended her for the operation. At this moment, he wanted to pound his fist through the wall—over and over again—but he wouldn't. Instead, he turned the shower's temperature all the way to cold, letting the icy water chill the hatred for his adversary into stone hard logic. Without realizing it at the time, the answer he had given to Mark's mother was the truth. He would not arrest Beth Coulter. She wasn't worth turning over for prosecution. Given a chance, he would kill her. Period.

To minimize the military's presence in the Warren's house, Axel decided the leather clothing would be a better choice, at least for today. He toweled off, pulled on the black pants, just as he heard a light knock on the door. He opened it to see Gina wearing a fuzzy bathrobe over blue pajamas.

She pushed her way in, shut the door, and then poked him in the chest with her finger as she spoke. "This is important. I need to tell you something about my brother. You must promise never to let him know I told you. Do you promise?"

Axel took her finger off his chest, led her to the bed, pushing on her shoulder until she sat down. He sat cross-legged on the floor so he could look at her. "Yes. I promise." He continued to hold her hand as she spoke at a break-neck pace in a hoarse whisper.

"I was a dancer—ballet—and I hurt my knee. I never stayed off it long enough to let it heal properly. It got to the point where

I couldn't stand on it anymore, much less dance. I had surgery to fix it. Long story short, I became addicted to the meds. Went all the way down the rabbit hole.

"Mark was away at college in Washington. He didn't know how bad I was. My parents called him. He came home. Went out alone—and found me in the worst place you can imagine—in the worst condition you can imagine—and I was being raped. My brother almost killed three guys. With his fists. After he brought me home, he locked me in my room for three days. When he opened the door to let me out, I told my parents I wanted to go to rehab. Then Mark went back to college and aced his finals.

"One of the guys that Mark maimed has had facial reconstruction—and do you know who he is? Our current sheriff. I'd bet that's the reason no deputy came to the hospital to take a report from the Lambert sisters." Gina slumped, as if she'd exhausted her last ounce of energy.

Axel spotted similarities from Mark's violent behavior in saving his sister, to his fierce actions in the lab on Luna. Good to know.

"This is a classified military incident, Gina. Which means it's preferable the local law enforcement not be involved." He grinned. "But I can fix the other thing."

"You can't let Mark near the sheriff."

"If it happens, I'll be with him. I'm his wingman."

"I'm twenty-five and still living with my parents." Her eyes brimmed with tears. "Because I'm afraid one of those guys might…come back. Mark asks why I stay here. I tell him because I'd feel guilty leaving Mom and Dad alone. I could never tell him the truth."

"If you give me their names—it won't ever happen."

She scuffed across the room in her fluffy blue slippers. Hovering over Eric's desk, she wrote on a slip of paper, came back and handed it to him.

"Consider it done." Axel tucked the note in his pocket.

"Now, what about my dad?"

"Maj. Torance has been saving soldiers, myself included, for as long as you've been alive. I have complete faith in his ability to heal your father and my friend, the soldier in the room next to his."

"You're not going to tell Mark—anything."

"Never."

"Okay." Gina threw her arms around his neck, giving him a long hug, before disappearing out the door.

Axel stretched out on the bed. He covered his eyes with his forearm, but he couldn't get the look on Gina's face out of his head. Today he'd witnessed a different side of her, compared to the first time he'd seen her. On the Luna vid screen she'd been bright-eyed, gorgeous in her yoga togs, high-spirited while talking with Mark. Since arriving in Portland, he'd seen her crying, haunted by memories of past abuse, and fearful not only of losing her father, but her brother's safety as well. She was tormented. Axel felt duty-bound to remove as much of her pain as possible.

Axel sat up and commed Ohashi. "How would you feel about doing some personal cyber sleuthing for me?"

"Are we catching bad guys?"

"Three."

"Oh, goody. I'm in."

"I want to know everything they've done wrong since the first grade, especially if it involves abuses of any kind against women. I have a feeling these scumbags are repeat offenders. And leave no trace." He gave her the three names, then turned out the light before closing his eyes.

***

Mark awoke at zero six hundred, on the dot. There were no messages on his tablet. He showered, dressed in leathers, t-shirt, shoulder holster, and gun. The second he opened the door, he smelled steak. He ran downstairs, taking three at a time, breezed into the kitchen to see Axel cooking—in a red BBQ apron.

Gina sat at the breakfast bar, in black floral yoga togs, drinking coffee and chatting with him as if they were old friends.

"Steak?"

"Coming right up, Sleeping Beauty." Axel flipped three sunny side eggs onto a plate, added a nice thick slab of beef from the fancy indoor grill, and slid it down the counter top.

"I didn't know you were so domesticated."

"I have many excellent qualities. Most will remain a secret." Axel winked at Gina.

Mark saw it. "Has anybody checked with the hospital?"

"I commed the major about an hour ago. He says Kamryn's nanites have kicked into high gear. She's off the critical list and on the mend. They might be transferring her back to the base tomorrow. Your dad's neural readouts show his nanite protocol is progressing nicely. We've been ordered not to go to the hospital before ten hundred because Torance is taking a cat nap."

"That's excellent news." Mark felt lighthearted as he poured a mug of coffee. He sat next to Gina, sliced off a hunk of steak, and stuffed it in his mouth. "Umm, good. When did you learn to cook?"

"I spent the last three years of high school summer vacations as a fry cook."

"What's in the pot?" Mark pointed with his fork to an industrial-sized soup pot on the stove behind Axel.

"Chili for the troops. All they brought were energy bars and MREs. Those get old quick unless you're in combat."

"That's not going to feed all of them."

"I can make more. Your mom's pantry looks like a grocery

store."

"Well, good morning boys and girl." Leslie Warren smiled from the doorway, dressed in a gray tweed jacket over black pants. "It's wonderful to see my kids in the kitchen again. You, too, Axel—oh, what smells so good?"

"He made steak and eggs, Mom. I told him you wouldn't mind. Soldiers need a hearty breakfast."

"Axel, I officially give you the keys to my kitchen." Leslie kissed both her children on their cheeks. After pouring her coffee, she leaned against the counter watching everyone. "And thank you for sending the major's update about Dave's condition to my tablet. Yesterday seems like a bad dream. I know it's not over, but things look so different this morning.

"We need to contact Dave's associates to let them know he's on emergency leave. His patients will have to be rescheduled or switched to another doctor. These are children and their parents. None of them are going to be happy about that.

"I don't want to put a damper on things, however, I have a few more questions. I wasn't prepared for what happened yesterday. If I know what might happen, then I'm better able to handle it—going forward."

Leslie looked at Axel. "Last night Mark told us the person who attacked his father had been caught. Will this woman continue to send people after us? Could Gina or I still be in danger?"

Mark started to answer.

His mom held her hand up to stop him, while continuing to gaze at Axel.

"Well, ma'am, I don't have a crystal ball...my guess is there's a fifty percent chance another attempt will be made. That's why we haven't left."

"I won't put myself or my daughter at risk. However, I also have a practice, patients, employees. Gina has a business, with classes and clients. What are we supposed to do?"

"I've already sent a situation report to my commanding officer, Maj. Buchanan. I'm certain she's in a meeting right now hammering out a plan to provide security and keep everyone safe until the threat can be neutralized."

Mark had hoped the morning would start out better than last night had ended. It had, but not by much. His father's injury was only the beginning of events that morphed into the military's ongoing Operation Pandora. With the apprehension of an enemy cyborg attacker, followed by an accomplice who tried to murder an NCO, Mark's family was now under the protection of armored troops. Since he wasn't running this operation, he had no say in what happened next. Somewhere in a far-off location, a major, or colonel, or general would make decisions directly impacting his family. Mark didn't like this situation. Not one damned bit.

An alert pinged on both men's tablets.

Axel caught the message on his first. He turned away from the women, sent a hand signal for Mark to be silent.

Mark glanced down, except he didn't understand what the five stars showing on the screen meant.

"I think the lieutenant outside might need a break. Let's go see what she wants." Axel tossed off the apron, moved toward the back door while grabbing his jacket.

Mark followed Axel across the backyard. "Five stars?"

"Someone on the Wanted List has been spotted. You get one guess who."

"Are you sure it's her?"

"Why would they be sending us this alert if it wasn't?"

A female soldier stepped out of the tree line on the backside of the house. Her armor reflected the camouflaged colors of the wooded surroundings.

"Lieutenant Inga Nazarova, this is Capt. Mark Warren. His father was the one attacked last night. His mother and sister are in the house. Did you get the alert?"

"Affirmative, Sergeant. Follow me. We've got a little vid conference set up back here with two of our commanding officers from the base."

A small vid screen had been wedged in between a tree fork. It showed a split image of Harben and Buchanan in their respective offices.

"Sirs, Sgt. Von Radach and Capt. Warren reporting."

Harben wasted no time. "Our facial recognition software caught an image it flagged as Beth Coulter leaving the Space Station just hours ago. She was almost unrecognizable because she was wearing the disguise of an older man with a beard, who we've since identified as a station employee. Using his account, fingerprints, and ID, she booked passage back to Terra, with Las Vegas as the destination. We must assume he has met with foul play and have initiated a search of the Space Station. The private transport craft has already landed on Terra. We are searching every database for any trace of her there, and on any flights leaving since she arrived.

"There was one anomaly. After her flight had left, people started getting sick on the station. Some bug was going around causing diarrhea. From the highest concentration of victims, they traced it back to a pathogen spread through the air ducts. It's been identified as RD-59. Capt. Warren, you have an extensive chemical background. Can you offer any explanation for this?"

"Sir, the first thing that comes to mind is RD-59 induces diarrhea, but RX-59 causes delirium. These are not street drugs. Depending on where and how they're stored in a lab, it's possible an inexperienced person might mistake one for the other. Without knowing what else Beth Coulter might have access to, an immediate inventory of the military's Special Pathogens Laboratory would be mandatory. And I guess we all know air ducts are her preferred method of delivery."

"Thank you, Captain. I'll forward this information to Gen. Dimitrios at HQ right away."

"Sir, I need to know what's going to happen to my family."

"I fully understand your concern, Captain. The plans are being finalized. You will be notified soon, in person, not by electronic means. Harben out."

His image disappeared from the screen, which held the expanded view of Buchanan.

"Nazarova, I want to reiterate your direct orders to provide protection to every member of Warren's family until you are relieved. Am I clear?"

"Yes, ma'am, Maj. Buchanan."

Chapter 15

At ten hundred on the dot, Torance welcomed the Warren family into his patent's room. Dave's coloring had returned to normal. His small contusions were about seventy-five percent healed. He had a day's growth of beard, and his hair had started to grow back, courtesy of the nanites.

Axel excused himself to visit Kamryn. The shadow of an armored soldier stood guard in a corner of her room. She lay motionless, eyes closed, peaceful as if sleeping, except for the extensive bandaging that covered the left side of her neck. The machines at bedside were busy with readouts of her neural, heart and nanite functions. Axel gently grasped her arm in a warrior's greeting.

She squeezed his arm a little in return. Her eyes fluttered, opened to slits, blinked, then opened half way. She focused on him, trying to smile.

"I've signed you up for a marathon when we get back to base. So don't get comfy here."

She chuckled. "Drugs."

"Oh, yeah. The major's got some good ones. Battlefield drugs are the best. They make you feel so good you don't want to get well."

"Uh-huh."

He bent over, whispering in her ear. "I'm so sorry, Kam."

She pinched him.

"Okay. No more emotional drivel."

"Sitrep?"

"Well, Mark's father is improving. Oh yeah, Beth Coulter was flagged leaving the Space Station in a man's disguise—using his fingerprints—so he's dead. She landed in Las Vegas. What do you suppose she's going to do there? Play a little roulette? Maybe see a show? Or, commit another murder, assume a new identity and hop the next shuttle to Portland?"

"Nooo." Kamryn lifted her head off the pillow.

Axel placed a finger on her forehead, lightly pushing her back down. He knew she would have gotten out of bed if she hadn't been hooked up to machines and full of drugs.

Kamryn shot him a meaningful look. "Catch bad guys."

"I know you want to. Don't worry. Lt. Nazarova's whole platoon landed last night. They're on protection detail. The brass takes it personal when a member of an officer's family is damn near beaten to death to pressure him into giving up military secrets. And one of their best sergeant's is shot apprehending an accomplice to the TMD's Most Wanted." He stroked her shoulder and stood there until she closed her eyes.

Mark walked up behind him. "How is she?"

"Drugged to the max, she still wanted to get up and go after Beth Coulter when I said she'd been spotted coming back to Terra. Kamryn's a damned good soldier. I respect her. I'm amazed she's still alive."

"Torance likes her. He called her a "peach." He'll take good care of her."

The cyber Ohashi entered. "Sergeant. A moment?"

"Sure." Axel stepped away from the bedside, while Mark wandered back into his father's room.

"I have that data you requested." The cyber specialist dropped a data chip into his pocket. "It reads like a crime novel. Two of them should have been castrated years ago. The third one is sneakier, but not much better. I don't understand how he got to be sheriff. I'm sure there's more that hasn't been documented. And you're not going to believe this—the deputy who responded to the call for Mr. Warren? Well, he's the sheriff's cousin."

"No shit."

"I left no trace, but you can't stick that chip into any military device to view it. I'd recommend a private system." She waggled her eyebrows. "Temporarily disconnected from everything else."

"Thanks, Ohashi. I owe you one."

"No." She made a slicing motion with her hand. "Justice will be thanks enough."

"Justice it is then."

***

Torance had waited until all the visitors were gone before he established a vid link with Harben and Dimitrios. The doctor was unhappy about having to transport his patients. In wartime, on the battlefield, in combat—yes—he could see the rationale. But not here—not now.

They would both heal. However, the doctor had not been entirely honest with David Warren's family about how long it might take before he would be back to normal. There could be some residual damage to what was inside the skull. He hesitated to tell Mark, since neural implants happened to be one of the repair options. And currently, those didn't have the best reputation.

Kamryn Fleming was a different story. As head wounds were the most complicated, neck wounds were some of the most problematic. Although she might wear her uniform again, she might not wear armor. Those units were in a class by themselves. You didn't need medals when you wore armor. It was your medal.

The vid connection came into focus with a split screen between Harben and Dimitrios.

"Do you have an update on the injured?" The colonel didn't look happy. He rarely did these days.

The doctor shared his prognosis with concerns for each

patient, even walking around putting their faces on the screen, along with their monitoring readouts. "They can be transported, but just because something can happen, doesn't mean it should.

"David Warren, his wife, and daughter all have practices. They're professionals in this community. If he's sent outside the area, his family will have to decide whether to desert their livelihoods to travel with him or abandon him in favor of staying here to make a living. Either way, when Warren's tour is up—considering everything that's happened to him, not to mention the attempted murder of his father—I would expect him to take his Ph.D. and run to the private sector. If he's still alive."

"Very well, Major." Dimitrios leaned forward; his usual salty demeanor had been replaced today with an unusual serenity. "Let's break for lunch. We'll reconnect in an hour."

The vid screen went dark.

The major knew Dimitrios well enough that his mood changes meant something alarming was on the horizon, and nobody was going to like it.

Ohashi poked her head into the room. "Sir?"

The doctor motioned for her to enter.

"We received an update on the Space Station incident. A container with liquefied human remains was found. They don't have a DNA match yet. Since Beth Coulter was using a man's ID and fingerprints—that has to be what's left of him, right?"

"*Araña viuda negra.*"

"And that is?"

"Spanish for Black Widow Spider."

"In New Zealand, they're called Redbacks." She shivered. "Nasty little things."

"We have a pathological serial killer on our hands, with a body count mounting by the hour."

Her tablet pinged. "You probably need to sit down for this one, sir."

The doctor sank into a chair. "Continue."

"With the transient population of Las Vegas, dead bodies aren't unusual. I flagged any report of a corpse remotely similar, and one just came up. A body bag with liquefied remains was discovered in a hotel's service elevator."

"Wait," he said, pointing a finger in the air. "Check the records on her flight to Las Vegas. I want an ID on her seatmate. See if that person had a reservation anywhere, then if anyone with the same name boarded another flight."

Ohashi rushed out, returning with a large tablet. Her fingers flew over the touchscreen, programming algorithms to produce the data requested by Torance. "Okay, now all we have to do is wait."

"Think I'll go get a quick bite to eat."

The large tablet buzzed. "Wow. The man from the station, Joseph Scheinberg, sat next to Tessa Underhill on the flight to Las Vegas. Her reservation was at the same hotel where they found the bag of liquefied remains. Six hours later, she also boarded flight N-965 to...Portland. Shit, sir. It's already landed."

"Immediately encrypt this data. Send it Priority One to Deering, Harben, Buchanan, and Dimitrios at HQ, plus Axel and Mark. We must keep the Warren women safe—but do not alert them. Find the location of the nearest shuttle; we may need it. Now."

He dashed out searching for the other cyber specialist. Found her dozing in the waiting room. "Deering."

Her eyes popped open. "Sir?"

The doctor snagged her by the arm, explaining the situation while steering her back to Dave Warren's room. "Send that data to every armored soldier at the Warren residence. Then get our facial recognition program working on everyone that got off that N-965 flight. I want to know what she looks like and where she went. You've got three minutes."

Torance ran to splash water on his face, finger combed his hair, and grabbed three cups of coffee from the machine. As he returned, both cybers had news. He offered them coffee, swung the chair into the corner to rest on, while listening to their updates.

Ohashi began, "Dimitrios is sending a shuttle to transport the Warren family, excluding the captain, to HQ. He says this is non-negotiable. It will also be dropping off three undercover operatives to impersonate Mr. Warren and his family. They will set up residence in the home and act as decoys for any future attempts by Beth Coulter or any of her agents." She hesitated. "Uh, sir, he did add that if it makes you happy, you can scan them all for neural implants when they get here."

Torance snorted and muttered a derogatory comment about the general's heritage under his breath.

Not to be overlooked, Deering cleared her throat in a dramatic manner. "I have the image from Tessa Underhill's ID. And an image of the person disguised as her, exiting the docking bay here about two hours ago. I'm transferring them to Ohashi's screen so you can see them enlarged side by side. On the left is the ID. On the right is the human at the shuttle port. I'm going to enlarge the left side of each face so you can see the difference in the faceprints. The distance between facial landmarks such as eyes, noses, and lips are nodal points. The human face has about eighty points. You can clearly see the variance. It's a good makeup job, however, the underlying bone structure is all wrong." She removed the ID image. "Now this is an image of Beth Coulter from her CAMRI badge of three weeks ago. It's a match."

"Do you have an image of the man, Josef Scheinberg?"

"Yes, sir." She inserted his ID between the two females on the screen.

"Amazing. She's a chameleon—for both sexes—that takes talent. It's a long shot but try researching back twenty-five years for anyone in the makeup, cosmetic, theater, vid production or entertainment industries. See if you can come up with a match for her faceprint.

Ohashi's small tablet pinged. "The incoming shuttle's ETA is twenty-six minutes, sir. Should I recall the captain and his family now?"

"Yes, but give no explanation—encrypt the message Priority One to Warren and Von Radach."

***

They'd just finished lunch at one of Leslie Warren's favorite Japanese restaurants when the Priority One message pinged on both military tablets. Mark tried to act as if he wasn't worried about the message, but the tightness in his stomach wouldn't go away. He felt compelled to present a confident façade to his family without knowing exactly what was happening—or why. He looked at Axel, who only shrugged and shook his head. Their orders stipulated a return to the hospital. Nothing more.

Minutes later everyone had gathered in Dave Warren's room to await the explanation.

The doctor wrote something on a piece of paper and passed it around. It read, "Warren family shuttled to HQ."

Mark mouthed the word "Why?"

"Your father's improving, except he needs specialized care not available at this hospital." The doctor pressed a finger to his lips, refusing to utter another word.

The Warren women seemed confused. They huddled together next to Dave Warren's bedside, waiting for the unknown.

A new uniformed doctor entered the room. She led two medics guiding a floating shiny cryopod. Were it not for her military bearing; she could have been mistaken for a mature model, with elegant features and shoulder-length silver hair.

Torance visibly brightened at seeing the new doctor. "Major Le Berre, I can't think of anyone I'd rather turn a patient over to than you."

The colleagues exchanged *faire la bise*, or kisses on both cheeks in the French custom.

"Quickly," she instructed the transfer of Dave Warren into the pod. The medics programmed all the settings and closed the lid. "So happy to see you again *mon cher*. I will send an ETA on TD. Come now, we must hurry."

Torance signaled for everyone to follow them out, up to the rooftop and into the shuttle. The medics situated the pod, carefully monitoring all the readouts flashing over the transparent faceplate.

Mark hugged his mother and sister goodbye, not knowing when he'd be seeing them again. He was about to insist on more information before letting them go when three people from the front of the shuttle walked toward him. They looked…remarkably like his mother, sister, and father.

Torance greeted them as he scanned each one for neural implants. Once they had been cleared, he motioned the male into the empty pod laying just inside the open hatch. The man climbed in and settled his frame within the confines of the metal cocoon.

At once, Mark understood what was happening. These three strangers were to impersonate his family while the Warren's were whisked away out of danger to the most safeguarded location in North America. He breathed a sigh of relief—until a new thought hit him like a sledgehammer. He grabbed Axel by the shoulder and whispered sharply, "She's here, isn't she?"

Axel gave a quick nod, verifying he had prior knowledge of this new game plan.

Mark felt anger rising in his chest. "What else aren't you telling me?"

"That's about all I know. Things are extremely fluid right

now. We'll be briefed when we get to your house."

Torance left the shuttle, taking everyone with him that was staying, including the three new additions to the Portland TMD contingent. The entire group congregated in Dave Warren's old room to switch out armored soldiers guiding the cryopod for regular hospital interns. Next, the entourage moved downstairs and out the emergency entrance where the pod was loaded into an EMS vehicle, then delivered to the Warren's home.

They were met inside by Nazarova. "The house has been swept for electronic devices and will be on a regular basis going forward. Also, a surveillance and alarm system has been installed on the structure and outlying perimeter." She smiled with pride. "If you decide to order a pizza, the delivery boy's going to be scanned for neural implants, blacklisted biomaterials and fifty-three different kinds of weapons."

"Outstanding." Mark had no idea what his mom would say when she returned. If it caught Beth Coulter, then it was worth it.

Every military tablet pinged with encrypted instructions for a vid conference.

Nazarova flipped on the large screen in the Warren's living room. They waited for the TMD insignia to materialize, followed by the split images of Harben and Dimitrios.

"Beth Coulter murdered a Space Station employee named Josef Scheinberg," Dimitrios spoke through gritted teeth, his coloring a sheer cherry red. "She cut off his fingerprints and liquefied his remains. The person she sat next to coming back to Terra was murdered in the same fashion. She has now assumed the identity of Tessa Underhill. This is the faceprint from the Portland spaceport where she landed this morning." An inconspicuous middle-aged brunette appeared on the screen. It could have been the face of a next door neighbor, kindergarten teacher, or librarian. Just not a killer.

"The Warren family was removed to avert the opportunity of

another attack. They cannot be used to coerce Capt. Warren into giving up any information. Except now, Capt. Warren, you are a decoy, along with the three undercover agents that have been embedded as your family. This predator wants what you have, Captain—so we've prepared a gift for her. A chip with massive amounts of cybernetic and terraforming data. However, this chip is formatted to be read exclusively by military systems, which means she'll have to be on a TMD base to access the data. Don't worry—it's flagged. The instant she opens the chip we know her location. Plus, it self-corrupts if anyone tries to make a copy. Just to put your mind at ease, not only is it encrypted, it's all obsolete data. Not a byte of useful information." Dimitrios gestured for Harben to proceed with his part of the update.

"An interrogation of last night's prisoner, the cyborg's human accomplice, revealed Beth Coulter has two more operatives in your area. Their identities were unknown. As of now, all TMD personnel have been scanned for neural implants—with an alarming number of unsanctioned devices being discovered. They've all been removed. It won't prevent a civilian with an implant from wearing a counterfeit uniform and impersonating a member of the military. So you must be on your guard. Don't take anything for granted.

"On a different note, the interrogation of the owners of the Malaysian cyborg plant revealed Beth Coulter had acquired another plant in India, which is not yet operational. Since titanium is one of the main elements, we've flagged those shipments and various other components to that particular location, as well. This new site will be under surveillance twenty-four/seven. It will never become functional.

"To recap here. Beth Coulter will contact you, Warren, or send one of her operatives. Your orders are to bargain—with the devil if need be—for the safety of your family using the data chip we've provided. We don't believe you'll be getting a second chance to get this right. So you'd better do a damned good job the first time around."

"Yes, sir. I understand." Mark understood all too well. They were using him as "chum" to bait the waters in hopes of luring their prime shark, otherwise known as Beth Coulter, to Portland. At the moment, he was too angry to be afraid. He still felt the enormous weight of this responsibility as it settled on his shoulders.

Chapter 16

The man standing in for his father approached Mark and handed him a small data chip. "You can call me Alpha. We never use real names on assignment. We studied a schematic of the house on the way, so we're familiar with the layout. I'm going upstairs to monitor the perimeter if that's okay with you."

"Sure."

"Hi, Mark," the woman said. "I'm Beta. I went over the dossier on your mother, so I know she's a professional. Do you know if she'd contacted her office manager to let them know to reschedule her patients?"

"No, I don't think she did. We should send them a message."

"Fine. I'll have the cyber Deering take care of that. Now, does she cook? Should I go see what I can make for dinner?"

"Be my guest. But I think you might have to fight Sgt. Von Radach for that position. My mom gave him keys to her kitchen this morning."

"Well, Sergeant, aren't you full of surprises?" Beta hooked her arm in Axel's. "Let's see what we can rustle up in this kitchen, shall we?" She led him away with the authority of a commanding officer, or a mom.

"I'm Charlie," the younger woman said. "This is such a change from what I normally do. Most of the time I have to portray the girlfriend of some scumbag weapons dealer, or a prostitute. So I consider this a righteous assignment, especially if we acquire the target. We were briefed on her crimes. I've never seen anyone with so many warrants. She's one wicked female."

Mark drew her aside, speaking in a confidential tone. "Can you tell me if her crimes also included being complicit in the destruction of the Europa mission?"

164

She nodded, then murmured. "Yes. I believe they were waiting on confirmation of some new information about neural implants before a determination was made on those charges. Your brother, Eric, was on that mission, right? I'm sorry for your loss, Mark. You have my word. We will do everything in our power to bring her down. For Eric and your father."

Mark collapsed on the couch. A warm rush of vindication washed over him. Finally, he had the answer he needed. His brother plus 151 other military scientists had been added to Beth Coulter's growing list of victims. From his second day on Luna, when Eva's friend had pointed to neuroscience, Mark had suspected Beth Coulter of orchestrating the annihilation of all those lives. Now, so did the Terran Military Defense. She would forfeit her life for the ones she had taken. Mark Warren swore he would sacrifice his life to be a part of her demise.

He went upstairs in search of Alpha, his father's stand-in. Mark found him sitting at the small desk in his parent's bedroom, looking at a vid screen with multiple views of the outer perimeter of the house. The man turned when Mark entered.

"I can't afford to screw this up, so I can't let my feelings toward her jeopardize whatever situation arises."

"You're a scientist, which means you have an extensive background in math. Do you play games—like chess or cards?"

In spite of himself, Mark's lips twisted into a lopsided grin. "Yeah, both."

"If you're good at chess, then you know there's a calculated strategy—tactics, you have to be able to visualize numerous moves ahead. It involves superior problem solving, logical analysis, and undeterred focus. You must employ the ability to be offensive and defensive at the same time to stay ahead of your opponent's moves.

"Playing poker takes slightly different talents. Reading people's 'tells' and adjusting your play to fit the opposition as well as the situation can catch your opponent off guard. Dumping your ego so you can focus on the game can be just as important as spotting specific patterns.

"Besides, Mark, you have an embedded geolocator, right?" He pressed a finger behind his right ear. "Everyone in my unit does, too. As far as we know, they're undetectable to enemy scanners. Your movements are being tracked twenty-four/seven. Just so you're aware—in the event it's removed, an alarm signal is sent out system-wide. The cavalry, or a shuttle, or a warship will respond. It depends on where you are and what kind of assignment you're on. Make no mistake, the TMD will come running."

"How do you see this playing out? Do you three have some sort of game plan?"

"We're mostly window dressing, to create the illusion of your real family. Your father was injured—not killed. That outcome would have been counterproductive. Coulter initiated a move to let you know she was serious. It's simple—if you don't want anyone else hurt, then give her what she wants. She won't be the one to contact you—for obvious reasons. Since there are two operatives here, one of them will approach you. Whatever communications you have with them will be monitored by Coulter. She knows your personality. You need to maintain the same behavior for her to believe you're bargaining in all honesty for the safety of your family."

"You have any idea when this will happen?"

"Soon, I would think. She's experienced some setbacks. I imagine she needs the data to move forward. That's what brought her here. She's not leaving anything to chance this time."

"I may have to lock myself in a room to get my head straight."

"It's not just about your family. It's for Terra's future in space, so—no pressure."

"Well, you might have oversold it with that last comment. I

don't know what playbook you're working out of, but the welfare of my family plus the future of Terra's space exploration don't equate to "no pressure." Mark wanted a drink, but he didn't trust himself. This was the ultimate high-stakes game. He couldn't win by playing fast and loose now.

"You worked with her for a year, didn't you? Just be what she expects. You'll do fine."

"Yeah, thanks." Mark nodded at his father's stand-in, turned to leave, then a thought struck him. Beth Coulter had deluded, hustled, and scammed him. Because she wanted what was in his head—and Eva's. If she could have created the formulas, she would have. That gave him the upper hand. Okay—now he was motivated. He descended the stairs two at a time, deciding to check on progress in the kitchen.

The doorbell rang. Mark veered off to answer the front door.

A short, balding older man dressed in khaki from head to foot, looking like anybody's grandfather, stood on the walkway. He held the leash to a small brown dog.

"Can I help you?"

"I saw the EMS vehicle bring Dave Warren home. I hope he's all right. You're his son, aren't you? Mark, is it?"

Mark stepped outside, closing the door behind him. "Yes, I am. Dad was in an accident."

"So sorry to hear that. I'm John Sands from up the street. Just out walking Gus here." He gestured at the bulldog on his leash. "Thought I stop to see—"

Behind him, the door opened a crack. "Mark, Mom needs you." His sister's stand-in poked her head out a little.

"Thanks for stopping by, Mr. Sands." He stuck out his hand. Reluctantly, the man shook it. Mark turned, went back inside and shut the door.

The room chilled. Everyone had gathered with anxious looks on their faces.

"Scan my hand," Mark whispered. "I didn't recognize that man. He called the dog Gus, except it was a girl dog. What about the new home surveillance system? Is it working? Did it pick up anything?"

Nazarova produced a utility-sized scanner. She passed it over both sides of Mark's hand, then flipped on the large vid screen and uploaded the data.

They watched it coalesce into almost a full handprint, which quickly linked to a faceprint taken from the new home security system, plus a DNA match. Seconds later a ribbon ran across the bottom of the screen with the message a neural implant had been detected in the most recent visitor.

"He's not John Sands. Face, fingers, DNA—all belong to Carson Adelle of Beaverton, Oregon, about seven miles outside of Portland. And he has a neural implant." Nazarova verified the information, then sent it to HQ in Virginia. As an afterthought, she added, "I'm going to flag his ID. Coulter has a bad habit of killing people once she's through with them."

"Bingo!" Alpha, Dave Warren's stand-in, sounded excited. "Four out of four. A perfect match. Coulter isn't wasting any time. She wants those files. The old man was sent to make sure you and your family were here. Now she'll send someone else to threaten you into giving up the data."

"Oh, joy." Mark studied the five people around him. "Well, hell, I've got all of you to back me up. So what could go wrong?"

Nazarova stepped in front of him, a bit too close for comfort. "Don't go near the door again until everyone's in position and we've identified the person outside. There's always the possibility it could be a real neighbor."

"Roger that, Lieutenant." Mark backed up a couple of feet. Much to his relief, she turned and walked away.

***

Axel grabbed Mark by the arm, steering him into the teal-trimmed, dark gray downstairs bathroom for a private heart-to-heart. "You're lucky Nazarova didn't put bruises on you for opening the door without permission."

"I'm supposed to know this shit? Nobody told me there were rules." Mark sounded indignant, he looked lost.

"Damn, Mark. You're supposed to be the smartest one in the room. You can't figure that out?"

"In case you haven't noticed, I'm out of my realm here. I'm a scientist—not a spy or undercover operative. Besides, Alpha said they aren't here to do anything. They're just window dressing."

"Look—your family's safe—for now, but if you ever want them to come back here to resume their lives after all this is over, then you have to have a plan and stick to it." Axel tried to get his anger under control. He was losing the battle.

"What if...the next time you answer the door, a stranger injects you with neurotoxin, cuts out your geolocator on the way to the spaceport, then shoves you onto a private shuttle bound for India, or god knows where? In fifteen short minutes, you could be in the wind. How do I explain that to your family? Or my commanding officers?"

Mark slumped. "Just tell me what to do."

Axel wished Kamryn were here. Her undercover work for the DEA in Vancouver would have been invaluable. Then remembered one of her stories. "Where's the data chip?"

Mark fished it out of his pocket, handed it to Axel.

"Now, I need a two inch square of black fabric and a stapler."

Mark left for a few minutes. He returned with scissors in one hand, a black silk scarf wound around a stapler in the other.

"Take off your pants."

"Wait, what?"

"I'm going to staple a small pocket to the inside of the zipper on your pants. Put the chip in there, then staple it closed. If a scanner is passed over you, the chip is hidden behind the zipper. It won't be detected. Kamryn did this. She said it worked perfectly."

Mark grumbled as he followed Axel's orders. The bathroom wasn't small, but the movements of two large men made it feel like a closet.

"Put these back on." Axel handed the black leather pants back to Mark. "You may have to sleep in them for the next few days because you can't afford to be caught without the chip if something happens in the middle of the night. You're going to start sleeping in your vest, holster, and gun, with a knife in your boot."

Axel pulled a folding knife out of his right boot, offered it to Mark. "Ceramic blade. Wood handle. One hundred percent unscannable."

"Now, listen to me. This is what they drill into us if we're taken prisoner in combat: escape, memorize your surroundings, resist. Try not to eat or drink anything—it's drugged. To maintain your sanity, repeat a mantra, some word, phrase, or formula. As far as interrogations go, it's like answering a kid's questions about sex. Only tell them what they think they want to hear. So man up." Axel power-punched him in the arm, and not playfully. "Let's go have dinner."

As they headed to the kitchen, Mark asked. "If you're my wingman, won't you be coming with me, wherever I go?"

"I'll try like hell, but it normally doesn't work that way. If a single person comes to contact you here, he may just leave with the chip. The TMD will track it then close in on her when she tries to access the data. One operative isn't going to take a chance on abducting two people. Besides, two of us means one will be tortured and used to coerce the other—guess who gets mutilated."

The kitchen was empty. A double layer chocolate cake with chocolate icing sat on a special plate in the middle of the breakfast bar. One wedge had been removed.

"Beta thought you might like a taste of home, since your family wasn't here." Axel helped himself to a bowl of chili with a fat slice of warm toasted garlic bread. Mark did likewise, didn't eat much and was quiet.

***

Nazarova burst in the back door. She grabbed both men by the shoulders, propelling them into the living room. "Someone's approaching." She flipped on the vid screen to monitor the activity picked up by the new surveillance system.

The image of a tall, dark-skinned man using a cane limped up the walkway, and rang the bell.

Axel and Nazarova disappeared into the dining room.

Mark tried to mentally prepare himself for whatever was about to happen, remembering Harben's orders to "bargain with the devil if need be." He opened the door a crack.

"I'm sorry to bother you. Looking for the Warren's residence."

"You found it."

"I have a message for Capt. Mark Warren. Would that be you?"

"Yes."

"May I come in? It's rather personal."

Mark turned, checked to make sure the vid screen was off, then opened the door enough for the man to enter.

They stood several feet apart, assessing one another. The stranger wore shades of brown, with a herringbone plaid cap covering his salt-and-pepper hair. As opposed to the earlier dog walker, this man was relaxed, confident, meeting Mark's gaze without wavering.

"I'm just a messenger—an intermediary, if you will. My instructions were to tell you there won't be any more problems if a compromise can be reached. If you're in possession of the information and are prepared to give it to me, life will go back to normal, everything will be fine. If not…there will be additional consequences."

"The person who sent you here knows I'm not stupid. You don't get a damned thing unless she can figure out a way to assure me no one else will be harmed."

"Well, in that case. I must tell you the amount of one million credits has just been deposited in your account. A rather excessive amount for a captain in the military, wouldn't you say? The TMD will, no doubt, be extremely interested to know how you came by those funds.

"Again—blackmail? It wasn't enough she had my father assaulted. Now she's threatening to ruin my reputation, plus have me arrested for conspiring with the enemy."

"It's entirely your call, but you did say you weren't stupid."

"Don't move." Mark rushed into the kitchen, removed the data chip from its hiding place and returned to the stranger. "Here." He held out his fist, opened his fingers.

The man picked it up with a handkerchief and put it in his shirt pocket.

Mark took two long strides to the door, yanked it open. "Now get out," he fumed.

"Have a pleasant evening." The man turned, shuffled out the door and down the steps.

Behind him, the vid screen came on, showing the outside surveillance of the stranger lumbering off into the distance. Axel and Nazarova came out of their hiding place in the dining room.

"I hope one of you recorded all that audio because I sure don't want anyone ever accusing me of selling military secrets."

"Don't worry," Nazarova said. "We have video and audio of everything."

Mark sank to the couch, physically drained. He was happy the hand-off had transpired without a hitch. He still felt apprehensive. "I have a weird feeling about this, guys. Have you ever heard of Merton's Law of Unintended Consequences? Sometimes a strategy works…and sometimes it backfires."

Chapter 17

Mark hadn't known Nazarova was under orders to put the interior of the Warren residence under surveillance, as well as the exterior. In retrospect, he might have opposed the move. Now he was damned glad it had been done.

The lieutenant sent copies of the meeting to HQ in Virginia. "This time we only found one fingerprint with DNA from the doorbell, but enough to match with a confirmed faceprint. The scans also produced evidence of a neural implant. It identified the newest operative as one Otto Vickers, who lives about ten miles across town. So far, the records show no connection between the two agents, except being from similar age groups. I flagged his ID, too, because we can't afford to lose track of these people."

The three Warren stand-ins had come downstairs to view the vid replay. Alpha patted Mark on the back. "Good job, Captain. You're a natural. I wish they were all this easy."

It hadn't felt easy. There had been a war going on inside Mark. He had to fight the urge to grab Vickers around the throat and squeeze until the man passed out—or worse. He kept telling himself it would have been instant gratification. Satisfying, yes, but counterproductive to the goal of capturing Beth Coulter. "Will we be notified when she tries to access the data?"

"Possibly," Alpha said. "Or, they may wait until she's apprehended. Her whole network has to be dismantled. All the operatives must be identified and incarcerated, and the cyborgs neutralized."

"Can I contact my family—check on my dad?"

"HQ will contact you as soon as it's safe. When the threat has been eliminated."

Mark disliked his answer. "*No.* I want to talk to them. *Today.*"

He took a step closer to Alpha. "The TMD hired this woman. Stuck her in my lab. This is all their fault. I've been shot. Sent off-world. My research—hell, my whole life—has gone down the toilet. My father was damn near beaten to death. Now my family has been taken away, and their lives have been put in mortal jeopardy." Mark had reigned in his rage for hours. His fury was on the verge of exploding. He took another step closer to Alpha. "*Today*. I will speak with my family. *Today*." He took a half step forward, just inches from Alpha's face. Anger colored Mark's body language and tone. "Or, somebody here isn't going to like what happens next."

Everyone froze, while neither man gave ground.

"Mark." Axel approached him from the side, touching his shoulder. "Why don't we take a walk? Give them time to see if something can be arranged."

He grudgingly allowed Axel to drag him away from Alpha, through the house, and out the back door.

"You've got a lot of balls. That spy you just chewed out in there could probably kill you fifteen different ways without mussing up his hair." Exasperated, Axel shoved Mark, hard, making him stumble back a few feet.

Mark came at Axel in an instant, returning the shove with the same fierceness. They stood a yard apart, fists clenched, glaring at each other and ready for a fight. Until Mark took a deep breath and looked up at the sky. A waning crescent moon climbed above them. He could see Mars off in the distance. It was twilight in the Pacific high country. The weather had chilled. A thick scent of Christmas trees hung in the cold evening air.

"I'm not married. I don't have children. I had my work and my family, that's all. Now Beth Coulter has taken both of those away. Hate is eating away at me. I have dreams of killing her, Axel. *With these*." Mark held up his hands; fingers spread wide. "And I'd gladly suffer the consequences."

"I hear you. First, we have to catch Coulter. That's our goal. So you need to focus on what you can do to make it happen. But not just her—we need to take down all the facets of her organization, as well. We can't have her cyborgs running all over the planet causing chaos. Wouldn't you like to get your hands on one—to see what's under the hood?"

A glimmer of interest began to replace the desperation on Mark's face. "Yes. Yes, I would."

"Maybe things have calmed down for the evening. Why don't we go to the hospital? Check on Kamryn. Talk to the major."

***

Both tablets pinged as they headed back to the house. "Aw, shit." Axel checked the message, then broke into a run.

Mark was right behind him. "What's wrong?"

"The dog walker's dead."

"Coulter's getting ready to cut and run."

They burst into the house, running straight to the living room. Nazarova stood in front of Torance's image on the vid screen.

"When he was picked up, all our tablets started pinging like the bells of St. Mary's. The hospital's trauma shuttle had him here within minutes. He was DOA. Apparent heart failure. The TMD has officially taken possession of the body—enemy of the state—and I'm on my way down to assist with the autopsy when you contacted me."

Axel stepped forward. "Major, do you have information on the second man, an Otto Vickers? He left about an hour ago."

"Yes, we've received all his data from Nazarova."

Again, tablets pinged, simultaneously.

Torance read the message aloud. "Another DOA in transit to this hospital. Patient identified as…Otto Vickers—damn that was fast—they're dropping like locusts."

"Did he have the chip on him?" Axel asked. "Where was he found?"

"Downtown. He fell to the pavement on a street corner in clear view of numerous people. Personal effects were ID, credit card, a set of keys—no chip." Torance turned sideways. "Ohashi, contact Portland's spaceport. Check faceprints of all passengers who boarded in the last hour. Then monitor all flights out of every spaceport in a 500 mile radius. We can't afford to lose her now. We need to know where she's going. And send an update to HQ."

"She's burning all her bridges," Axel surmised. "By now she may suspect we've captured the cyborg from last night, plus his accomplice. She's not going to let that happen again. Send the shuttle, please, Major. We need a ride to the hospital."

"Will do. Torance out."

Axel rushed into the kitchen, seized the cake and went outside to wait for the shuttle.

"What are you doing with the cake?

"Torance has a sweet tooth. Besides, Petra gets grouchy when she's sleep-deprived. She and Ohashi will be up all night searching through faceprints, hunting for Coulter. We need to keep those women happy."

The shuttle whisked them to the hospital in no time where they were welcomed with hugs by two chocolate-starved Cyber specialists. Between bites, Petra told Axel that Torance was in the bowels of the hospital, assisting with the impromptu autopsy of the dog walker, Carson Adelle. The second unplanned procedure would be the autopsy of Otto Vickers.

Ohashi also said Torance instructed everyone touching the bodies to wear HazMat suits, as a precaution, given Coulter's penchant for chemicals. Afterward, both bodies would be sealed in cryopods and shipped to HQ for an in-depth forensic analysis.

"Thanks, ladies. Make sure you leave some cake for Torance. Now I need to check on Kamryn." Axel peeked around the corner of her door and was surprised to see her propped up in bed. "Well, look at you. Those nanites must be working double-time. You'll be ready for that marathon by the end of the week." Axel lightly caught her arm in a warrior's greeting.

Kamryn produced a crooked smile. "That whole side of my body is numb from the pain meds. It's a good thing they're not feeding me soup. I'd be lying in a puddle." She chuckled and winked at him. "Sitrep, please."

Axel stroked her hand while he gave her a play-by-play of the events since yesterday.

"Blue eyes is turning into a real badass." Her eyes sparkled. "Did he really get in the spook's face?"

"Yes, he did. I drug him outside and called him on it. There was a little shoving back and forth—it almost came to blows. But he simmered down. He's strong-willed. He's been pushed. Everybody's got a bottom line, Kam. I think he's on the edge."

"Send him in. I'll give him a pep talk."

Puzzled, Axel knitted his brows. "You sure?"

"Yup." Kamryn finger combed her short hair and smoothed the sheets over her chest.

Axel sent Mark in with a sliver of chocolate cake.

Eighteen minutes later Mark walked out of her room with a solemn face.

"What happened? Is she okay?"

When Mark walked down the hall without replying, Axel rushed into her room.

Kamryn was licking frosting off her fingers. She smiled at him. "Mark understands now. He'll keep his eye on the prize."

"What did you say to him?"

"I just told him a story. Then said...if he screwed up, you get to kick his ass again."

"Excellent—that works for me."

***

Torance exited the elevator, tired, sleepy, hungry, yet still in need of living human companionship. He rounded a corner, went straight to the coffee machine for a cup of caffeine, then headed for his favorite patient's room. Kamryn was asleep. He spotted a plate with…chocolate crumbs on it. He left to search for more of the same and heard giggling coming from the waiting room.

Petra waved at him. "Major, we have a surprise. Look." She pointed to a small end table where a platter held half a chocolate cake.

"Bless you, my children." He was suddenly filled with the spirit of the sugar gods. He wasted no time helping himself to a hunk of the cake, while he shared some of the less gruesome information from the two autopsies.

"I don't want any of you to come within miles of this monster—if you can help it. She's a Genghis Khan on steroids. She didn't have to be anywhere near these people to kill them. Coulter could have done it from Mars. Her latest victims had neural implants which seemed to have short-circuited. I'm not a neuroscientist, theoretically, it would send mixed messages to the heart to speed up then slow down, causing arrhythmia and death. Like being repeatedly hit with a stun baton. Something I believe you're familiar with."

"Yes, but I didn't die, Major."

"No, but you didn't have a mega dose of RX-45 coursing through your veins, either. I don't know how, or where she got her hands on that pathogen. I've sent an emergency update to HQ. It's been added to the list of viruses being audited at the Special Pathogens Laboratory. The TMD is conducting an official investigation of every person who ever stepped foot into that wing. First it was the undocumented neural implants in military personnel. Now it's deadly military grade pathogens that have been stolen from one of our most prestigious facilities. What's next?"

"Major?"

"Thoughts, Captain?"

"Sir, is the TMD the only Laboratory capable of creating these biological agents? Might they come from another source? Could Petra and Ohashi compile a list of scientists with the necessary degrees needed to create such viruses? Then cross reference that data with corporations or nations where they reside or work? Cast a broad net, so to speak. See what turns up. Maybe it was stolen from the TMD—maybe not. If there's another source, we've got bigger problems."

"Intriguing. All right, ladies, break time is over. Off you go. Check with HQ to see if there's been any movement on the new faceprint protocol."

After the women had scurried out of the waiting room, Torance indulged in another slice of cake. "Okay, you two, Nazarova commed me about the captain's issues with…not being able to contact his family."

Mark hung his head, like a puppy who'd been scolded for peeing on the carpet.

"Well," Axel said, "there might have been a difference of opinion. We got beyond it."

"They're fine."

Mark perked up. "Who's fine?"

"Major Simone Le Berre was the doctor who came to pick up your father and the man who shot Kamryn. I met the major in Paris years ago. We both spent a rotation there. We had a…personal relationship. I trust her. Besides," he said grinning. "I scanned Simone for a neural implant when she wasn't looking. Anyway, I've received a message your family is together, being well treated, and your dad is progressing nicely."

"Thank you, Major. When can I speak with them?"

"Unknown. Now, at least, we have a lifeline. And in my book, something is always better than nothing."

***

Before he forgot about it, Mark contacted The Chocolate Moose and spoke with Iris Lambert. "If you still make the cake called "Death by Chocolate" please have one delivered to Maj. Torance at the hospital tomorrow. You could bring something different every day after that as long as he's still here. Send me the bill."

"No worries, Mark. I gotcha covered. Uh...we've been thinking about your dad. And want you to know we're so sorry we didn't do more."

"No, no, no, Miss Lambert, on the contrary. If it weren't for both of you, my dad might be dead. You two have my family's everlasting gratitude. You ladies are angels—dipped in chocolate."

Mark went back into Kamryn's room. Axel sat at her bedside with half-closed eyes, his head nodding slowly forward. In the dimmed corner, an armored sentry stood guard, his protection unwavering. This was family. These were comrades. Born and bred on the battlefield—however it was defined. These were his people now. He felt it. Especially after listening to Kamryn's harrowing story of defeat and triumph. He would never again look at a soldier, male or female, with anything but the greatest respect.

Petra stuck her head in the room. She motioned for Mark to follow her. "Ohashi says she's found a suspicious irregularity. Maybe you should take a look." Petra led him to a small exam room where Ohashi sat in front of two vid screens, set up side by side. Unending rows of streaming data on one screen were being correlated by her algorithms on the other.

"Captain, at first I tried a correlation of chemistry engineering degrees within countries. I compared that list to corporations employing these degreed individuals. Then I narrowed the search parameters for any of those companies with a history of buying or selling biomaterials."

"You're a bona fide wizard, Ohashi."

"Wait!" She was breathless and barely able to control her enthusiasm. "I haven't finished yet."

"*Mea culpa.* Please proceed." Mark suspected her excitement was in direct response to the sugar content of her latest snack.

The two cybers exchanged knowing looks, grinning at each other, as Ohashi uttered one word, "Houston."

Mark felt like he'd been hit with a two-by-four. "Holy shit."

The gleam in the eyes of both women told him they knew the evidence was solid.

"What's the name of the company? Have you traced it? Of course, you have—what did you find?"

"BioKlon LLC is a German multinational engineering and electronics company headquartered in Gerlingen, near Stuttgart, Germany. Their one subsidiary in America happens to be in Houston."

"Who owns it?"

They both looked perturbed. "We don't know. This is the suspicious irregularity. Some government records seem to be missing."

"My money's on Beth Coulter. You're both promoted. And you can have chocolate cake every day for the rest of your lives." Mark wrapped an arm around each cyber and hugged so tight Petra squeaked.

"Sorry, sorry" He kissed her forehead. "Where's Torance? He needs to send this to HQ."

"He's taking a cat nap."

"Well, wake him up."

Both women shook their heads.

"I'll do it. Where is he?"

"Downstairs. He's lying on a gurney next to the dead bodies."

"Oh." Now Mark understood. He took Petra's arm, guiding her out of the small room. "Let's get Axel. You can brief him on the way. We'll wake him up. You don't have to stay."

They snuck into Kamryn's room. Mark tapped a dozing Axel on the shoulder, signaling for him to join them. Axel shook himself awake, got up and followed them out. Petra rattled off an update as she led them through the vanilla colored halls, down the elevator, around corners, then came to a stop. She pointed to a door.

Axel issued rapid-fire orders. "Check all flights bound for Houston since her first agent died. Include all connecting flights landing there. We can't rely strictly on faceprints anymore. Find every military facility in a 100 mile radius of Houston. I don't care what it is. Anything with a main frame that can read the data chip we gave her. We'll bring Torance up in a minute. Have the data ready for him to send to HQ."

Petra darted off, leaving them alone in front of the door.

Axel rubbed his stubble for a moment. "Okay, let's do this." He pulled the door handle. It opened with a sharp, high-pitched screech.

The major sat upright and damn near fell off the gurney. He glared at Mark and Axel. "Who'd dead now?"

"How about we get some coffee, Major. I'll give you a sitrep."

Torance yawned, rolled off the gurney. He trailed after them while listening to Axel. They stopped at the coffee machine, where the major got two cups, then continued to Ohashi's improvised office.

Ohashi and Petra presented Torance with the verified data. He approved it. Ohashi encrypted the update. Petra sent it to HQ.

Finally, they all began to relax.

"I have a thought." Mark leaned against the door frame. "I guarantee nobody's going to like it."

"Something else you want me to search for?"

"No, Ohashi, and you're a glutton for punishment." He paused. "It's just the more we know—the more I realize how much we don't know about Beth Coulter. The man who shot Kamryn said she had two more agents in Portland, which proved to be true—so far. What if there are more he didn't know about. We can't assume the immediate threat has been eliminated."

Chapter 18

Dimitrios sat stone-faced behind his desk on the vid screen, while Torance explained the results of their investigation of the BioKlon Laboratory in Houston. "According to its contracts, the North American plant designs, develops and sells neural implants only to the TMD plus three hospitals: Seattle, Los Angeles, and Washington, DC. There's no mention of pathogens, despite dozens of degreed experts we traced to that facility. The viruses she's employed may not have been stolen from us, but developed in-house by this group of specialists. According to my cybers, the preliminary investigations reveal all their records are encrypted by a security system that rivals our own.

"Sir, one more thing. The company's name is BioKlon. In German, it translates to Bio Clone, as in *cloning*. From the beginning, there's been a global ban on cloning humans among most nations, that doesn't mean it hasn't been done, somewhere, by someone. We would be wrong to assume Coulter hasn't broken this mandate as well, considering what we know she's been guilty of in the past.

"When we were on Luna, Warren told me he remembered hearing Coulter speaking German on her comm in the lab at CAMRI. She could have been conversing with Houston or Germany. If she's from Germany, maybe that's where she met the real Beth Coulter. I'd like my cybers to begin an in-depth background search. I'm told we'll need a special clearance. Or, you could initiate it from HQ."

Dimitrios's complexion was an unhealthy pink and rising. "It's a damn good thing the TMD isn't currently involved in any military conflicts. This Pandora's Box Operation is beginning to drain our resources. All we're doing is fixing one huge sink hole after another. The problems this bitch Coulter has caused are Machiavellian. Some of the most insidious situations I've had to deal with in my career."

"General, think of it as fighting a ground war—on someone else's terms. We are making headway. All unsanctioned TMD neural implants have been removed. The Malaysian plant was shut down—the Indian one will never open. Now she has the bogus data chip. Maybe a decision is made to expunge BioKlon at some point. She must be taken down on Terra soon—before she escapes again and turns this into a space war. We have proof she can wreak havoc in that realm too.

"You're right, Major." Dimitrios wiped his face with meaty fingers and unbuttoned the top of his uniform jacket. "We'll position a geosat over the facility, with drones to monitor the physical activity. I'll see to it our cybers make a push into every crevice of BioKlon. We'll go back fifty years using facial age regression software for anything digital still in the records for Coulter, or whoever the hell she is. Maybe there's more than one company in Germany—this could be her base of operations.

"By the way, how's our Warren holding up?"

"I've been watching him—closely. He's strong. If he wasn't, the attempted murder of his father might have derailed him. There have been a few minor issues with anger. He's working through them. Regular contact with his family would go a long way in mitigating these challenges."

"Thanks. I'll pass this along. Dimitrios out."

Torance looked to his left. "Did you get all that, ladies?"

"Yes, sir," they answered in unison.

"I've heard you two talking about piggybacking, haven't I?

"Oh." Petra exchanged a sheepish grin with Ohashi. "We didn't know you were listening."

"I'm old—not deaf."

Petra frowned. "You're mature, Major—not old. I personally

think mature men are more attractive than young, dumb, and hung."

Torance chuckled in spite of himself. "Good to know. Thank you for sharing. Now let's get back to the issue at hand. Can you and Ohashi piggyback off HQ while they're performing their searches into BioKlon? I want to know everything—in real time."

"Yes, we can." Ohashi steepled her half-gloved fingers together. "Every system has vulnerabilities. We assess their network and applications, then penetrate wherever we find defects."

"Do it." Torance left for coffee and a few moments of solitude. He longed for the comfort of his home surroundings. Secretly, he did find all the intrigue exciting. However, he didn't know how much longer he could keep up this pace.

He wanted to take his patient home, or back to base, and see to her recovery. But he was worried. He couldn't yet determine if Kamryn would be able to return to her unit. The physical qualifications for the armored assault unit were the most stringent in the TMD. He knew her entire medical history, including the horrific injuries she'd suffered while working undercover for the DEA. After recovering, Kamryn had resigned, then enlisted in the TMD. She worked like a fiend to qualify for the armored unit. And she passed. Maybe she could do it again. If not…well he had plenty of time before any alternative decisions had to be explored.

***

Axel's energy level had bottomed out. He either needed to eat or sleep. The waiting room's couch looked so inviting he couldn't resist. He sank into the corner, sprawled out until pinging from his tablet awoke him. He grabbed it, noting almost fifteen minutes has passed since he last checked. The incoming message originated with Buchanan. "Major, this is Von Radach. Is there a problem?"

"Sergeant, I wanted to contact you privately," she said. "There has been a development. We decided it's your call—whether or not to tell Warren. But Eva Jackson's brother was attacked in Brooklyn yesterday. His injuries were too severe. He died. He had a weapon. It had been discharged. So there could be a disabled cyborg roaming the streets of New York.

"How is Eva taking it?"

"She's devastated. He was the last of her family. I know Warren and Jackson had grown close in recent weeks. Torance has been informed. He has concerns about Warren being susceptible to survivor's guilt syndrome. His brother was killed. You, Jackson and Fleming, were gassed on Luna. His father attacked. Fleming shot. Now his family's been removed with a communications blackout. Not a pretty picture—for anyone. Remember, he wasn't a combat soldier, to begin with."

"Yes, ma'am. I won't tell him until we're on our way back to base. No reason to burden him with this."

"It's up to you, Sergeant. You know him better than anyone by this point. If you change your mind—check with Torance first. Buchanan out."

Stunned by the news, Axel sat motionless. A cold sadness enveloped him. His mind began to replay all the happy, angry, dangerous moments he'd shared with Eva, Kamryn, and Mark. They had bonded. The four of them were still alive, but for how long?

Everyone seemed to have high hopes this data chip plan would work. Coulter would be caught. That would be the end of it. Not true. The plan sucked. Since hearing it, Axel doubted Coulter would actually be the one fooled into using the chip. If recent setbacks were any indication, she'd hand it off to another unsuspecting operative with a neural implant, then send them in as a decoy. Any minute, he'd hear an attempt had been made, and the TMD had taken someone into custody. It wouldn't be Coulter. Not her style. She'd anticipate this trick.

Axel surmised she might do the exact opposite of what they expected. She'd stay in Portland to focus on another target. Who? Not Eva, she was protected in an out-of-state underground base. Kamryn had an armored guard. Axel wasn't a relative. He didn't have anything Coulter wanted. So it was Mark. He had to be the one with the big red X painted on his chest. Would Coulter come after him just to get even? Hell, yes, she would. Or, maybe Mark didn't know he had something—else—she wanted? Regardless, Axel had been given orders. Protect Capt. Mark Warren. He intended to complete his mission and try his damnedest not to die doing it.

Where was Mark? *Holy shit.* Axel jumped off the couch, sprinted down the hall to Kamryn's room, burst in the door. Everybody turned around to look at him, including Mark, who happened to be unpacking large bags of delicious smelling food.

"You hungry?" Mark smiled. "I cooked."

Kamryn sat propped up in bed, grinning from ear to ear, staring at a banana cream pie. The bed served as a table for the barbecued pork subs, baked beans, mini corn on the cobs, a pie for dessert, with a gallon of hard iced tea to wash it all down.

"Where did all this come from?"

"One of our neighbors owns Wolff's Smokehouse BBQ. I asked him to drop off a few leftovers on his way home."

Axel divided the pie into equal parts, plated a slice, handed it to Kamryn. He smiled watching her lick the filling off a spoon. The major, both cybers, Mark and the guard weren't wasting any time in helping themselves to the more nutritious parts of the feast. Axel hadn't eaten in hours. The food aromas released from the bags were overwhelming. He dove in before people started reaching for seconds. "Major, I assume you scanned it all for anything detrimental to our health."

"Affirmative. Even the alcohol content in the tea is less than six percent so everyone can partake, except my patient. Sorry, Kamryn, nanites don't like spirits."

"That's all right, doc. I'm more of a beer connoisseur, anyway."

While they ate, Axel decided to get opinions on the data chip maneuver. "Anybody have views on the probability of this chip ploy working."

The munching and crunching slowed to a halt.

Under her breath, Kamryn muttered, "Coulter's not dumb enough to fall for that kind of trick."

"My sentiments, exactly," Petra grumbled.

"Snowball's chance in hell," snorted Ohashi.

"Why didn't anybody tell me this before?" Mark asked, alarm now evident in his voice. "You all let me go through with a plan none of you thought would work? Some friends you guys are."

"Headquarters came up with the plan," Torance interjected. "It bought us time to remove your family, while enticing two more of Coulter's operatives into the open. Who, by the way, are dead. Even as we continued searching for ways to locate Coulter and bring her down. You keep forgetting we're in the military. We follow orders. In your lab at CAMRI, your research was funded by TMD. You wore a uniform, but it's as close as you came to being military. We live and breathe it twenty-four/seven."

"Okay, what now? Does anybody have a plan that will work?" Mark drilled everyone with a challenging look. When no one responded, he said, "Kamryn?"

"If it were me—I'd go on the offensive to target BioKlon. Working with hypotheticals here, let's say she is German, so there's a good chance that country is her home base. Which makes BioKlon the main source of her revenue. The facility in Houston is an alternate source. She's in our country, so an attack or threat to this facility is bound to get her attention and draw her resources away from you, Mark. For a while, anyway."

"Being on the offense for once sounds great," Axel responded before anyone else. "What kind of threat?"

"Something affecting everyone in the facility. Like a communicable disease, deadly pathogen, cache of drugs, threat to national security, or a fire. You know, something all-encompassing."

"Under the hypothetical heading, which scenario might lure her to Houston?"

"Fire. Nothing draws a moth like a flame. When a business goes up in a blaze, most authorities won't admit it, but they immediately suspect arson, either to conceal a previous crime or for insurance fraud. The investigators will work backward from there. The bigger the disaster, the higher the odds it was deliberate—excluding lightning strikes."

Ohashi had been following the conversation while feeding data into her tablet. "Houston is the lightning capital of Texas."

"Well, how 'bout that." A shadowy grin spread across Axel's face. He stood, motioned for Ohashi to follow him and without a word, they both left Kamryn's room. As they walked to the stairwell, Axel cautioned Ohashi, "Do you remember, Boss Lady, the shuttle pilot who flew us to CAMRI? Contact her—she owes me a favor. I need an act of god to wreak havoc on BioKlon. Last year we were cleaning up a little skirmish in South America, and we needed a diversion. She sent blasts of ionic pulse down from her shuttle that looked exactly like bolts of lightning."

"Oh, wow. That gives me time to send a RAT, a remote access Trojan, into their system. I can piggyback into Houston off a transmission from the German plant…uh-oh." She clasped a hand over her mouth.

"You're hacking the German BioKlon? I thought that was off limits?"

"Not hacking per se, just piggybacking off HQ."

"Whose idea was this?"

"Can't say."

"You don't have to. Our doctor is one sneaky bastard. Well, good. That should make things much easier. Can you do the same thing from Germany to Houston?"

She nodded. "I'll program it to send us a mega burst of data when the pulse...uh, lightning...strikes it. We'd have to take what we can get. It'd be more than we have now."

"Just so you're clear. We never had this conversation. If any of this gets out we both could be retired—to a military penitentiary. So, leave no trace, right?"

Ohashi's amber eyes danced with mischief. "Sergeant, I'm a Cyber Ninja. It's a good thing I wear a white hat. If I were pitching for the other team, the TMD would be in big trouble."

"No doubt." Axel extended his arm. Ohashi grasped it, sealing their clandestine game plan. "Let's make this happen. One natural phenomenon coming up."

***

Mark couldn't help but notice Axel and Ohashi as they entered Kamryn's room. Their body language radiated with a controlled excitement. Mark snagged Axel's arm, guiding him into a corner. "What's up?"

"Are you always this suspicious?"

"Have you forgotten one of my parents is a shrink? I grew up being analyzed. I know duplicitous behavior when I see it. So, what are you and Ohashi scheming on?"

Axel thumped him on the chest. "Do you want to go to jail again?"

"Not especially."

"If we get caught, that's where we're headed."

"I haven't liked a single plan someone else has thought of so far, beginning with sending me to the moon. Why would I like this one any better?"

Axel squared his shoulders. "Because I've had your back since day one. So you're just going to have to trust me."

Funny thing. He did trust Axel—had since the day they'd met. Mark could do without the chest thumping and ass kicking, but they'd become…friends—more like family, warts and all. Maybe they piss you off sometimes, but they are bound to you, like you are to them. Good, bad, or ugly. Right, wrong, or indifferent. This was the relationship he and Eric had shared. Without Mark's knowledge, Axel had nonetheless stepped into the gaping void left by Eric's death. A brother. A badass brother.

"If you were me, Axel, would you let others decide what happens to you?"

"If they were qualified, yes. My background and training make me imminently qualified. Did you question me at CAMRI?"

"No."

"Then I've proven I can do my job. Have a little faith."

"I do. It's Coulter that has me worried."

Chapter 19

The rain inundated Houston right on time. Ionized storm cells had gathered, blanketing the entire area. If Axel could have counted on an exact natural strike of lightning to the BioKlon facility, he wouldn't have needed assistance from Boss Lady and her shuttle. Updates from the North American Weather Bureau forecast a widespread soaking for Houston with the rain coming in two rounds—one moving in now, another later that night.

Axel checked the time. It was almost noon. They'd already been in Portland for more than thirty-eight hours. Maybe they could go back to Mark's house, get some rest, clean up and return in plenty of time before the shuttle would be in place for the lightning assist. Axel hoped the potential damage to the plant would draw Coulter away from Portland, in time for them to return to base.

Ohashi's piggyback maneuver on HQ's hack into the German based BioKlon would enable a duplicate maneuver into Houston. With any luck, by tomorrow morning they might have enough proof to close down both plants. This was war. Not the conventional kind, but war all the same. The only thing that counted was winning. Headquarters' wouldn't care how they came by the information if it helped them tighten the noose around Beth Coulter.

All seven of them were in Kamryn's room when their tablets pinged. Everyone checked their messages. The fabricated data chip had been used in Seattle. The female in possession of the chip had died when authorities tried to apprehend her. The dead woman had been identified as a sixty-three-year-old grandmother from Tacoma. Not Beth Coulter.

Profanity turned the air blue, with the major being the

guiltiest by far. Axel had never heard Torance string so many expletives together before. If the situation hadn't been so serious, he might have laughed.

"The bitch is murdering the elderly," Torance shouted. People got out of his way as he began pacing back and forth, waving his hands in the air. "Both bodies downstairs are the same age. There's a pattern here. She has to be getting her victims from the same pool."

When his tablet pinged, but no one else's did, he stalked out of the room. A few moments later, he returned. "I've been ordered to bring Kamryn back to base. A shuttle will be here in twenty minutes. We'll drop the captain off so he can secure his family's residence, and another shuttle will transport the rest of you back with Nazarova's troops. It's time to go home." He slumped into a chair beside the bed, shoulders sagging; the anger drained from his face.

Without a word, Petra began packing up her equipment, as did Ohashi. The guard commed the ER to send up a hover gurney.

Axel approached Kamryn from the far side, giving Torance plenty of space. He reached for her hand. "I'll come check on you when we get back."

"We were getting close—weren't we?" Her eyes glistened.

"Yes. It's not over, though. We can still work on our plans from the base."

"It won't be the same."

He leaned over and whispered. "No, Kam. This is war. We don't quit until all our enemies are dead."

Mark came to stand by Axel. "I'll bring Eva to visit. You two have a lot of catching up to do."

At the mention of Eva's name, Axel remembered Mark still didn't know about her brother's death. He should tell Mark now so he could process it before they got back. Torance ought to be there, too. No time like the present. "Major, join us for some coffee?"

They walked toward the end of the T-shaped hall where the large closet sized machine stood.

"Mark, there's something we need to tell you about Eva."

"I've got this, Sergeant," Torance intervened. "It seems Jackson's brother was targeted, the same as your father. They found his body not long ago. There's evidence he fought with his attacker. The authorities found a discharged weapon near the scene, which is probably the reason he was mortally injured. He didn't make it. However, it looks like he may have damaged his assailant."

Mark mouthed a word that stuck in his throat. "Why wasn't I told?"

"Because," Axel said, "you were dealing with your father's injuries, taking care of your family, and being prepped to hand off the data chip to Coulter's agents. So command made the decision to delay informing you until we were scheduled to leave. Only the major and I knew, no one else. Due to your friendship with Jackson, command thought this message should be delivered by one of us."

"I understand," Mark said, resigned. "She's alone now. All her family's gone."

"A Chaplain and grief counselors are providing support," Torance offered. "The TMD will take care of...everything."

"There must be something we can do."

"Spending time with her, Mark, is the best way to show you care."

When they all had coffee, Torance produced a leather-encased flask. He poured some of the cognac colored liquid into his cup, then theirs.

"To Eva's brother, Dion." Mark lifted his cup.

"To Scarlotti." Axel now felt the dead weighing him down twofold.

"To the grandmother, that died in Seattle today, instead of Coulter." Torance shook his head in disgust.

They all drank.

Again, Mark lifted his cup. "To my brother, Eric Warren, and all 152 crew members of the Europa mission."

The three men emptied their cups. The dark moment seemed to last forever.

An unusual noise invaded the silence. It caused Axel to turn around. He saw a silver ball the size of a large egg rolling along the floor toward them.

He recognized it. "Shock grenade!" Axel spun to face both men, grabbed their shoulders, forcing all of them to the floor.

A contained explosion rocked the hallway. The blast was meant to disorient—not to kill. Axel had experienced them before. Since he wasn't wearing armor, it wouldn't be near as easy this time. He saw stars. His ears were ringing. He didn't know where the shock grenade had come from. But he knew who'd sent it.

Coulter.

They were being abducted. Which meant somebody was going to be tortured. *Shit.* He had to move fast. In a few seconds, it would be too late.

He felt adrenalin flooding through his system. His instincts told him they were in mortal danger. He must survive at all costs.

Kill or be killed.

Axel got to his knees, reached out until he touched a shape on either side. Axel seized body parts. In a superhuman effort, he stood and began dragging his friends in the direction they were facing when the blast went off.

With repeated blinking, his vision began to clear. The instant he could focus, Axel dropped the bodies. He drew both guns, turned and aimed back down the hallway.

The blaring sound of an emergency alarm began filtering

through the fog in his mind. His hearing was returning. Human screams grew in intensity. He glanced around to see the two cybers plus Kamryn's armored guard, all running at him with guns drawn.

A second shock grenade rolled straight for them. The armored guard shot a stream of foam at the orb, rendering it inert.

Two new male figures in pale green scrubs appeared in the hall from a doorway about thirty feet beyond the coffee machine. They advanced in a deliberate fashion. No emotions registered on their faces. They were large. They were cyborgs.

In close combat, your enemy's face was a prime target. Axel aimed at the eyes of the cyborg on his left, fired both his pulse weapon and handgun. He managed to destroy one eye. After a momentary stumble, the damned thing kept on coming.

Mark, now conscious, had risen to stand beside Axel, shooting at the eyes of the cyborg on the right.

As their enemies approached, one tossed a couple more shock grenades down the corridor toward the armored guard. The one advancing on Axel flung a couple more at him.

"Incoming." Axel dove on top of the major, who had remained unconsciousness. On the floor, an acrid smell filled the air, stinging Axel's nose, eyes, and throat. It was the last thing he recalled.

***

Mark kept firing at both oncoming cyborgs until his pulse weapon died. He'd counted the shots fired from his handgun and saved the last one until the cyborg on the right was close enough to spit on. He shot it in the right eye. It stumbled. For a brief moment, Mark thought it would fall on them. It corrected, grabbed him by the collar bone, turned and ran to the nearest stairwell, dragging him along.

As Mark struggled to get free, the cyborg's grasp tightened like a vice. He felt pain searing through his nervous system. The cyborg hefted Mark over his shoulder while it descended the stairwell, taking multiple steps at a time. The jostling made it hard to catch his breath. He felt close to passing out.

Everything stopped. The cyborg flopped him on a hover gurney, jabbed a syringe into his thigh and covered him from head to toe with a sheet. His pain melted away. He sensed the movement of being loaded into a conveyance, accompanied by the sounds of traffic.

When his mind cleared, Axel was his first thought, Torance his second. Mark hadn't seen what happened to either of them. There had been two cyborgs. If one had come for him, had the other one captured Axel? Could he be here, too?

He tried to move the sheet away from his eyes. He couldn't. He didn't remember being restrained. What if the injection had been drugs—laced with a paralytic, or some sort of neuromuscular blocking agent? He tried to make a noise. Nothing more than a grunt escaped his lips. He kept trying until he uttered a hoarse whisper resembling "azo." Hopeless. He wouldn't be talking until the drugs wore off.

Again, everything stopped. He heard sounds of feet moving, followed by a feeling of weightlessness, which meant they were transferring him...to what? A shuttle door slid open. *Oh, crap.* He knew that noise. He was going airborne. *Damn, damn, damn.* They were transporting him to another location. On Terra? Or into space?

Something snagged the sheet, pulling it away from his face. He caught a glimpse of another gurney being carried into the shuttle. A familiar arm dangled off the side—Axel!

His friend's words rang in his ears. "...abducting two people means one will be tortured and used to coerce the other—guess who gets mutilated."

No. He would not allow that to happen. He'd negotiate, bargain, cajole, lie, hell, he'd do anything to save Axel. Except. Even if he gave Coulter all his classified formulas for augmented human cyborgs—past, present, and future—she'd never let him go free. *No.* She'd turn him into one of her neural implanted marionettes. Or just kill him. Axel, too.

Something had been bothering him. From the recesses of his drugged mind, it dawned on Mark these cyborgs hadn't said a single word since they'd left the hospital. They didn't converse. The first one at CAMRI hadn't spoken. His father's attacker hadn't either. Maybe they couldn't.

No wonder she wanted augmented humans.

How could he best use this information against Coulter? He needed to devise a plan before they arrived at their destination. Wherever that was.

***

The hospital's ER doctor had bandaged a cut on Torance's forehead, checked his vital signs, pronounced him alive—and an ass. The hospital physician left Kamryn's room cursing the TMD, muttering that doctors made the worst patients.

The major rolled up his sleeve and self-injected a dose of SP-27. His color returned, as did the rest of his mental facilities, before reporting live on vid to Dimitrios.

Flanked by the cybers, Torance stood, covered in a fine yellow power residue from the grenades, while relating the firefight, and abduction. He omitted the part about being unconscious. "We were prepping Sgt. Fleming for transport back to base, when two enemy cyborgs overpowered us with multiple shock grenades. Within seconds, they'd kidnapped Warren and Von Radach.

"The cybers rushed to activate the embedded geolocator

chips in our men. Hospital surveillance showed the cyborgs loading them into a hearse, which we tracked to a private tarmac. They've been airborne for sixteen minutes. We're transmitting their geosat data to you now. The enemy shuttle's exact destination is unknown. As you can see, its current heading is straight for Houston. If Coulter escaped our net, she may also be on that shuttle, or maybe she's already there.

"All TMD in Portland are hereby ordered back to your home base before something else happens. We'll be monitoring both men's geosat locations from HQ. I'm mobilizing a battalion out of the Sixth TMD in San Antonio as we speak. Lieutenant Colonel Maeve Sorayne will be commanding. She'll get the job done and bring our people home—even if she has to level that damned BioKlon plant to do it." Perspiration beaded on the general's forehead as he tugged at his uniform collar.

"Sir, if I may…Coulter couldn't have known about the tracking devices; otherwise, they would've been removed. If they go offline, she's found them, which puts our men in mortal danger.

"Also, we have reason to believe there's a large cache of highly combustible biochemicals in this facility. You can confirm it by checking shipments received from specific manufacturers.

"And, need I remind you, they produce the neural implants Coulter's so fond of using to control her victims. It would be insane to think a good percentage of those employees didn't have them, wouldn't you say?"

The general's face glistened. His meaty fingers curled into tight fists. "If there's any more information you wish to share, major, a memo with bullet points would be good."

"Sir, we've been working on this since CAMRI was attacked and have a plethora of data Sorayne might find useful. Once she's up to speed, have her contact me if she has questions."

"Fine. Now if you'll permit me—Dimitrios out."

Torrance turned to Ohashi. "Show me this Sorayne."

She pressed keys, bringing up a head to toe image of a tall, striking woman of indeterminate age, with short spiky platinum hair.

"Magnify."

Ohashi enlarged the face by a factor of five.

Under his breath, Torrance murmured, "One green eye. One blue eye."

"Oh, yeah, look at that."

"I recognize her. Australia. Six years ago. The APPNEX Campaign. She died on my table. Twice. Extensive damage. She underwent augmentation. She's a...cyborg.

"Really? First one I've seen. That's what Warren designs, isn't it? Augmentation? For humans, I mean."

"He does, indeed."

"Do you think she'll remember you?"

"Without a doubt." Torrance recalled the miserable conditions of the CSH, Combat Surgical Hospital in the middle of Australia, where he'd had to amputate what remained of her left leg and left arm. Sorayne opted for augmentation over prosthetics. At the time, a heroic choice for a female officer. And now...she was a colonel, who had garnered praise from Dimitrios.

If she knew of Warren's research, it might give her impetus to make sure he came out of this alive.

"Major, our ride's here."

Torrance turned. "You ladies ready to get the hell out of Portland?"

"Yes, sir."

"All right soldier," he motioned to the armored guard. "Let's take my patient home."

They placed Kamryn on the hover gurney, carried her through the halls, then up the elevator to the roof. Their shuttle waited, hatch open, and full of Nazarova's armored troops. It was a tight fit, but the craft lifted off with everyone aboard.

When the ship touched down, the door swung open to the gray frigid air of their North Dakota tarmac. Harben stood in front of the medics, who waited to offload Kamryn's gurney. After the formalities, both cybers accompanied the officers back to the colonel's office, where Buchanan joined them for a full debriefing.

Afterward, Torance singled him out. "Sir, how is Capt. Jackson doing?"

"Not well. I'm glad you're back. Maybe your presence—and Fleming's—will be what she needs right now." As Harben eased into his chair, a sadness crept into his voice. "This never should have happened. These scientists enlisted in the military to do research for the good of humanity. They *are* soldiers in the strictest sense of the word. They are *not* combat troops and as such were never supposed to be in harm's way. Not only have they been attacked, but members of their families have been maimed, and now one is dead. All because of a fat little megalomaniac who's not afraid of getting her hands dirty." Now he cupped his head. "Give me a straight up battle and boot me to the front lines. I'd welcome that—to this—dealing with the misery brought on by greed and corruption."

He could see Harben was distressed. "Sir, we may have more of a tactical advantage than you're aware of."

He gestured for Torance to sit. "Well, out with it. I'm ready for some *good* news."

"I know the commanding officer Dimitrios is sending to retrieve our people." He proceeded to explain their history, which brought raised eyebrows, with a glimmer of hope to Harben's face. "Also, there's an approaching thunderstorm. Lightning is about to strike the Houston area at any moment." Torance intimated a TMD shuttle might be able to assist in the electrostatic fireworks. It could deliver pinpoint damage to the

BioKlon plant, forcing the evacuation of all personnel—into a trap laid by Colonel Sorayne.

Hope had spread across Harben's face. He commed his assistant in the anteroom. "Keller, get Dimitrios on the vid for me. We have new Intel."

Chapter 20

Mark awoke in a panic, his mind in a state of confusion and his heart beating like a jackhammer. He scanned the dark surroundings. Axel's limp arm hung from beneath his sheet.

Oh, thank god they were still together. But where were they? Why hadn't Axel regained consciousness? Had he been given a heavier dose or different drugs altogether?

Mark tried to move his hands. He could, although his fine motor skills were sluggish. He started moving his extremities to increase circulation and blood flow to the brain for better concentration.

He tried to talk. "Axel." *Yes*—at least his vocal chords worked. Although it brought no response from his friend.

A slight vibration swayed him for a second. *Oh, shit.* If they were in the shuttle, maybe they had landed. Where? In Houston?

Faraway voices grew louder. His arm worked enough to drag the sheet back over his face. He lay motionless, forcing himself into a calm state with shallow breathing.

The hatch swung open.

"You get the one on the right," a voice said. "We'll get the other one."

Mark felt his gurney being moved.

"How much farther? This one weighs a ton."

"D level, Lab 438. This way. We need to take the elevator."

Mark committed that information to memory. D level might equate to a fourth floor. Lab 438 implied it was one damned big place.

He came to rest on some sort of surface. The footsteps disappeared. Mark pulled the sheet away from one eye. He saw Axel. They were each laying on island workstations in a large dark lab. *Alone? Maybe.* A lab meant experiments. Or in Axel's mind, torture.

Should he try to wake up Axel? Should they escape now, or wait? No. Axel had drummed it into him.

I must survive at all costs. Kill or be killed.

Mark eased off the island, making sure he could walk before moving toward Axel. After checking for a pulse, he heaved a sigh of relief. "Wake up Sleeping Beauty."

On command, Axel opened his eyes. He winked at Mark and flashed a big toothy smile.

"How long have you been awake?" Mark searched the cabinets for items to stuff under the sheets.

"Long enough to hear somebody call me heavy." Axel followed his lead.

"He was just teasing—you're as light as a feather." Mark piled lots of supplies on the islands, padded them with hand towels then draped sheets over the decoy shapes.

"You know HQ's been tracking us, right?" Alex pointed to his neck.

"Yeah, I remembered about the chips. It doesn't help us in here. Do you want to be turned into an experiment, or tortured?"

"Hell, no."

"Well, then it's time to go."

On the way out, Axel pulled the knife out of his left boot and slid it in his belt. He pointed to Mark's boot.

Mark withdrew the ceramic knife from his boot, embarrassed he hadn't remembered Axel giving it to him.

Axel darted to a dark corner, grabbed a broom and snapped the handle in half over his knee. "Baton—comes in handy." He opened the door, peered out, checking for foot traffic.

"Go left," Mark whispered.

Axel slid out, staying close to the wall.

As Mark followed, he could see they were on a walkway with

a metal railing as the only barrier to falling four stories below. The men scurried along the passageway to the stairwell exit. Inside, they paused for a moment.

"Were you awake all the way up here?"

"Yes."

"I wasn't. Which way do we turn at the bottom?"

"Keep turning left," Mark said, "until we're out."

"Then which way?

"I don't know. I wasn't piloting the shuttle."

"We were on a shuttle?"

Exasperated, Mark turned to Axel, ready to hurl some choice words, just as an enormous clap of thunder exploded overhead. "Rain?"

"And lots of lightning." Axel had a glint in his eyes that matched the wicked grin on his face.

While hurrying down three flights of stairs, Axel enlightened Mark about the weather forecast and the favor Boss Lady would be repaying. His plans hadn't counted on him being inside the building when it happened.

At the bottom, they hesitated. Thunder rumble overhead, followed by the sharp, loud cracking noises of lightning.

"Should we wait in here, or make a run for it?"

Axel looked around. "This is a cement stairwell. We should be safe. If we get company, neutralize them and follow me." He looked straight at Mark. "Do you understand?"

"Yes," Mark said without any hesitation. "I've got your back."

They stood in silence behind the door to the ground floor, listening to the thunder clapping all around the building.

"Axel..."

"Don't tell me you have to pee."

"Why bring us all the way here, then leave us up there alone?"

"That bothers me, too."

"Coulter's planning has been meticulous—until now."

"Shit happens. Or maybe we're finally making some headway."

"I don't—"

Thunder crashed, drowning out Mark's voice. Multiple electrostatic impulses filled the air with the smell of ozone and burnt hair. A few seconds later, the door burst open.

A group of six or eight men invaded their hiding place.

Axel sprang into action using surprise to overwhelm them. His makeshift baton became a club to render them unconscious and his knife to disable them.

Trying to evade Axel, one fat man made the mistake of coming at Mark instead. He slashed at the fat man. Blood spurted from the cut.

The fat man staggered backward.

Mark rammed the heel of his left palm into the fat man's nose while slashing across his chest with the blade.

The fat man went down bleeding, while another taller one circled around Mark trying to dodge his knife.

Mark swerved just in time to see him fire a gun. He ducked, threw the knife, which landed up to the hilt in the tall man's stomach.

The tall man dropped the gun as he crumbled to the ground.

Mark dove for the weapon, snatched it midair, turned, and began shooting at anything still moving.

"Now!" Axel pulled the door open, sprang out and veered left.

Mark trailed behind him, bending to retrieve the knife from the tall man's mid-section before joining Axel.

They hurried toward a stream of employees rushing for an open exit leading outside. Slowing to blend in with the others, they were close enough to see torrents of rain pouring down, when two large cyborgs appeared off to the right.

Mark zeroed in on their faces. Damn if they didn't look like the same two from Portland; each one missing an eye. Mark thrust the gun at Axel, pointed to his eyes, then to the cyborgs. Axel passed the baton to Mark, grabbed his sleeve, pulling him though the flow of people to the far side.

"When I start shooting, you run like hell. Don't stop, no matter what."

The cyborgs moved toward them, pushing people out of the way like they were paper dolls.

Axel aimed at the nearest one. He fired two shots. They found their mark, blinding the cyborg. Its momentum continued driving it forward. Without sight, it listed to the left and into a terrified group of screaming employees behind them.

Mark heard two more shots as he plowed into a tight bunch of people, trying to force himself through the bottleneck at the doorway. Out of nowhere, he felt weightless. Something had lifted him into the air. Two metal hands were squeezing his ribcage. He tried to twist around to jab the knife or baton into the cyborg's eye. He couldn't move. Mark heard more shots being fired. Now he was scared. He curled into a ball to avoid being hit, praying Axel didn't shoot him instead of the cyborg. From his elevation, Mark could see people scrambling out of their way as the cyborg turned to run farther back into the plant.

Thunder continued to boom. Several lightning bolts struck the ground outside. Mark felt an enormous charge of electricity surge through the air. The level of human shouting rose to a cacophony of fear and confusion.

Axel raced past the cyborg. Thirty feet ahead, he spun, took aim, and began shooting.

Frozen in place, Mark felt the projectiles zinging past him. Until, at last, a shot pierced its one remaining eye. The cyborg lurched, stumbled, then wavered before it fell forward—on top of him.

***

Armored TMD soldiers rushed into the plant by the dozens. A loud raspy voice announced, "Halt by order of the Terran Military Defense, or you will be shot."

Almost everyone stopped in their tracks. Those that didn't were stunned into submission. One armored soldier jogged straight toward him.

Axel put his gun on the ground, to avoid being mistaken as the enemy. "Sir," he called out, "my captain's underneath this cyborg." As the soldier neared, Axel recognized the rank of lieutenant colonel emblazoned on the armor.

The officer thumbed up the mirrored faceplate, revealing feminine features. She bent down on one knee, lifted the hulking metal frame enough for Axel to drag an unconscious Mark free. The female colonel grunted as she finished heaving the inoperative cyborg over onto its back.

Axel was impressed. "Thank you, ma'am. He's Capt. Mark Warren. I'm Sgt. Axel Von Radach, Tactical Assault Group, ZULU-2 Base, North Dakota.

"Colonel Maeve Sorayne, Sixth Tactical, San Antonio." Kneeling beside Mark, she passed her arm over his body, scanning him with the sensors built into her armor. "I know who you are. I'm here to bring you home. Or did you think we were just passing by and decided to drop in for a visit?" She commed her medics for a retrieval. "He has several broken ribs and a flesh wound—in the groin."

"I did not shoot him in the groin, ma'am."

"I'll take your word for it, Sergeant—but he might not." She pointed a gauntleted finger at Axel. "Is any of that blood yours?"

He looked down at his uniform. The word bloodbath came to mind. It covered him. Streaks of crimson still wet, saturated both his shirt and pants. "Oh, no, ma'am. It's an occupational hazard—protecting the captain, here. We were attacked while escaping. Things got a little messy. If you're interested—there's a pile of bodies in the ground floor stairwell. A few may need medical attention."

She commed more medics for another retrieval. "You hiding bodies anywhere else?"

"No, ma'am. Just the bunch in there and these two cyborgs. We weren't here long enough to do any more damage." He liked this lady colonel. He flashed her one of his wholesome smiles.

Two medics in dove gray ballistic-proof bodysuits secured Mark to a hover gurney. Axel retrieved the knife Mark dropped, stuffed it in his boot before following them outside into a light drizzle. Two large black TMD shuttles hung suspended in the sky overhead. On the ground sat a silver spacecraft, half the size of a regulation shuttle. It bore the Medical Corps' insignia of a red caduceus encircled by gold stars. Once they had boarded he turned to close the hatch. Sorayne stopped him. She had a corporal and a cyber corps specialist in tow.

"Change of plans. We've been ordered to Headquarters. Personal debriefing with Dimitrios. You'd better harness up. This is going to be an express flight."

"Has our base been notified of the new destination?"

"Yes, they have. When we get to HQ, they'll be joining us on vid. You'll be able to communicate with them then."

"I don't suppose your people found Beth Coulter in there, did they?"

"Not yet. They have orders to scour the plant for her. They'll faceprint every single human. We're also searching for any underground tunnels which might have been used as a means of escape. We're accessing BioKlon's system now and should have answers to whatever questions the general has by the time we get to HQ"

One of the medics passed a handheld scanner over him, making sure Axel's body wasn't leaking any of the dark red fluids spattering his bedraggled, yellow tinged uniform.

Axel looked over at Mark, now covered in cuts and bruises. "How's the Captain doing?"

"Unconscious, but good. He's full of pain meds and nanites."

He turned to Sorayne. Her helmet sat on the floor between her boots. He watched as she finger combed her short spiky platinum hair while rattling off instructions to her aides. Axel saw a handsome woman, strong, confident, and a sense of humor similar to his own. Then he noticed her unusual eyes. A unique woman, indeed.

"Ma'am, I've been up for over forty-two hours. If I'm to meet the general, I should probably be coherent, or at least awake. And what are the chances of me getting a clean uniform?"

"Your report will carry more weight if you look like you've just come from the battle. We can help with the..." she paused, sending a questioning glance to the medic.

"Uh...dehydration?" he volunteered.

"Yes, see to it the Sergeant is hydrated."

Axel wasted no time in unbuttoning his shirt, stripping it off and offering his bicep for an injection of "hydration".

With the syringe in hand, the medic seemed perplexed.

"You're not getting anywhere near my ass with that syringe."

He smirked. "This might sting."

"If it does—so will you." Axel didn't feel so much as a pinprick. He leaned back, waiting for the drugs to sharpen his perceptions and powers of recall. The day's events flashed through his mind as if he was watching a vid. Colors seemed brighter. He could smell his sweat. He stared at his hands, focused on the pulse throbbing in his veins.

"Sergeant."

"Ma'am?"

"Do you intend on meeting the general half naked? We touchdown in ten."

"Minutes?"

"Seconds."

"Yes, ma'am." He dressed while remembering Dimitrios's imposing image on the vid back at CAMRI. That was the only time he'd seen the general. Torance hadn't been intimidated, neither had Monroe. Except...they'd been thousands of miles away—not up close and personal.

As the hatch opened to the hospital's rooftop, a short Eurasian doctor flanked by two orderlies waited in the cool evening breeze. The hem of his white lab coat fluttered against his major's uniform. After transferring all medical data to the doctor's tablet, the medics returned to their shuttle. Everyone else followed the doctor down to a private room on the third floor. Axel was surprised to find Dimitrios along with several aides waiting for them. Once formalities were out of the way, Sorayne spoke with him nonstop for several minutes while nurses cut off Mark's clothing.

The doctor examining Mark declared, "This man needs to go for a full body scan to rule out concussion, punctured lung, or any other internal damage not previously identified."

Axel stepped into the doctor's space, towering over him. "I'll be coming, too. Where he goes—I go."

"As you wish. Follow me."

The industrial-sized scanner showed Mark was healthy as an ox. Except for two fractured ribs. And a tiny flesh wound to the inner thigh, not the groin, as stated by Sorayne.

Axel was extremely relieved to hear he hadn't shot Mark in the balls, or somewhere worse. Regardless, he'd never hear the end of it anyway. Axel would have to come up with a doozy of a story about how it happened. Blame it on Mark squirming around. Or, a ricochet. Yeah, that would work.

Mark regained consciousness back in the private room.

Axel laid a hand on his shoulder to calm the alarm registering in his eyes. "Detoured to HQ," he whispered. "Dimitrios is over there."

Mark swiveled his head, caught sight of the large man and rolled his eyes.

"Don't worry. I've got this covered." Axel hoped his false bravado sounded convincing. He kept a furtive eye on the general. Dimitrios looked about the same age as Torance, but with silver at his temples, shorter and a good twenty pounds heavier. Red piping trimmed his steel gray uniform; its mandarin collar disappeared into the general's thick neck.

Sorayne's cyber specialist was showing a live vid stream of BioKlon's plant to Dimitrios as the colonel continued her verbal report. Moments later, she and Dimitrios strolled over to Mark's bed. Axel offered a crisp salute; Mark's was more lackluster, his movements seemed uncoordinated.

"Well, you men have certainly opened up a nest of vipers at BioKlon. The Terran Military Defense thanks you—of course. I don't think you planned on getting kidnapped to do it. Still, it's results that count." Dimitrios pulled up a chair and made himself comfortable. "Warren, I want to hear all about these metal cyborgs."

He looked up at Axel with a gleam in his eyes. "And Sgt. Von Radach, I want to hear about the trail of bodies you left—and don't leave out any of the gory details."

Axel wasn't sure, but he thought Sorayne might have given him a wink.

Chapter 21

In the last six hours, Axel had reported in to his base, showered, slept, donned a clean uniform, and consumed a five-star breakfast. He felt excellent—but naked. He had no comm unit or tablet. Without these devices, he felt cut off from the rest of the world.

At the door to Mark's room, he stood watching a pair of nurses while they fluffed pillows and acted captivated by Mark's blond, blue-eyed charms—and body art.

Spotting Axel, Mark bolted upright. "You shot me in the...soft parts," he said, amending his words in deference to the women.

The nurses scurried out.

"Not true. It had to be a ricochet." Axel chuckled. "Anyway, it was nowhere near anything important."

"Be careful I don't return the favor one of these days."

They lapsed into a game of one-upmanship, ridiculing each other while tossing four letter words back and forth with the speed of a hockey puck. All to relieve the tension of another life-threatening experience.

"I'm beginning to think you injure yourself on purpose, so nurses will fawn all over you."

"Jealous?"

Axel ignored the remark. "Have you spoken with your family?"

"No, but they're here." Mark brightened. "The doctor's coming by any minute to discharge me. Then we can go see them."

"We?"

"I'm not going alone—not with broken ribs and cuts and

bruises. I wish Kamryn were here to work her magic."

"I do, too."

A solemn moment passed between them. Axel handed the ceramic knife back to him and pointed to his boot. "It served you well once—it may again."

Right on cue, Mark's doctor entered. Behind him, an orderly carried a freshly pressed uniform.

Axel whispered, "When's the last time you had pain meds?"

"I don't remember."

The physician completed a cursory examination. Before he authorized his patient's release, Axel stepped forward.

"Capt. Warren is going to visit his father, who's also a patient in this hospital. I believe it would alarm his family if he were visibly in pain."

Muscles around the doctor's eyes twitched. He walked out.

"You enjoy throwing your weight around."

"So?"

The doctor returned with an injector, which he pressed to Mark's bicep. "Now, you are both released."

The orderly helped Mark into his uniform, intimidated by Axel's watchful stare. He finished just as Sorayne arrived.

Axel had found her handsome in armor yesterday, she looked twice as appealing out of it. Her platinum hair and unusual eyes contrasted sharply with the dress uniform she wore that morning; fitted gray tunic skimming over long, lean trousers, which seemed to accentuate her feminine physique.

"I'm here to escort you to see your father. Then we'll be delivering you back to your base."

Axel thought he saw a half grin tweaking at her lips. One of those 'I know something you don't know' smug looks people have a hard time hiding.

As they trailed behind her through the maze of corridors, Axel kept an eye on Mark, making sure he showed no signs of distress.

Sorayne stopped abruptly, gesturing to an open door.

Mark glanced at Axel, who nodded, then they both entered.

Mr. Warren was alert, sitting up in bed, facial lacerations almost healed, with a new growth of blond hair covering his head—thanks to the nanites. The Warren women ran to Mark, welcoming him with hugs and kisses.

Good thing Axel had anticipated the need for pain meds; otherwise, Mark would've been on his knees by now.

The visit lasted for about twenty minutes with father and son not hesitant in the least at showing affection for each other. The Warren women bursting with excitement at having the family united again.

Behind them, someone cleared their throat. Everyone turned to see Dimitrios and Sorayne in the doorway.

The general began, "I want to apologize to the entire Warren family for the injuries you've suffered as a result of a classified operation I cannot explain, now or possibly ever. The Terran Military Defense will provide all medical care to Mr. David Warren for the remainder of your life, sir. Moreover, we will reimburse everyone monetarily for the impact this truly unfortunate event has caused."

Sorayne flipped opened the hinged lid of a small black box. Dimitrios pulled out a star dangling from a striped ribbon.

"It is my honor to show our gratitude to Capt. Mark Warren by awarding you the Silver Star for extraordinary heroism while engaged against an enemy of the Terran Military Defense." After pinning the medal on Mark, the general shook his hand.

Sorayne repeated her actions, as did Dimitrios while he stepped in front of Axel, who took a deep breath and stared straight ahead.

"It is my honor to show our gratitude to Sgt. Axel Von Radach by awarding you the Silver Star for extraordinary heroism while engaged against an enemy of the Terran Military Defense." He pinned the medal on Axel and shook his hand. Axel was stunned and proud beyond belief, yet—humbled by the recognition.

Sorayne first shook Mark's hand, then Axel's, congratulating them both.

"I hate to cut short these formalities, however, we are sorely pressed for time. There's a ship waiting for these two soldiers."

After quick but sad goodbyes, all four Terran military personnel left for the tarmac.

At a corridor intersection, Dimitrios stopped. He pointed a finger to the left. "A ship to your base is in that direction." He waved a hand toward the right. "This way will lead you to a ship bound for Germany to join forces with TMD Euro Command to take down BioKlon headquarters in Gerlingen. They could benefit from your combined knowledge of cyborgs and chemicals. It's your choice."

Axel had a crushing urge to grab Mark by the shoulder and run for the ship to Germany...but he wouldn't. He was the wingman. It was Mark's call. It had been from the beginning.

Mark took Dimitrios by the arm, leading him away for a private conversation. They both returned in somber agreement. "General, it would be a privilege to assist with dismantling BioKlon. My hope is that it also results in the apprehension or death of Beth Coulter."

"God speed, to you both. If you'll follow Col. Sorayne, she's going in that direction."

Sorayne hurried toward the far exit with Axel and Mark close behind.

Axel asked, "You want to arrest Coulter?"

"Hell, no. I want to kill her."

"Did you tell that to Dimitrios?"

"No," Mark said. "If I don't come back, I made him promise

he'd be the one to tell my mother."

They burst through a door straight out onto the tarmac. A massive, deadly looking silver warship hovered, bristling with half a dozen weapons to the fore and a pair aft just behind the nacelles. Terran Space Command lettering and insignia flowed in blue down its side, ending with tail number SS-N78. Two black armor-clad soldiers with rifles stood waiting by the open hatch.

Sorayne jumped into the craft, turned, motioned them inside. When met with a surprised look on their faces, she said. "Did you think I wasn't going? *I'm* in command. These are *my* troops. Though, I may have asked Dimitrios to twist your arms."

Astonished, Mark asked, "The medals, too?"

"Oh no. Those were his idea. You earned them fair and square."

As they harnessed up for liftoff, Axel frowned at the sight of rows of shiny black-clad soldiers. "No armor—no combat."

"I can fix that." She gestured to an aide. "Corporal, once we level off, show my two new consultants to the armor locker, please."

***

"Oh, I want one of these." Marks eyes lit up like a kid at Christmas.

Axel hammered him in the chest with a finger. "No. This is *not* a toy. You have to *earn* it."

"Well, I got my ribs fractured, so I've *earned* a spin in this one."

"Step back. Watch and learn."

Mark engaged the part of his brain that memorized sequences, committing to memory the exact succession of movements Axel completed to enter, assemble and secure his set of armor.

"Now you try."

Mark turned around and stepped backward into his shell. He locked the boots first, as he'd seen Axel do, then worked his way up the legs, torso, arms, finishing at the shoulders. The servos created an airtight seal, which automatically engaged a temperature regulating system. It was a good thing he wasn't claustrophobic; still, this would take some getting used to.

They moved around, bent over, kneeled, stretched, spared until Mark could accomplish these simple feats with comparative ease.

Sorayne emerged in her armor in time to see Mark thump Axel in the chest. "Dr. Warren, you break it—you buy it."

"How much?"

"More than you can afford."

"Maybe not."

Axel shot him a questioning look.

Mark lowered his voice, "Remember the million credits in my account—courtesy of Coulter when she tried to blackmail me into giving her the data chip? I transferred them into a special fund. In case of my untimely demise, it goes to my family."

Before Axel had a chance to comment, Sorayne motioned them over to a group of six soldiers, half of them women. "These are the officers leading my troops. They've been briefed about BioKlon—with schematics of the plant. You've both had experiences with the cyborgs and the agents she's used that's even more valuable."

In a warning tone, Mark said, "Do not remove your helmets for any reason. It's well documented that Coulter has a habit of using pathogens, viruses, tranq gas, paralytics, and lethal chemicals that liquefy human bodies. A dispersing system for any one of these agents could be triggered the minute you enter the plant.

"I understand no tunnels were found in Houston. Don't let that fool you. Underground passageways exist all over Europe. Just because they're not on the schematic, doesn't mean they don't exist."

He covered every bit of pertinent information, finishing with, "...I've encountered these cyborgs three times. Never once have I heard them utter a sound. Which leads me to believe they were unable to communicate independently. They only followed programming. German cyborgs might be the same, or they could be upgrades."

Axel stepped forward. "Coulter is treacherous, pathological, lethal—she will kill you. Don't put anything past her. She's about five foot three, weighs close to 150 and can disguise her appearance to look like a man as well as a woman, so you must disable everyone first, then faceprint all humans, without fail.

"Now about cyborgs—from experience, taking one down is not easy. Pulse weapons don't seem to work. Projectile weapons do—so aim for the eyes. We've also seen evidence an old 12-gauge shotgun took off a cyborg's foot at the ankle joint. Another option is the polymer foam setting on an M906. It worked to neutralize one of these cyborgs. Start at the head and work down—you might have to work in tandem."

While Axel continued his briefing, Mark backed away from the group, looking for Sorayne. He spotted her leaning against a bulkhead double-checking her weapons while keeping an eye on the group dynamics. Not quite comfortable in his armor yet, Mark approached her with precise movements, careful not to trip in clear view of an audience. "Colonel, I'm sure you've been briefed on Operation Pandora—care to share what you hope to accomplish at Gerlingen, once we arrive?"

"Personally? I'd like to level the place. However, my orders are to secure all data, disable all personnel, segregate those with neural implants, and neutralize Coulter. Not necessarily in that order."

"I thought this was a joint operation with the Euro Command?"

She snorted. "They've opted for a supporting role—the exterior is their AOR, area of responsibility and have set up a security perimeter surrounding the plant. They're going to guard the gate and cut the power. Then after everything is over, pick up the prisoners. That way, if anything goes wrong, they can blame it on us."

Mark had been scrutinizing her hands as they worked on the weapons while she spoke. "You're augmented, and very adept at concealing it."

"I wondered if you'd be able to tell."

"I knew the minute you shook my hand this morning. I think you wanted me to know."

She cracked a smile. "Dimitrios handpicked me for this operation on purpose. He was aware you designed human cyborgs—and I am one. He assumed I'd have a personal stake in making sure you stayed alive."

"I've only been working in this field for about a year and a half. I only do upgrades."

"I have your upgrades. New left arm and leg—six months ago. I am the product of your genius, Dr. Warren. You've made me what I am today."

"Have you experienced any discomfort? Were there any problems with integration? Is there any slippage in the rotational torque?" He stopped short, realizing his rapid-fire questions had been unacceptable on several counts. "I'm sorry, please forgive me. I…I rarely get to speak with a recipient." He felt his face getting hot—his mom said his cheeks were the color of cotton candy when he got embarrassed.

"Not a problem, Dr. Warren. Ask away. I don't mind at all."

He hesitated, now more in control of his curiosity. Without

hurrying, he paced his questions from a list that had been growing in his mind as he created new designs for limbs, hands, and fingers, always wondering about the actual assimilation of the new appendages. Sorayne even rolled up her sleeves so he could compare her arms. "The strength and elasticity in your subdermal tissue are incredible."

"In the beginning, a few people were far less than complimentary of my new attributes. However, after a couple of broken arms, the message got around, '*Don't badmouth Maeve*'." A wicked smile tweaked at her lips. "Nowadays all the comments are positive. Oh, I'm sure some still say things behind my back—none to my face."

Mark felt an enormous admiration for this woman; she'd triumphed over pain and ridicule to succeed where few others had. He also held the same admiration for Sgt. Kamryn Fleming, who'd overcome torture, then endured severe pain to earn a coveted position in the armored unit. Then there was Axel. Badass Sgt. Axel Von Radach. By now, he believed Axel had probably been born a badass. Mark admired—and respected—Axel. He was a friend...like a brother—a brother-in-arms. A brother with a gun, who had your back, was the best kind of brother to have. He had to tell these people, while he still had the chance.

"I'm sure Dimitrios has the greatest respect for you, as I do, to get the job done, ma'am. Regardless of any secondary motive, you might suspect. It's an honor, Col. Sorayne." Mark saluted her, not an easy thing for him to do in armor.

She waved back a salute, tilting her head; platinum hair spiked to perfection, staring at him with her green and blue eyes.

He returned to the group of officers, who were engaged in debating the finer points of urban warfare.

Axel drew him aside. "I saw you getting cozy with Sorayne back there. You planning on making a move?"

"No. Fraternization is a violation of the Uniform Code of Military Justice, Sergeant. I'm surprised you don't know that."

"Well, it didn't stop you on Luna with Lt. McDonnell—a general's daughter."

"Whatever happened between us was not *entirely* my idea." A thought blossomed in his mind. "Wait…you weren't watching me. You were watching the colonel; *you* have a thing for *her*? Oh, crap. That would be fraternization."

"I didn't say that."

"You don't have to." He laughed. "It's written all over your face."

Static buzzed from the ship's PA system. A female voice warned over the comm, "Heads up people. Helmets on. Lock and load. Touchdown in five minutes."

Sorayne joined Mark and Axel. "The comms in your helmets are synced to the officers and mine. Everyone has their orders. You two are consultants only. You'll be the last ones off the ship and the first ones to return. You will not put yourselves in harm's way, or I will shoot you myself."

Soldiers hastened to their assigned seats preparing their troops for the chaos of combat.

Axel secured his helmet, instructing Mark as he completed each step. Mark accomplished the procedure without a mistake. Axel checked the connections, then spoke to him over the helmet's comm, "Mark, no cowboy bullshit today—you understand?"

"Yeah—I got it. Just a consultant. No shooting. No killing." Against his better judgment, Mark still found himself hoping against all odds that Beth Coulter was here. An overriding sense of excitement kicked in with the realization his journey for revenge might be ending.

Inside his helmet, Mark heard Sorayne's voice issuing commands, "Touchdown in twenty seconds. Euro Command has just cut the power. The plant is dark. Set all your internal sensors to detect toxic compounds. Scan all doors for pathogens before entering. All Cybers to the mainframe server room. Alpha platoon will enter from the roof. Beta from the ground main entrance. Charlie encircling to the right. Delta to the left. No one leaves."

The hatch opened. Black-clad armored troops spilled out onto the rooftop. The hatch remained opened as the ship angled around, descending to within inches of the ground. Armored soldiers poured out into the darkness of a German evening. The main artery of soldiers breached the plant's front door. The other two branches split right and left, surrounding the building.

Mark followed the last soldier out. They raced inside. His helmet optics adjusted to the dark. Everything with a heat source glowed in night vision green. Bodies littered the floor. Since no fluids were present, he presumed they'd all been stunned, not shot.

A loud explosion detonated, drawing everyone's attention to the far end of the building.

As he turned to look, Mark saw a movement in his peripheral vision. A streak of green fleeing around a corner. He spun toward the escaping form and raced after it, down a short hallway, around another bend and through a doorway, which was flung shut immediately. Mark reached the metal door. With one jerk, it came off its hinges. He was thrilled. He'd graduated to the rank of supersoldier.

From behind, Axel yelled, "Stop..."

But it was too late.

Mark had already taken two steps into the room and tumbled down a large open metal shaft.

Chapter 22

Axel had fallen for much too long. He was deep underground. As the angle of descent lessened, he slowed down, then shot out of the tube onto the ground, rolling twenty feet or more before crashing into Mark. He chinned a spot inside the helmet to comm in private, blocking any sound from escaping. "I told you to *stop!*"

"I would have—if I hadn't fallen in the hole first," Mark said.

"Where were you going?"

"I saw somebody jump up and run off. I tried to catch them."

Sitting in the dark underground tunnel, they saw the green glow of heavily armed mercenaries running toward them. They couldn't retreat. They couldn't go forward. They were trapped.

"Don't move. We're outnumbered and outgunned," Axel commanded. "Follow my lead. You're a corporal. Use a fake name." Axel rushed to send Sorayne a sitrep, including his armor's internal GPS coordinates.

A large thickset man broke out of the pack. He motioned with his thumb for them to raise their faceplates. Moving the barrel of his rifle, he signaled for them to stand and walk in front of him.

The mercs were recognizable at a glance by long hair, beards, and facial scars—their employment benefits did not include military grade nanites. Ten of them carried rifles with bandoliers of explosives strapped over their paramilitary gear. No cyborgs among them.

As they trudged along, Alex stole a glance at Mark. He looked anxious, out of his realm, unsure of himself. It had to be an act. Mark swaggered when he was injured, sober, drunk—even after Axel had kicked his ass. Except...when he'd talked about his brother dying, and when he'd first seen his father in the hospital. This situation came nowhere near those, so yes, he was acting. Good. Theatrics could help when they created a diversion. Axel kept searching for an avenue of escape. There weren't any. Even if Mark knew how to use the weapons in his armor, they might have been able to take out some of the mercs, but not ten.

The leader barked orders. A few men ran forward to swing wide a pair of steel doors. They entered an enormous cavern where a pale bronze-colored spacecraft rested on pylons. He estimated it was fifty feet long and thirty feet wide, which made it a private business-sized craft. He looked up. Far above, stars shone through a large circular opening in the ceiling.

In less than a minute, they were all aboard. The elegant blue interior bore no resemblance to military ships; built more for comfort, with separate compartments to keep the lower echelons from interacting with the hierarchy.

The hatch was sealed. Time for a diversion had passed. Too late for an escape. Axel felt a sinking feeling in the pit of his stomach. They were seated five feet apart, with mercs guarding them at gunpoint. The ship vibrated as it gained altitude. It pitched right, nose up, with an increase in speed. These people weren't wasting any time. No doubt about it—an emergency takeoff. He had no idea where they were being taken. Or why they hadn't been questioned, much less interrogated. But he knew one thing. They were prisoners. *Shit.* Prisoners got tortured.

He caught a questioning look from Mark. Axel responded by mouthing "Sorayne." He had to let Mark think help was on the way, if only to keep him from doing anything else reckless.

Coulter knew the TMD had seized the North American plant. She must have suspected the German plant was next. The fact people were still there mystified Axel. Everyone had more than enough time to run. Unless…the remaining employees had neural implants and been programmed to destroy data and inventory…at their own peril? Or to create her own diversion? *Damn. A smoke screen. While she vanished.*

Sorayne must have learned this by now. Axel had to figure out a way to send her a message anyway. He needed to wait for just the right moment.

***

The longer Mark sat with a gun pointed at him, the worse he felt. It was all his fault they were prisoners on a spacecraft bound for an unknown destination. To complicate matters, there was no way to tell if they were headed for another Terran location or outer space. But he needed to work on projected outcomes to this scenario, rather than wallowing in self-disgust.

Had Coulter been at the plant, she would never have stayed until the last minute. She wouldn't be on this ship. After the attack on CAMRI, she had fled to the Space Station. Coulter might go there again.

Most flights leaving Terra stopped at the Space Station before journeying to Mars. Maybe this vessel would meet up with her there.

No one here knew their identity—yet. When they did, his future would be very unpleasant. And that of Axel, too.

He'd gained insight to Axel's aversion to torture. They must find a way to either get off at the Station, or cause damage to this ship to prevent it from leaving. In hindsight, he should have taken a few courses in Aerospace Engineering. Well, a hole anywhere in a spaceship would have to be good enough. He could jump the guards, grab two grenades. He stopped himself, stifling the urge to commit another stupid mistake when he remembered that Axel had said, "Follow my lead."

The floor shuddered under his boots, forcing him back to reality. The ship had landed. The mercenaries' stocky leader issued orders. Men responded by forming two lines in front of the hatch, except for the pair pointing guns at them. Were they offloading, or loading more people? On the outside chance Coulter might board this ship, Mark obscured his line of sight to keep from being recognized. He kept a watchful eye on Axel, waiting for him to make a move.

Through the opening, he caught the unmistakable smell of ocean air. Not much time had passed since leaving the German plant. They were on a coastline, he had no idea whether it was the North Sea, the Mediterranean, or the Atlantic.

New people climbed steps into the ship. The mercenaries separated into a barricade, forcing the newcomers to enter single file. They looked like teenagers but acted oddly dumbfounded and glassy-eyed. Several dozen dressed in white ballistic-proof jumpsuits.

In the flurry of activity, the men guarding them were distracted for a moment. He observed Axel flip down his faceplate, then a few seconds later back up again—just long enough to send a silent message to Sorayne.

A female wearing the same clothing as the youngsters came from the front of the craft to meet them.

Mark was terror-stricken. His heart stopped. Beth Coulter stood less than fifteen feet away from him, except she looked thirty or forty years younger.

A clone. She had cloned herself. From her manner of greeting, the others too.

He turned to Axel for confirmation.

Axel stared in disbelief at this new version of Coulter, the color draining from his face.

Damn, damn, damn. The name BioKlon hadn't been a misnomer after all, but a harbinger of prophetical magnitude. Coulter had added cloned humans to her list of malicious creations. He was almost afraid to consider if these were the only ones. What if she'd made not just one—but multiples of herself? *Oh, crap.* What a repugnant thought. And what of these other young people? They had no mothers, fathers, siblings, families. What futures awaited them? *Holy...*Coulter was literally planning on world-building with metal cyborgs, plus her neural implants—now add her clones to the mix—she planned to *populate* the outer reaches. She still needed Eva's terraforming and his human augmentation research.

Waves of nausea struck Mark, pinning him back against his seat. A prolonged episode of hyperventilation followed. *No, no, no.*

It was all a hallucination. It couldn't be real. He strained to open his eyes. A young Beth Coulter stood in clear view; a testament to aberrant science. Coulter's Machiavellian aptitude was limitless. Mark bowed his head, vowing to Eric, that her crimes against humanity would not go unpunished. He watched as she led the group away.

The ship vibrated underfoot while it rose straight up for several minutes, then banked left and continued to climb.

His vivid memories of recent space travel told him they weren't bound for another Terran destination. If they were headed for the Space Station—or farther, he hoped the TMD wouldn't blow this ship out of the sky with two of their own aboard, but would have a trap in place before they docked. Private spacecraft didn't come with onboard weapons, although Coulter's mercenaries might have found a way around that legality.

***

On the Indian spaceship, *Star of Jaipur*, Beth Coulter paced back and forth fuming with rage. Her VIP stateroom lay in shambles. She hurled profanities nonstop at the Terran Military

Defense until the vid on her desk pinged. She stalked across the room to answer it.

A man with extensive facial scarring dressed in paramilitary gear, scowled at her from the screen. "We have everyone aboard, plus two armored TMD prisoners. Our ETA to the Space Station is one hour and eleven minutes."

"I am transmitting clearance codes for your arrival now, Krupic." She sent the codes she'd stolen on her last visit to the Space Station, confident they would be accepted, as they had been for the *Star of Jaipur*. "You will dock adjacent to us in B-17. Now transfer me to Abrina."

The cloned version of Beth Coulter appeared on her screen. "Abrina here. What are your orders?"

Beth gazed at her progeny with a critical eye. She could find no flaws. "Gather your coterie and prep them for transfer to my ship, which will take them for a longer journey to a new home."

"It will be done."

"Of that I am sure. Coulter out." As the screen faded to black, a smug expression replaced the anger on her face. Despite the recent setbacks caused by the TMD, manufacturing of cyborgs and neural implants continued at her plants in Brazil and Bolivia. The biotech facility in Peru was a hidden gem, producing clonal offspring to which her corporation claimed sole ownership. Two dozen pubescent youngsters from that facility were already on board, soon to be joined by the group from Germany. All of them fitted with pre-programmed neural implants. This portion of her grand plan was well on its way to fruition.

She commed her vessel. "Captain Dolkar, another ship is docking within the hour. We will be acquiring fifty passengers. Provisions will be required. You will depart as soon as everyone is aboard. I am sending you a departure code now."

"Yes, madam...but it is rather irregular the clearance code is not coming from the STC command center, especially since we're are traveling to the Martian Colony."

"No, it's not irregular at all."

She changed into clothing more appropriate for a prolonged space journey. After leaving her cabin, she strolled through the barrack-style quarters of her new clones, making sure they were acclimating to their surroundings, before stopping for coffee in the galley. At the appointed time, she zigzagged through the ship to the airlock, which connected to the boarding area. Indian crew members were there waiting for the hatchway to complete its sealing procedure. The door opened with a hissing of air.

Abrina herded the gaggle of young people into the corridor, followed by mercenaries escorting the large armor-clad prisoners.

"Put them in the brig," Beth said, waving at the black armor. "You." She pointed at a crew member. "Take these people to the barracks. The rest of you men," she beckoned to the mercenaries, "follow me to the Briefing Room."

Both Capt. Dolkar and his XO, Commander Bhatti, sat at the rectangular gray metal table. They stood as she entered. "Madam," Dolkar said, "we shall be under way in five minutes. Do you have any further orders before we report to the bridge?"

"See to it the prisoners in the brig are under heavy guard at all times."

He nodded, handed down her directive to his XO and they both left.

"I didn't instruct you to take prisoners, Krupic."

"It not easy to kill man in armor. Noisy. Lots of ammunition. Draws attention. Much faster and quieter to take prisoners. You can count armor as asset."

She knew Krupic was right. The soldiers inside the armor were assets as well. They would make good candidates for implants. She would have sent them back as unsuspecting operatives, after altering their memories. But that was no longer an option, since the TMD had adopted new scanning procedures to detect implants. Just another setback after the CAMRI debacle.

She moved toward the door. "I'll take a look at these two new specimens."

Krupic spread his hands, halting her. "My men have not eaten since yesterday."

"I'll have the captain send a cook to the galley." From the table's console, she keyed a message to the bridge. "We'll get everyone fed—while we go visit the brig."

They wound through the corridors searching for a small alcove with one gated holding cell. A single crewman armed with a pulse rifle stood guard, visibly intimidated by the black armored soldiers. The prisoners were almost the same size as one of her cyborgs, their stance aggressive and menacing even from behind the bars. She nodded at Krupic to take the lead.

"Remove helmets. Identify yourselves."

Neither one responded.

Krupic took the guard's weapon. Motioned for him to leave. "I kill this one. Then the other one will talk." He raised the rifle, thumbing the safety off.

The soldier unsealed his helmet, lifting it off in slow motion. He stared down at them with an impenetrable insolence.

"Speak."

"Sergeant Ricco Scarlotti, TMD, Sixth Tactical."

"Now you."

The second armored soldier moved up to stand beside the first. He too drew out the process of removing his helmet.

Beth Coulter could not believe her eyes. A laugh escaped her lips, and another, until she was consumed with laughter. Moments passed before her mirth was contained. "Nice of you to join the party, Mark. Let's get you out of that outfit and up to the Med Lab where we can have a nice private conversation."

"No," Mark said flatly.

She spun toward Krupic, drilling him with a look. "Do whatever you have to. Just get him to Med Lab. *Make it quick.*" Her delight froze solid by an innate cold-blooded hatred for this blond, blue-eyed male rival. She *despised* him—on so many levels.

Beth Coulter raced through the ship to her cabin. After finding the required medical supplies, the Med Lab was her next stop. She'd wasted too much precious time and resources trying to acquire his research—plus her million credits had *vanished.* Hostility and loathing threatened to choke her before she reached the lab. Her mind whirling with possibilities. She'd embed an implant, then turn him into a eunuch. First, she would extract the data locked away in his brain.

She heard them coming and pressed herself against the wall next to the door.

At gun point, Krupic brought in his uncooperative prisoner. Mark was younger, taller and outweighed him, but both men were wounded and breathing hard.

Without warning, she sprung toward Mark, jabbing him with a syringe of paralytic. Before he crumbled to the floor, they guided him to the centralized medpod, and attached the limb restraints. "Where's the other one?"

"On floor in cell."

"Dead?"

"Not yet."

"Do not kill him. He can be useful." Now gazing down at her nemesis, she keyed instructions to lower the clear cryo cover, as an added precaution against escape.

Chapter 23

Torance and Buchanan, stood in Harben's office glaring at the split images of Dimitrios and Sorayne on the vid screen.

"We're still trailing them," Sorayne said. "From Gerlingen to Amsterdam to the Space Station. They left using counterfeit departure codes twenty minutes ago on an Indian ship called *Star of Jaipur*. I also received visual confirmation *Beth Coulter is on the ship*."

Astonishment registered on all three officer's faces.

Torance was the first to recover. "Colonel, we've been monitoring their armor's vital signs. They're no longer wearing it. Coulter could already have them dissolving in body bags or could be hacking them to pieces by—"

Harben broke in: "Since their ship has left, the casualty threat to the station is nonexistent. What are you waiting for, Sorayne? *Christmas?*"

"All right, Harben, that's enough," Dimitrios said. "Sorayne has two warships following them in stealth mode. Two more stationed directly in their path to Mars. Instead of blowing them up in space, we've commandeered the BioKlon ship they brought to the station and will try using it to board the *Star of Jaipur* on some fabricated reason."

"Furthermore," Sorayne said, "there are *clones* on the Indian ship. Three dozen or more. Young people."

Torance struggled to comprehend her statement. "*Clones? Kids?* Coulter's cloned human beings?" He reached for the desk to steady himself, feeling weak-kneed. "General, killing children is *murder...*"

"Major, I wear the same uniform you do. I follow orders, like everyone else. My orders came from the Prime Council. That ship does *not* reach Mars, regardless of who lives or dies. Dimitrios out."

The screen filled with Sorayne's image. "You three know your people. Do you think they could still be alive?"

Harben and Buchanan replied in unison, "Yes."

Torance sank into a chair as energy bled out of him. "If it were the two of them, against a normal adversary, I would agree. *However*—Coulter is a pathological megalomaniac. She wants Warren's research. Which he won't give her. So she'll use Von Radach as leverage, like she did with Mark's father. After she has the data, there will be no reason to keep them alive. She will kill them. Because she *enjoys* it." With arms on knees, he cupped his head and emitted a helpless sigh.

Buchanan rested a hand on his shoulder. She gazed at Sorayne's image. "Warren's brother was on the Europa Mission. He's aware Coulter sent a virus to the neural implants on some of those scientists and arranged the ship's destruction. One of Von Radach's men died when her mercenaries attacked CAMRI. He holds her responsible for that man's death. If either one gets the chance—I believe they will kill her. Even if it means they die in the process."

"I understand." Sorayne nodded. "Thank you, Major. If it's within my power, I will bring them back alive. Uh—one more thing. How smart is Dr. Warren?"

Torance raised his head. "The exact score isn't in his file. But it borders on genius, maybe Nobel Prize winner category. Why?"

"How smart is Coulter—by comparison?"

"Well, she wouldn't have targeted Warren's research, or Jackson's either, if she could have created the data herself. So, Coulter's not in his league. Again—why?"

"I'm on the BioKlon vessel now. We're approaching the *Star of Jaipur*. I *am* going to board that ship. Sorayne Out."

A spark of hope coursed through Torance. Deep within his

memories, a line of Greek mythology surfaced, "*From the Kingdom of the Dark, I shall carry them over the River Styx.*" He prayed Sorayne wasn't on a suicide mission, and would bring back the two soldiers he was in fear of losing.

***

Mark awoke feeling like he had a hangover. He had a bad taste in his mouth and hoped he hadn't done anything stupid. Not that it would have been the first time. He tried to move. Nothing happened. Oh well, at least he hadn't fallen off the bed. His head throbbed, more so with every passing moment.

Something pierced his neck. A blinding flash of white-hot light shot through his brain. He yelled. His eyes flew open.

Someone laughed behind him.

He tried to turn around. Restraints. He'd been restrained before and knew how it felt. *Oh damn.* It all came to him. A gazillion thoughts to sort out in three nanoseconds. He. Axel. Prisoners. Ship. Clones. Coulter. Kill. Her.

"Party time, Mark." Coulter handed scissors to Krupic.

The mercenary's right eye was almost swollen shut, courtesy of Mark's well-placed left hook. He freaked as Krupic moved closer until he saw the man was only cutting off his shirt.

"What is this? Body art? How infantile."

"Not babyish," Krupic muttered. "I have four."

She scanned Mark's torso. "He's got fractured ribs."

Krupic shrugged. "I don't know my strength."

She attached electrodes to Mark's chest, and hooked the wires into a machine, which blinked colored lights. "I have a treat for you." She held up another needle for him to see, tapped it twice. "It's an update on sodium thiopental, an old earth drug, better known as Truth Serum." She jabbed it in his bicep. "In less than fifteen minutes, you'll be telling me every secret of your boring, pathetic life, and the data I need for human augmentation."

Fear spread through his mind like a flu virus in winter, turning all his thoughts to mush. Save one: The spy had told him to: *do what she expected.* She knew the person he used to be. Not what he had become.

He tried not to relax, but couldn't help it. In the back of his mind, he remembered being restrained before, but he'd broken out of them. Could he do it again? Pain—he must inflict pain. His head had stopped throbbing, and his ribs didn't hurt anymore. He closed his eyes, forgot about everything, and started drifting off. In his dream, he pictured formulas from blackboards, textbooks, tablets and vid screens. He imagined himself as a server farm, giving her an info dump which could take years to sort through. He hoped to live that long.

A searing pain brought him back to consciousness. He looked around, fearful one of his limbs had been sawed off.

"You're not going to fool me with this garbage," Coulter screamed. Cursing at him, she paced around the room, infuriated, waving her arms in anger. She scurried over to the machine, keyed in new settings, stood clear to watch the results.

Sudden agony—so severe tears ran down the side of Mark's face. This time he used the pain. Heaving and pulling with every ounce of muscle Axel had pushed him into building with every lap around the gym, every weight lifted, every time he'd gotten thrown on the mat and struggled to stand up again. He yanked at the base of the straps until screws started to pull away from metal plates.

"I'll give you a few minutes to get you head out of your ass, and we'll try again." She keyed the machine off, composing herself as she left the room.

Mark was suffering. It was damn near impossible to breathe, think, or plan his next move. As of now, he had a first-hand understanding of Axel's aversion to torture.

A few of Krupic's men had helped put Axel on the floor before removing Mark from the cell. He worried his friend's injuries might be more serious than he'd first thought. If Axel didn't make it—*no*—he was one badass soldier; he would make it through this. They both would. But Mark had to do one thing first: *Kill Coulter*.

His pain subsided. The ability to concentrate became easier. His ribs still made breathing difficult. With renewed effort, he started weakening the connection between the screws and the metal plates to his restraints. He had to be ready to lunge at the first opportunity, knowing he wouldn't get a second.

Coulter hadn't returned. There must be a reason. It must be important to keep her from coming back to torture him.

Then a thought trickled through his damaged brain: The TMD. *Hallelujah*. The military had been tracking them. They were coming to the rescue.

***

Axel's last message to Sorayne had been during the confusion in the cell when the merc's turned over guard duty to the new crewman. Liberation—or annihilation—would happen in dark space before this ship reached Mars. Axel leaned toward rescue. However, the TMD had a history of overkill, so the outcome was iffy at best.

Krupic had ordered them out of their armor before delivering Mark to Coulter. Because they'd refused, the merc had called for help, using multiple stun batons to garner cooperation. He'd inflicted an overabundance of punishment for their noncompliance. While Axel had been put down, Krupic had dragged Mark off to Coulter. Axel had remained on the floor, injured, but able to fight. He feigned unconsciousness, waiting for a chance to spring an attack. Two empty suits of polished black armor stood in the corner, immobile yet ready for action.

Moments ago, the crewman guard had been relieved by a short, young twenty-year-old merc with crooked teeth. Half his group had the mean street look of homeless youth. Except for the leader and a few others, who were older, taller, heavier men and experienced fighters. They'd taught the younger ones how to handle weapons, except the guns hadn't yet become an extension of their being. He could use this to his benefit. One slip in concentration by the kid would be all Axel needed.

Coulter charged into the room. She pointed at Axel. "Get him up. Bring him to the Med Lab. *Shackled*."

The young merc commed for assistance. Two more rushed in with batons to provide backup. His guard unlocked the cell door.

Axel uncoiled, striking them with a speed they had not anticipated. All three were out cold in as many seconds. He stunned them with heavy doses to keep them out. After removing their comm units, he looped one over his ear to monitor their communications, took their weapons, stepped into his armor, and attached his helmet on the way out. Exhilaration flooded through Axel as the armor wrapped around him. To better blend in with the ship's corridors, he changed the armor's color from black to urban gray. He was in control and ready to do battle.

Okay, Coulter…you wanted me—I'm coming to get you.

He set the pulse weapons to silent kill, strapped a rifle to each arm, slung one across his chest and went hunting.

He turned the corner, running straight into a merc. He shot him, stuffed the body in a wall panel and kept going.

The next two targets were young ship's crewmen.

"Where's the Med Lab?"

"D-down one l-level and, uh, aft." The skinny youth pointed farther down the passageway.

Using discretion, he smashed their comms, squeezed both

into a storage closet, then sealed the door shut with his armor's laser.

Monitoring the chatter on the borrowed comm, he ducked into a Lav as several more mercs approached. One opened the door. Axel pressed the rifle barrel against his body, pulled the trigger, pulling him in. The merc crumpled. He flushed the dead man's comm.

Axel stepped out. "Who's next?"

Both mercs turned toward him.

He shot them.

Lav's were always busy places, so he dragged all three down to a trash receptacle and got rid of them.

The distance to the end looked like thirty feet, with one more corner at the end before descending to the Med Lab level.

To his left, an older man stepped out a doorway. Before he could close the door, Axel shoved him back inside. He was the captain. Tall for an Indian, with black hair and a full beard, who seemed oddly resigned to the situation.

"Where's your first officer?"

"On the bridge."

"Why are you here?"

"I've just finished dinner." He waved at a tray with covered plates on his table.

Axel backed up, lifted the cover, passed his arm scanner over the food. It didn't smell appetizing. The word "fish" appeared in his readout.

"Comm your XO. Tell him the fish gave you indigestion. You'll be up when you feel better. Word for word."

The captain followed Axel's orders to the letter.

He pointed to the captain's vid screen. "Are your transmissions monitored from the bridge, or anywhere else on this ship?"

"I cannot say, as I have never been on this ship before. I was on holiday in Mumbai when I was approached with an offer of a substantial sum for only a quick trip to Mars, no questions asked."

"Very well." Axel zapped him with a heavy dose of the stun baton. He laid the captain on the bed while sending another message to Sorayne.

***

Beth Coulter stopped at her cabin for a few of her more exotic medical supplies. She hadn't expected Mark to be so damned stubborn. Something new to hate about him. He just needed the appropriate incentive: his research, for someone else's life. The soldier taken prisoner with Mark wasn't a relative, but he'd have to suffice. Dismembering the man in front of Mark would ensure he gave her the correct data this time. On her way back to Med Lab, she commed Krupic with orders to have the prisoner there when she arrived. No reason to draw this out.

She peered around the opening. The room was empty, except for Mark, who lay unconscious on the center pod. Frustration mounting, she commed Krupic again and learned the prisoner had escaped.

"No..." She screamed, ranting obscenities in several languages. Blinded by rage, she grabbed a scalpel from her bag, and slashed at Mark's thigh.

He awoke with terror in his eyes, stared at the blood oozing from two slits in his pants. *"You bitch—you crazy bitch..."* He roared like a wounded beast, straining to get off the pod and attack her.

Startled, she involuntarily backed away.

Krupic appeared at the door, hesitated while assessing the situation. "The prisoner is in armor. He killed four of my men." He held up fingers to emphasize the number. "Three more are in coma."

"*What?* Don't blame me. *You* brought him aboard."

"He is expert. In armor, he can kill every person on ship. One by one.

"You have weapons. Kill him *first*."

"Our weapons not good against armor. We have grenades, yes, but they blow hole in ship."

"Then you must get him to surrender. Threaten to kill Warren—this one here."

He summoned his last two men. The final trace of conscience passed over Krupic's face as he touched his comm again, "TMD soldier Scarlotti. Warren is in Med Lab. You surrender. Or he dies."

"I'm warning you," she said. "They better get here before he does."

She turned back to Mark, sneering. "Bitch, you say? Shame on you. I thought you were brought up better than that."

"I was taught not to call women names. That doesn't apply to you. Because you're not one."

"If I were a man, I'd be called strong, decisive, persistent, goal-oriented…"

"No, Coulter. You're a homicidal, power-hungry, vicious, grotesque, short, fat, malignant *cancer*. You're not *even* human."

Incensed, she ran at him again, scalpel held high, ready to strike.

Krupic thrust his rifle barrel between them, warding off her assault.

"Get out of my way," she hissed through clenched teeth.

"If you kill him, the soldier never surrenders. We *all* die."

Still enraged, she rummaged through her chemicals for an ultra-toxic nerve agent, plus another dose of MX-3, the Truth Serum. With extreme care, she inserted each vial into an injector. Her anger was out of control. She knew it. Mark had a perverse talent for goading her. No one else had ever spoken to her in that manner.

Two of Krupic's men burst into the room. She blanched. They wouldn't last long—too young and expendable—fresh meat for the TMD killing machine.

Beth took a position on the far side of Mark, both injectors in hand, above his heart.

Krupic posted a man next to Mark, while he and the other one flanked the doorway, waiting for the soldier's arrival.

"For this to work, I threaten to kill Mark if he doesn't cooperate, but you must get the soldier out of armor and tied down."

"When he sees you have injured this one, soldier thinks you mean to kill Warren, either way."

She hurried around the Lab, using towels to mop up the rivulets of blood dripping onto the floor. To stem the flow, she smeared surgical adhesive on both cuts.

"Not much of a nurse, are you?" Mark continued taunting her. "Your bedside manner sucks. You're no more a doctor than your hired lackeys. Do they know what happened to your last bunch of mercenaries? All dead—every single one. I saw them blown to bits by the TMD."

"Shut up, you imbecile." Beth looked around, powerless to escape the looks of distrust and hostility growing on the faces of the only protectors she had left.

"You want *my research*, so I can't be the imbecile here. You on the other hand..."

Returning to Mark's left side, she pulled the two injectors out of her pockets, holding them inches above his heart. She glared down at the object of her contempt. "One kills you. One shuts you up. Your choice."

Suddenly, the young mercenary across from her sailed into the air like an acrobat, then flew backward against the wall, fell with a thud.

Everyone watched it happen. What followed was the unmistakable stench of scorched flesh.

Mark let out a low rumbling laugh. "One down. Three to go." He winked at her.

Chapter 24

As the others recovered from the startling death of the young mercenary, Mark worked to loosen the restraints. Although his pod was perpendicular to the doorway, he'd been so preoccupied with trying to distract his captors that he hadn't kept an eye on the entrance. With Axel's stealth, Mark might not have seen him anyway. He no longer had any moral qualms about neutralizing his enemies; all these people fit into that category.

"Mikhail…" shrieked the other young mercenary as he turned away from the door.

"No," Krupic barked. "Stay put."

The kid ignored Krupic, abandoning his post, running around the back side to check on his friend.

Mark picked up a faint vibration just before another invisible cloud of burnt flesh filled the air.

Krupic circled back in the opposite direction to the spot where both bodies lay in a heap. Staying clear of the pathway to the door, he nudged them with his rifle barrel, to no avail. Neither one moved or made a sound.

Mentally Mark felt elated, physically he was exhausted. Words were his only weapons. He'd keep using them as long as he could. "Two down. Two to go."

Coulter and Krupic were on different sides of the room, with Mark in the middle.

Mark yelled, "She's on your right—he's to the left."

The mercenary aimed his rifle at Mark's leg. "Soldier, surrender, or I shoot your man's kneecap in three seconds. If you do not, I shoot the other kneecap. One…Two…Thr—"

A giant figure in gray armor appeared in clear view: Mirrored faceplate down. Rifles strapped to each arm. A mean as hell looking badass, intended to strike terror into the souls of his enemies.

Krupic stepped closer to Mark until the muzzle of his rifle touched the kneecap in question.

Mark's elation evaporated. His heart sank to the lowest point since his father had been attacked. He wanted to keep his kneecap, but not at the expense of Axel giving in to Krupic's demands. Now they were *both* prisoners.

Coulter had been hiding behind his pod. She stood now, positioning the injectors over his chest. "I have two injectors. One with a nerve agent, the other with a paralytic. Remove your armor, or he gets both."

Axel began unwinding the straps around his left arm to remove the rifle, repeating the process on his right arm.

Mark hated watching Axel yield—sacrificing himself—to a psychopath and her hired gunman. Guilt and remorse would choke him to death sooner than anything Coulter had planned.

After lifting his faceplate, he moved away from the entrance, unfastened each segment with precise movements—almost as if stalling, or delaying the inevitable—before stepping out of the armor. In uniform, he was no less an imposing sight; taller, younger, powerful, full of coiled energy.

"Get him tied down."

Krupic hesitated to withdraw the rifle from Mark's knee. "Lay down there." He motioned to a duplicate pod across the room. "Strap one hand down."

Axel backed away, not taking his eyes off Coulter or Krupic, sending his two targets an 'I-could-kill-you-with-my-bare-hands' glare. He reached around, felt for the pod. Easing one leg over the corner, he half sat with one leg still on the floor. He smiled at the mercenary, beckoning with his index finger. "You do it."

Mark remembered him making the same move on Luna when

he was egging on the thugs.

In half a second, Krupic had swung his rifle around to Axel and fired, hitting him in the leg. Axel growled, grabbed his leg, falling forward off the pod onto the floor. Krupic fired again, hitting him in the arm.

Mark was stunned. His mind went blank.

"I will kill your dog, piece by piece," Krupic said, without a trace of emotion.

In the same tone, Coulter said, "Give me what I want, Mark, or watch him bleed out."

He felt light headed, cold and clammy. The sound of his own heartbeat pounded in his ears, while Axel lay bleeding on the floor. Krupic was going to kill his friend, leaving Coulter to kill him.

Mark closed his eyes, summoning all the strength he had left, pulling at the restraints. To his surprise, the left one gave way. *Almost.* He focused on the right side, wrenching with every single ounce of force he could muster. Thread stripped off the screws. The metal brackets separated as his fist lifted off the pod's surface.

***

Axel was in pain; a feeling he recognized like an old enemy, something fought in the past and overcome. Cheating death did have its limits, but he wasn't dead, yet. With his eyes closed to bare slits, he tried to monitor the activity between the three people above him. His captors were arguing, paying no attention to either he or Mark.

A slight movement caught his attention. Mark's forearm moved an inch or so off the pod. The metal looked fatigued, twisted, as though the screws no longer held it together. If Mark got loose—they might have a chance.

The ship's PA system buzzed in Med Lab. A male voice spoke: "Madam Coulter, we are being hailed by your BioKlon ship. Their captain wishes to speak with you."

"Oh, what now?" She took a couple of steps to the wall. Slipping the injectors in her pocket, she pressed a button and responded, "Why?"

"He didn't say. Do you wish to take this in your cabin?"

"No, transfer it to me here."

"Very well, transferring, go ahead BioKlon…"

"Madam Coulter, this is Captain Yilmaz. We have a problem. After leaving the Space Station, we were…detained—by a Terran Space Command warship. I was informed the docking and departure codes you gave us were counterfeit. They're waiting for us back at the Station. They say I cannot return to Terra until this matter is settled. We have the Station's Deputy Consul aboard to take your statement. We must dock with the *Star of Jaipur,* so Miss Sorayne can notarize your deposition."

When Axel heard "Sorayne" his pulse increased. He glanced at Mark for confirmation. He blinked. *Yes.*

"Is this really necessary? Can't we do it on vid?"

"Madam, I have a family back on Terra, so I'm following Space Command's orders."

"Where are you and how long will it take you to reach us?"

"At present speed, we'll reach you in ten minutes. We've already sent docking coordinates to your captain. Yilmaz out."

Axel had one last move to make. The timing had to be perfect.

Coulter paused.

Axel bent into a fetal position, snatched the knife out of his boot with his one good arm, then threw it into Krupic's back. It pierced his left lung.

At that defining moment, every movement was reduced to slow motion.

Mark sat up. He yanked at the straps. Both his arms broke

free of the restraints, sending pieces of metal flying through the air.

Krupic recovered from the shock. Furious, he looked back over his shoulder at Axel, still on the floor: an easy target. He turned facing Axel.

Mark grabbed the knife hidden in his boot, threw his arm wide, slashing Krupic across the right jugular.

A stream of blood spurted out a few feet.

Mark ducked.

Krupic's knees buckled. He fell.

Coulter was sliding down the wall, trying to hide.

Mark caught sight of her. He threw the knife at her midsection. It landed up to the hilt.

Axel watched her drop the last few inches, hitting the floor with a "splot" noise. Her eyes widened and her mouth formed a small "O."

Everything returned to normal speed.

"*Finito*," Axel said in a raspy voice.

Mark shook his head. "I'm not done."

"Well, you'd better hurry. The cavalry's coming."

***

Mark's ribs made it difficult to bend over and relieve the dead mercenary of his rifle. He shot the two restraints off his ankles, flexing his legs before trying to stand on them. He took a few steps, limping from the cuts to his leg, accompanied by a good deal of discomfort in his ribs now that he was moving around. He knelt in the widening puddle of Axel's blood, propped him up against the pod. "Are there meds in that armor like the one you had?"

"Yes. Seam on the left bicep."

Mark stumbled over to the armor, found the hidden pocket,

withdrew the envelope, then brought it to Axel.

He ripped the package open with his teeth, jabbed the syringe into his thigh. "Hand me a rifle. Then go."

Mark gave him the weapon. "You sure?"

"Yeah." Axel smiled, happy, drugged and hugging the rifle like a baby. "Looking forward to seeing that colonel again. She's hot as hell."

Mark went to Coulter, checked her pulse. *Still alive—excellent.* He remembered doing the same thing when Axel had carried her back into their lab. He'd been worried about her then. He was ashamed of himself for ever having had those feelings. Too late. In the past. He'd fix all that now. Mark fished in her pockets for the two injectors. He identified the paralytic and gave her a small amount. "A taste of your own medicine, bitch."

He went to the armor, opened it, and stepped in backwards. It closed around him. He sealed it from the bottom up, looking at Axel, making sure he did it right. As he picked up the helmet, Mark straightened, gave the best salute of his military career to Axel, then simply said, "Friend." He slipped the helmet on, picked up Coulter, tucked her under his left arm, and limped out.

Behind him, he heard Axel say, "Wait...Mark?"

Upon their arrival to the *Star of Jaipur*, he'd memorized the way to the Med Lab, in case he needed to retrace the path. Every so often Mark looked back to make sure no one was following them. He noticed Coulter was leaking body fluids. He continued through the passageways, holding on to her with a vice-like grip. He limped through it, leaving a streaked trail of blood. He hadn't seen a single person. *Strange.*

The suit's bio-monitoring system sensed his injured physical condition. It adjusted an oxygen-rich air supply that helped clear his mind.

"Coulter, I need to explain a few things to you, before it's too late." He put her down beside the hatchway of the airlock chamber. He gazed at the keypad, flipped the helmet's faceplate down. *Voilà*. Fingerprint residue glowed a dim green on several numbers. All he had to do was figure out the correct sequence. He thumbed the faceplate back up. After the fifth combination, the keypad blinked. He turned the wheel and lifted the lever, pulling the heavy door open. He dragged her inside the ten-by-ten chamber, securing the door behind them.

"The first one is: I don't pretend to understand the universe. For as long as humans have been on Terra, we've only seen an infinitesimal bit with our own eyes. What I do know, is that morality is part of our genetic makeup. In my heart, I know there is justice. I don't always have faith my fellow humans can decide on the righteous path justice should take against evil. And you are evil. Personified."

Two jet packs were encased in the wall. Following the posted instructions, he took one out, stepped into it, drawing up the straps, and attaching them to the shoulder and chest harness. Once everything was secure, he scanned the procedures for operating its controls. *Okay—good to go.*

He checked Coulter again. *She had a pulse.* Her eyes were tracking him. To her, it must have seemed like forever. In reality, only a few minutes had passed.

He grabbed a railing along the wall, and took a knee in front of her, noticing the trickle of blood oozing down her abdomen between her legs onto the floor. She looked pallid. "The second one is, I've decided to space you."

Her eyes grew enormous. She looked as if she might be pleading with him not to go through with it.

"My brother, Eric Warren, was on the Europa Mission. I'm going to offer your sacrifice as a gift to all 152 murdered souls. They will watch your journey to hell for the rest of eternity. If need be, I'll follow you to hell myself, just to make sure you get there."

He stood, looking through the porthole to the outside. The ship had stopped. He must hurry. "The third one is, I could tell you what's going to happen when we take our little space walk. For instance, you might survive for about three minutes, but I doubt it—you're in sad shape. Your tongue's going to freeze. Your body's going to swell to twice its normal size. You're going to urinate, projectile vomit, defecate, then experience dramatic seizures. Then you're going to suffer cardiac arrest and die. I could tell you all that, but I'm not going to. I've decided to let you experience it first-hand. Fear only exists to be conquered. Can you see, Coulter? I have conquered my fear. Willing to kill is one thing—willing to die is another. Today—it ends here."

Mark sealed his faceplate, helmet, gauntlets, and keyed the same numerical sequence into the pad to the outer hatch. He picked up Coulter, then withdrew the knife from her midsection, which unplugged the severed vessels, allowing the wound to bleed in earnest. He tossed the knife on the floor. It belonged to Axel; he might want it back.

Mark pressed the button. The hatch slid into the right side of the hull. He swung Coulter out in front of him, holding on to her with one hand, while he pressed the control to the jet pack with the other. He kept his eyes on her as they sailed into the vast emptiness of space together. One short spurt, a longer one, another one. He talked to her. She couldn't hear him. He did it anyway. "My family's free now. They can go back home to live their lives. Not worry or look over their shoulders at shadows or strange noises. Axel's free. I hope they get to him soon and patch him up. He was a good friend. No—more like a brother." He tried to swallow. It stuck in his throat. Tears welled in his eyes, spilled out, running down his cheek, slowing as they reached his chin.

He looked at Coulter. She was dead. It was done. He let her go.

Pressing the pack's control again, he sailed farther out into space. A wonderful blanket of peace engulfed him. He looked out at the stars, started humming a long forgotten lullaby his mom had sung a lifetime ago.

"Dr. Warren."

"Mom?"

"No, Mark. It's Sorayne. Maeve. Remember me?"

"Uh-huh."

"It's time to come back inside now."

"I don't know how."

"Okay. I'll come get you."

A small figure floated toward him growing in size as it approached. A light appeared in the faceplate. He could see part of a woman's face. "Maeve. Sorayne?"

"Yes, Mark. Let's go back inside. Check on Axel, okay?" She attached her tether to his jet pack harness.

"Axel thinks you're hot as hell. He said so."

"I think he's hot, too, but don't tell him."

They sailed toward the ship much faster than he'd left it.

***

Torance sat next to Sorayne. Both wore anxious expressions. They watched from the overhead viewing booth as a team of surgeons worked on Axel. His blood loss had been on the fringe of what a human could lose without dying. The damage done by the mercenary had been extensive, shattering both left humerus and femur bones beyond repair—even by nanites. Augmentation was the only option.

Sorayne spoke softly, "When I ordered my pilot to land at the closest Combat Hospital, I had no idea it would be their home base."

"Good that you did," Torance said. "We're the best on the Northern continent. Soldiers from all over are transferred to us.

Besides, they have friends here—a support system. They'll heal quicker."

"How's Dr. Warren doing?" she asked.

"He never ceases to amaze me. It's a wonder he's still sane. We've identified seventeen different chemicals in his system. He had significant injuries to his wrists and ankles, which means he was restrained *and tortured.* We've administered a new nanite protocol for his ribs. Repaired his leg wounds in the correct manner. After ten hours of sleep, plus the breakfast of an Olympic weightlifter, he's up walking around this morning." Torance chuckled. "He submitted to a halo interrogation, but told the young sergeant that he'd break her 'friggin' arm if she came near him with a needle. Anyway, he doesn't remember much of what transpired once Coulter had him under her control. He swears he didn't give her any of his research. We can't prove it."

"We began monitoring her transmissions before they departed the station. No data left the ship, so I'd say he's in the clear." She looked down at the surgery theater. "Does he know what's happening to Axel?

"Yes, I told him." Torance let out an audible sigh, hunching his shoulders over, resting elbows on his knees.

"And his response…"

"He shook my hand and said, 'Everything's going to be all right, you'll see.'"

"Where is he now?"

"With Capt. Eva Jackson, the other scientist, and Sgt. Kamryn Fleming, Axel's counterpart. Kamryn was shot apprehending a cyborg's accomplice. She's still recovering. Sad. She won't be returning to her armored unit. Now, neither she nor Axel will. You, along with a handful of others are the only augments still allowed to serve on Terra."

Chapter 25

Mark hugged Eva like a long-lost friend. He repeated the greeting with Kamryn, Petra, even Ohashi. He was shirtless, wearing a two-day growth of beard, various contusions, lacerations, ugly bruises, with bandaged wrists and ankles. The women had gathered in his room after breakfast to welcome him "home." Kamryn and Ohashi took chairs. Eva and Petra sat beside him on the bed.

Because they pleaded, he gave them a play-by-play rundown on "The Harrowing Misadventures of Axel and Mark." He tried to keep it light, making jokes, leaving out the gorier details, plus his part in Coulter's demise. Although, he suspected they already knew. News travels fast in an underground military complex.

In typical Petra style, she asked, "You saw her. The young Coulter—the clone?"

"Yes. I did."

With a look, she urged him to elaborate.

"Younger, thinner, following orders, in charge of the others." In a not so typical tone, he added, "So scary, I almost puked."

Mark got up, drank half a pitcher of water, then sat down again. Looking straight at Kamryn, he said, "I can't explain how responsible I feel about you being shot—now Axel too, much less what happened to my father."

"No, Mark," Eva said in a decisive tone. "It was Coulter. She had my brother killed. She ordered all these other things, and more. I cannot blame myself for Dion's death. I won't allow you to bear the guilt for what she did to your dad, or anyone else."

"She's right," Kamryn chimed in. "How dare you try to take credit for my war wound. I could have gotten this on foreign soil. Instead, I got it here, keeping people safe in my own country. If you try this with Axel, he's going to kick your, ah… well, you know."

"You can't go back to your unit. Axel can't either."

"We are soldiers, Mark. We wear our wounds with honor. They make us who we are. We are warriors." In a softer tone, she added, "Let it go. I have."

Every tablet pinged.

Kamryn read the message aloud. "Axel's out of surgery. We can see him in a couple of hours."

A collective sigh of relief filled the room.

"Well, I would've eased into this, but I'm sensing a deadline. Here's my news: When my tour is up in two months, I'm leaving the military. I was planning on opening a business back in Oregon. Not any longer. Santa's coming early this year." He tried but failed to hide his smile.

The ladies looked at each other, their eyebrows raised.

"I have a proposition for you."

They giggled.

"Back in college, I started investing in the stock market. With the new tablet they issued me this morning, I accessed my private accounts, and found I'd been contacted by some attorneys who represent a company that wants to purchase a certain stock I have."

"Are you going to sell it?" Petra ran a hand though her new indigo blue tipped hair.

"Yes…and my proposition is: I want you to join me in a business venture. The startup capital is not a problem. For this to work, I need *all of you* onboard with this—*as partners*." He made eye contact with each woman, emphasizing the serious nature of his proposal, remaining silent to let it sink in.

"On Luna, Eva and I began to compare theories about Coulter, and why she wanted our research. We pooled our knowledge, devising a plan to seek out information from a network of our colleagues who also had suspicions about how the Europa Mission might have been destroyed. That's when Axel and Kamryn became full partners. From there, we sifted through clues, finally coming up with a working hypothesis. Then you— Petra and Ohashi—became integral to tracking down the leads. You also pulled our asses out of more than one fire until we tied Coulter to BioKlon. *This is astounding.* The TMD had been working on it for a year, yet we came up with answers in a fraction of the time."

He stood, limping as he wandered around. "We're excellent at what we do, but together—as a unit, a team—we're better. *So much better.*"

"A team...to do what?" Kamryn asked, showing some interest.

"Coulter had the plant in Malaysia—now closed. The plant she intended to open in India—now closed. Both BioKlons— now closed. Her corporate ship flew us to Amsterdam to pick up clones. We need to start there. Search for holdings, chemical shipments, genetic engineering or cryopod purchases. I'd bet my life there are more plants. We've no idea what kinds of research she was using them for. How many more ships did she have? Where are they now? Could there be another Coulter clone ready to take over?" He stopped, taking in the grim expressions on their faces. *"Too much?"*

The women exchanged glances.

Eva squirmed around to look at him with a Mona Lisa smile on her petite bronze face. "I know you, Mark. You already have a plan. What is it?"

"I negotiate an agreement with the TMD, buy the BioKlon ship taken into custody, plus every future ship which is confiscated—there's no way to retrofit them for military use— including my pick of BioKlon research equipment. Selling this stuff at auction would be their only option, except it's a lengthy process. Once we have the ship, next is the equipment, then we need a location for a Lab. Then we're in business. You ladies choose a location. Anywhere is fine with me. Eva, if you'd rather handle the Terran side—be in charge of research—great. Petra and Ohashi, you both have cyber specialties. You get to choose your own titles. Kamryn, Axel and I will hunt down the leads— boots on the ground stuff. We just need a pilot."

No one said anything. It dragged on.

Kamryn stood.

Mark thought she was going to walk out.

Instead, she extended her hand in a dignified, solemn manner. "I'm in."

The other women stared, taken by surprise.

Eva asked, "What should we call it?"

"Wait..." Petra closed her eyes, tilting her head toward the ceiling. "I know: M.A.V.R.E.K. an acronym, or a portmanteau. A combination of Mark, Axel, with an E added—for Eric."

"Perfect," said Ohashi.

***

Axel and Mark were wrestling in the gym. Transparent sleeves protected the new skin growth on Axel's left arm and leg. They had stripped down to trunks. At the mat's edge lay a heap of exercise togs, towels, water bottles. Axel was healing fast, due to the nanite protocol, boosted by his extreme self-imposed exercise regime. Nowadays, he'd rather have his brain flooded with endorphins than battlefield drugs. Although officially discharged, Orthopedics' would not sign his release until he finished rehab.

They spotted a familiar figure walking toward them.

She waved.

They waved back.

The gorgeous, platinum-haired woman wore a colonel's uniform. She, with the one blue eye and one green eye, walked with a military stride that was so sexy it raised Axel's libido.

"I happened to be flying by. Thought I'd stop to check on you two." Her gaze rested on Axel. "I see you've been exercising more muscles besides the ones you sit on."

Axel stared at her.

"So...you've officially been discharged, Sgt. Von Radach?"

"Yes, ma'am. They're keeping me here until I finish rehab. Orthopedics wants to make sure I'm good to go before they release me."

"Well, then, why don't I take you to lunch." She leaned closer, whispering in his ear, "And maybe I can find you a pilot."

He fought the urge to pull her close.

Mark whistled.

Axel turned around in time to catch the clothes Mark pitched at him. He stepped into the pants, and pulled the t-shirt over his head.

Sorayne picked up his sleeved arm, draping it over hers while they walked out of the gym together. As they started toward the dining hall, she stopped him. "Didn't I tell you? We're having lunch in Winnipeg. I have a meeting. I'll bring you home afterward. Not to worry."

No way was he going anywhere outside with a fine-looking female colonel in sweaty exercise togs.

"My ride's on the tarmac. See you in ten minutes?"

He ran to his quarters, took a two minute shower, dressed in leather clothes, then broke the land speed record for making it to the exit in time.

A sleek silver ship with the requisite blue Space Command insignia hovered on the tarmac.

Axel jumped in, closing the hatch. They were the only passengers. He eased into the seat facing her.

"I haven't seen you awake since my people boarded the *Star of Jaipur*. Why don't you start from there? Bring me up to date…Axel."

He did as she requested. He didn't leave anything out. From one soldier to another, one augment to another. The unvarnished truth. Period. He spoke. She listened, like kindred souls who had known each other for a long time, but had only just met.

In Winnipeg, they parted when she entered a skyscraper downtown, with plans to meet there in two hours.

Axel took out his tablet, found what he wanted, then called to make sure the tattoo artist could do what he asked. He hailed a car for the drive, showed the tattoo artist the image, got it done, and was back in front of the building with five minutes to spare. He watched the traffic until she approached him from behind, threading her arm through his.

"How about some lunch?"

He nodded, staring at her again.

She walked him into the next building, up to the desk, and received a card. They went up to a suite on the twenty-fifth floor with a breathtaking panoramic view.

"I'll be right back," she said, leaving him at the window. In a bit, she returned wearing a white towel.

He walked over and kissed her as he had never kissed another woman, and she kissed him back. Maeve Sorayne looked, felt, and now tasted different than any of the others. She was unique.

The towel slipped to the floor.

He picked her up and carried her to the bed.

***

Under a clear noonday sun, Mark stood on the icy tarmac, gazing at his first spacecraft. He was certain there would be more. Petra had used coercion, in the form of chocolate cake and a case of beer, for the privilege of designing the logo, which she ordered emblazoned on both sides: Royal blue outstretched eagle wings fifteen feet wide, with three-dimensional gold letters spelling MAVREK, superimposed over them. A dramatic visual against the pale bronze hull.

True to her word, Sorayne had recommended two pilots; one male, the other female. Both were former Space Command who'd suffered wounds requiring augmentation, as such, were no longer certified for military spaceflight. Conversely, Mark considered it a fringe benefit, not a drawback.

He'd scheduled a test flight of their new ship, using the male to pilot and female as copilot on the outbound trip, and reversing roles for the return. This weekend was the maiden voyage in their new ship to Lexington, Kentucky. They were on a scouting mission for the home office of MAVREK Enterprises. The TMD Headquarters were 350 miles east, in Richmond, Virginia. Close enough, without being too close.

Once everyone arrived, the pilots boarded first. The women followed, sending out squeals of delight with comments on the posh blue interior, the meeting room, and both Lavs; a world apart from what they were used to in the military. Although it held six passengers today, it could carry fifty or more if necessary.

A male voice announced over the ship's comm, "Test flight of *MAVREK I*, ready for liftoff."

Everyone applauded. They strapped in while Mark produced a chilled bottle of champagne with plastic cups. He toasted them, "To my friends."

They bubbled with excitement about the new venture, new location, and this new direction for their lives. Mark sat back, watching his colleagues—partners—his family, enjoying a blissful moment after experiencing more than their share of sad ones. He reflected on his own life. He was a scientist who had become a soldier, a path he would never have envisioned. Although he'd taken some lives, he'd saved some as well. He chose not to dwell on the past. He heard the echo of his father's voice, "Deal with it—and persevere."

Back in Portland, his dad, mom, and sister were happy, healthy and back to work.

Gina had bought a condo, which in a strange twist of fate, coincided with a series of events that shocked Portland to its foundation. A law enforcement probe originating in New Zealand had tied the Sheriff, Harold Blackwell, along with a couple of his old friends, to an International Child Pornography Ring. They were behind bars awaiting trial. Alas, the media had already tried and convicted them.

Karma's a bitch.

Mark relaxed, leaned back, closed his eyes, listening to the jovial chatter.

Mid-flight, Ohashi screamed, "*Holy crap!* Facial recognition software just identified an image of a young Coulter on the Space Station. What should we do, Mark?"

"*Don't lose her*—whatever you do—don't lose her. She's an engineered psychopath who enjoys killing—believe me."

Mark raced to the pilot's cabin. "Change of plans—we're diverting to the Space Station. We need to be there five minutes ago."

Both pilots turned toward him smiling like they'd been given a bonus. The brown-skinned man said, "That's what we're trained to do, sir. Get you there quick. Get you home safe."

The blonde woman said, "Go strap in. We'll double-time it."

Mark rushed back to the passenger cabin.

Neither Kamryn nor Axel were in their seats.

Petra had moved over to sit beside Ohashi. Both had their large tablets open while working feverishly to learn when she'd arrived, on which ship, and where she was going.

"Should we contact the TMD?" Ohashi asked, her fingers zipping across the screen.

"No. Not yet." Mark said. "They should be monitoring the Station. Plus, there are always warships at the Spacedock ready to go anywhere—anytime. Instead, we'll contact Sorayne when we have more information."

"*Found it*," Petra cried. "A ship. Same type as ours. Just one digit off in the serial number. Registered to a Peruvian company called *BioSíntesis*, based in Cusco, Peru."

"Petra," Mark said, reaching out to touch her knee, "search this ship's manufacturer for serial numbers sequentially similar to ours. Begin in South America, then work outward. I need to know if we're dealing with a single ship—or a fleet."

"Ohashi," he said, "start a new search in the adjacent countries for the same corporate name or the equivalent in that indigenous language. Also, cast the same type of blanket search we did before, including chemical shipments, genetic engineering or cryopod purchases. If the Peruvian facility is manufacturing clones, there might be a sister plant somewhere close—making cyborgs."

"Ladies," Mark said, "cover every avenue you can think of. Keep in mind—if she leaves the Station on the identified ship, she might be returning to Peru. We may have to divert again to follow it."

"Peru is one of the few countries that haven't banned human cloning," Eva volunteered.

Axel and Kamryn trudged back with armloads of sidearms, rifles, grenades, plus a couple of nasty-looking rocket launchers.

Mark pointed at the rocket launchers. "Really?"

"In case all hell breaks loose," Axel said, sounding energized at the prospect.

"Should I ask where these came from?"

"I know a woman—who knows a guy." Axel offered no

details.

"*The ship's leaving,*" Petra cried again.

"Is Coulter on it?"

"Yes."

"Where are they going?"

"Wait…wait…Bolivia."

"Ohashi, sister plants in Bolivia?"

She snapped her fingers. "Well, look at that. Yep, in Sucre, 600 miles southeast of Cusco. It's called *BioMetalurgia.*"

"Name of the corporation?"

"Bio S.A."

"How many other plants—in which countries—how many ships?"

"One more plant, 850 miles south in Córdoba, Argentina, called *BioEstar.*" Ohashi added, "Each plant has its own ship."

"Okay, now, we have to decide what to do next," Mark said. "This morning we left on a weekend trip to hunt for a home office on Terra. All of a sudden, we're hunting down a psychopathic clone in outer space. Everyone must decide what kind of commitment they're willing to make. Because these people don't play games."

Eva stood. She picked out the smallest holster and spoke while strapping it on. "Have I ever given you any reason to believe that I wouldn't do whatever it takes to put an end to this?"

"No, you haven't, Eva. And I'm sorry if I insinuated otherwise."

"I saw what they did to you on Luna. Then I saw what happened to you on that ship. You've changed. You look older. You sound more decisive. There's less swagger and more resolve in your step. You might have had goals before, now you have a purpose. You've matured, Mark." She chose a gun, slipped it into the holster. "We've all changed. Besides, you're all the family I have left." She walked over, hugged him and sat down.

The whole group followed her lead. Axel passed on the hugging.

"Now we contact Sorayne. I'll leave that to you." Mark motioned toward Axel. "Make sure you tell her not to blow up any of those ships. They belong to us now."

He got up and headed to the pilot's cabin. "I need to tell them we're diverting again—to Bolivia."

When Mark had tackled the cyborg, he'd interrupted a chain of events which could have altered humanities space faring capabilities. Coulter hadn't succeeded in stealing the augmentation or terraforming research. But if she had, Terra's future would have suffered. Although they might be going to Bolivia, the *Star of Jaipur* had been headed to Mars; he had a feeling it would be their next destination. That distant world was on the edge of the future.

The End

Acknowledgements

All the characters in this novel wish to thank the author, Andria Stone, for giving them a voice (applaud!) and they can hardly wait until she turns them loose again in the next episode. (They also hope she doesn't kill any of them off.)

Now the Author wishes to thank Amanda Ryan as Beta Reader, Tiffany Shand as Editor, and Carolyn Farias as Proofreader, who helped shape this story. Their time, care and influence were invaluable.

***

The New *Edge Of The Future* Audiobook,
narrated by Nic Barta, is now available.

***

Before You Go…the next adventure of the MAVREK team,
Edge of the Stars
is finished and will be out soon. They're all harnessed up
and waiting for liftoff!

Reviews matter!
Thank you for reading *Edge Of The Future*.
If you enjoyed the escapades of the MAVREK characters,
please leave them a sterling review.

Connect with Me:

Follow me on Goodreads: https://
www.goodreads.com/author/show/16574927.Andria_Stone

Author Website:
http://www.andriastonenovels.com

CPSIA information can be obtained
at www.ICGtesting.com
Printed in the USA
LVHW081055040822
725112LV00004B/370